# STARS TO STEER BY

## SAM ZITTER

PublishAmerica
Baltimore

First printing

ISBN: 1-59286-603-4
PUBLISHED BY PUBLISHAMERICA BOOK PUBLISHERS
www.publishamerica.com
Baltimore

Printed in the United States of America

# DEDICATION

This book is being published posthumously. Were the author alive, he would surely have dedicated it to his beloved family—his wife of 50 years, his children, and his cherished grandchildren. Under the circumstances we are dedicating it to him, in loving appreciation of the many ways in which his compassion, his integrity, and his unstinting devotion to what he believed to be right have helped each of us in steering the course of our individual stars.

The Zitter Family

# ACKNOWLEDGMENTS

Following the death of the author, this novel was readied for publication primarily by his wife, Sarai, ably assisted by his daughter Sherry. But it takes many generous helping hands to complete such a task, and we cannot possibly name all of them.

We give particular thanks to our friend Bruno Chmiel and to our nephew Dave Allen, without whose technical assistance we would still be bogged down with the computer. Our cousin Eve Sorel provided invaluable and much-appreciated editorial skills. And our publisher graciously provided the extra time and assistance which Sam's death amidst these proceedings necessitated. Help came from many other sources, too numerous to mention. You know who you are; know also how much you are appreciated.

And finally, we must acknowledge one another. The mutual support we shared during these difficult times is what truly made it all possible and rewarding.

The Zitter Family

# CHAPTER I
# SIXTH SENSE

## *Martin—1993*

"I came as fast as I could, David," I murmured to the oxygen-masked face as I leaned over my brother in the hospital bed.

The eyelids twitched without opening, and I bent closer. A moment later I glimpsed his dark brown eyes and felt the pain mirrored there. Then the lids closed.

He needed a cheery nudge. "Can't be serious, young man. You're not in Intensive Care."

I leaned back and wrestled my worry. My brother is in damn good health for seventy-one years old. But he's a paraplegic, and when polio ravaged his legs and his spine as a small child, it also short-changed his lungs. I looked around and was not encouraged. Thin tubes looped down to David from both sides. The I.V. dripped with uncaring monotony. Oxygen hissed into the bluish mask, whose shape struck me as a grotesque parody of Mardi Gras clownery. What if David didn't make it? An icicle pricked my heart.

He'd better get better. Eight years older, he helped ease the terrors of my childhood, the teenage torments, my stumbling steps to self-confidence.

The pain of Anita still throbs after all these years. At nineteen, my first real love. Feverish kisses, aching separations. Then to open a door and find her whiteness pinned down on the bed by another, her chestnut hair sprawled across the pillow like Medusa. David, you pulled the hot spear from my heart. You somehow soothed the wound till the agony began to subside. You're disabled, but you have the power to lift me up.

My brother's eyes suddenly opened and focused on me in a melancholy way. I gave him a broad smile.

"You sure know how to fool a guy," I said. "Charlene phoned to say Uncle Abe is being rushed to Carmel Hospital. So I jump on the next plane. And I find you here too—in the next room! What are you trying to do to me?"

The corners of David's eyes showed laugh wrinkles. He couldn't talk with the mask on. But he didn't have to. Our minds touched.

9

Doctor Kahn slid back the curtain around David's bed. I trailed him out of the room. "How is my brother, Doctor?"

He put his hand on my shoulder. "Not to worry, Mr. Richman. No reason why David shouldn't beat his respiratory infection in a few days. We just have to reduce that heavy congestion in his lungs."

Relieved, I went back in. David smiled lightly, looking human again with his oxygen mask off. I asked, "Shouldn't this go back on?"

"The doc said I could do without it for fifteen minutes. I hate masks. Masks are the faces people wear when they're hiding their real feelings."

I chuckled. "Philosophy already. Now we know you're better."

My brother had a way of saying a lot in a little. He's talked about people masking their faces to conceal the pain inflicted by an unfeeling spouse, boss or acquaintance. Many bottle up their vulnerability till it twists their inner selves into something they themselves hate.

David gave me a warm look. "Glad you're here, Martin. What about Uncle Abe?"

"He's also improved. I'd say the worst is over."

The door suddenly burst open and Charlene Richman surged in like an aircraft carrier steaming head-on. Big vertically as well as horizontally —upward of three hundred pounds—her bulk tapered down to trim ankles. Her cherub face was artfully camouflaged to roll back her forty-one years. Some tinting marvel ignited her hair to a passionate red.

My sister-in-law bore down on David's bedside, seized his hand and cried, "Davy, Davy, are you all right? What do the doctors say?" Her voice was raspy from a sore throat.

"Charlene," I said, "Should you be so close to David right now when you both are loaded with germs?"

She ignored me and continued ladling her confectioned concerns. "Sweetie, I'm terribly upset over your condition, okay? You know your lungs are weak to start with. I'm sick with worry, okay?"

David pumped himself up to sound better than he was. And he had a way of turning the point around. He squeezed her palm. "Charlene, shouldn't you be in bed getting rid of that cold so you'll be in shape to care for me when I come home?"

It wasn't easy, but his gentle persuasion made so much sense that she soon left.

I try not to hate. But face it—Charlene's a bitch. I hate her, but I hide it, for David's sake.

I shadowed his bedside all night long, and was heartened to see improvement by noon. David's voice was weak, but his brain sharp. How many people do you know who love to hone their minds on ideas? My brother and I could spend endless hours in intellectual jousting, like now.

I was upset over the headline that NASA was getting another fifteen billion dollars this year. "All that taxpayers' money being shot up into the sky when we've got so many problems here on Earth."

David was a cosmic thinker. "If Queen Isabella thought that way, would we be here? Could anyone of her day possibly imagine today's United States—the world's bread-basket, the world's industrial leader? Out there among our planetary neighbors we'll discover undreamed-of wonders for uplifting our society." He took a sip of water and grinned. "To misquote Shakespeare: Our future is in the stars, dear Brutus."

We were brought back to earth by the necessary interruptions. Blood pressure. Siphoning off blood for testing. What irritated me, though, was the technician who turned David over and pounded away on his back with cupped palms like a bass drum tattoo. "It's a bronchial treatment," the man explained, "to loosen the congestion in the lungs."

David didn't complain, but his knuckles gripping the railing were white, and pain flashed in his eyes. I thought, *They don't do bloodletting, but this is medieval torture, brought up to date.*

Worn out by all these recuperative assists, David drifted off. But his nap was fractured only ten minutes later by a nurse asking him to expel phlegm into a cup. David's coughs yielded only feeble croaks. "Keep trying," she said. "We need a sample to test."

The dinner tray arrived, and I fed David his first real food in thirty-six hours. He tried for a phlegm sample but lacked the lung power. Just as he began to doze again, the technician returned for another bout of backslapping, pounding more intensely. The bed rocked and the walls reverberated. David grimaced and groans escaped his mouth. I curbed my impulse to bean the technician with the water jug.

Standard treatment, I suppose. But for a guy with lousy lungs?

I settled back to read the newspaper while David rested. I remembered the day I was heading out for a paper and discovered my wallet had disappeared. A friend had just left, and my wallet was right there on the table after I had loaned him a twenty. I never saw that friend or my wallet again. More than the money or the nuisance of card replacements was my anguish of betrayal.

When I poured out my soul to David that evening, he had a story for me:

11

*A man searching around the world for what life is all about came to a fabled*
*guru sitting cross-legged in a Himalayan cave. "Oh great one," he asked*
*humbly, "where can one find meaning in life?"*

*The answer came in one word: "Wisdom."*

*"How can one achieve wisdom?"*

*The answer was another single word: "Experience."*

*"But how does one gain experience?"*

*The guru used two words: "Bad experience."*

Suddenly I heard David cough hard and gasp. He was gagging. I jumped up
and pulled his torso vertical, crying, "David, David!" Struggling for breath,
he turned fiery red. I pounded his back, but he was choking, his eyes rolling
in circles.

Frantic, I dashed to the nurses' station just outside the room, yelling,
"Help! Emergency! My brother can't breathe!"

The nurse flew into the room, took one look and signaled back to the
desk: "CODE BLUE! CODE BLUE!"

Within sixty seconds, a white-clad team of four appeared with the
equipment wagon, arms flailing around the bed as the nurse shoved me
outside and shut the door. Then Dr. Kahn darted into the room.

I was stunned. What skyscraper had fallen on me? I saw Alice, Charlene's
best friend, come out of Uncle Abe's room next door, where she'd
volunteered to watch over him. I shakily told her what happened. She
suggested we phone Charlene.

I said, "I'm sure they can clear David's throat. Why get his wife in an
uproar when she's sick herself?"

The door to David's room remained ominously closed. I listened outside,
but no sound penetrated, and a nurse shooed me away. Sweat formed on my
brow despite the air-conditioning. I glanced at my watch. Incredible—it's
fifteen minutes already!

Suddenly there was Charlene streaming toward us, hair disheveled and
robe askew over her nightgown. Alice must have called her out of bed at
home. "Well? Well?" she shrilled.

I tried to reassure her. But Charlene began a tormented screaming that
reverberated down the corridor. She tried to wrestle her way past a nurse to
attack David's closed door. A burly aide rushed over to restrain her, and she
was tugged down the hall to the waiting room. Alice and I followed, trying
to calm her.

A few minutes later, a somber Dr. Kahn appeared at the waiting room
door. My heart unhinged as I read his face. "We did everything we could to

save him. I'm sorry."

Charlene covered her eyes and let out a howl. I felt like I had just toppled off Nightmare Mountain. I grabbed the doctor by the arm. "How can that be? You said David was getting better. You said he'd be home soon!"

Dr. Kahn shook his head and sighed. "Things happen. Things we don't expect. Believe me—we did all we could."

Charlene tore out of the waiting room and up the corridor like a bull elephant, wailing wildly. Alice and I rushed in pursuit as she flung herself through the door and onto David's still body. She clung to him, hysterical, and shrilled, "Davy! Davy! Why did you leave me? What will I do without you? How will I live?"

Alice and I moved close to comfort her. With my arms around Charlene's shoulders for the first time in many months, our animosity was forgotten in the intensity of our common grief. She sobbed uncontrollably on my shoulder, while Alice alternately patted and stroked her back.

That evening the kitchen looked infuriatingly normal after my world had spun 180 degrees.

Charlene greeted a man at the door and introduced Lou Bianca as a dear friend and co-worker of David's. Tall, broad-shouldered and moving with a limp, he solemnly shook hands all around, expressing his sympathy. "I'm head of the Disabled Citizens League. David and Charlene founded it last year. I wanted David to be president, but he was too modest."

"I've asked Lou to give the eulogy for David at the funeral," declared Charlene.

Huh? My beloved brother, summarized by a guy I don't even know? But I bit my tongue and muttered, "I'd like to say a few words too."

As Charlene's friend Alice served another round of coffee, she asked, "What shall we do about Uncle Abe?"

"This is no time to tell a man who's in the hospital with heart problems," I said firmly. I dreaded to think how badly Abe would be shaken by losing David. He's been a father to David—and to me—since our dad died thirty years ago.

"It's going to be an overflow funeral," Charlene said. "Everybody knew David. He was the first to fight for the disabled. Maybe I'll have Mayor Gomez say a few words. He came to our wedding—remember?"

*I remembered. I remembered all too well. Newspaper headlines the next day proclaimed: "DISABLED RIGHTS LEADER, 69, MARRIES ASSOCIATE, 39." She was little more than half his age, but that wasn't the problem.*

13

*Such a joyful wedding: it was David's first chance at marital happiness. Then such unhappiness just one year later, when Charlene abandoned him. And remembering the conflict after he took her back—such irony.*

*The saint married the sinner. They say opposites attract, but I never understood why.*

I studied the forlorn expressions grouped around the kitchen table. *What can be more dismal,* I thought, *than the silence that follows the outpouring of grief after a death? What can be more inane than the random chatter we toss out to escape our own fears of mortality?*

Alice spoke up. "I don't understand why they couldn't revive David when he began choking."

"That's right," said Mike, Charlene's uncle. "A tracheotomy woulda cleared his windpipe. Why didn't they do it?"

I never cared much for Mike, a heavyset, overbearing personality with a beer belly. He's a car dealer, and you have the feeling he carries the 'deal' approach into his personal life.

"It was done," I said, wishing they would stop gnawing at a barren bone.

"What I don't understand," said Charlene, "is how come the doctor told David he was going home soon."

"Really?" said Mike sharply. "Then maybe they didn't handle the case properly. Sounds like malpractice is involved."

*"Malpractice?"* cried Charlene, her voice rising. "You mean my Davy died because some bastard was *negligent*?"

Mike's voice took on an ugly undertone. "Happens all the time. And Martin just said there was no reason for David to die." He stared at Charlene. "I'd say you have a case. I'll call Phil for you right now."

I was bewildered by this turn in the conversation just two hours after my brother's death. Phil Fox is an ambulance-chasing lawyer, some relative of Mike's. In a moment I heard Mike speaking animatedly on the phone.

Dumbly I stared upward at a solitary fly buzzing near the ceiling. My brain felt like a vast hollow cavern, tormented by a ridiculous rubber ball which wouldn't stop bouncing. Of all people, David, who wouldn't lend himself to such a charade when alive, was now being dragged in as a corpse.

"Phil says you got a good case," Uncle Mike was briefing Charlene. "But I gotta phone the hospital right away not to release the body to the undertaker. Gotta arrange for an autopsy."

Charlene gritted her teeth. "Let's get those sonsabitches!"

"If a doctor is negligent and lets somebody die," Alice said piously, "we've got to expose him."

As Uncle Mike moved back to the phone, Lou Bianca took Charlene by the elbow and motioned to me. "Please," he said. "May I have a word with you two in the next room?"

Seating himself between us, Lou spoke softly. "Look," he said. "I know you're both very upset. But stop and think. Do you really want David's body cut up into a hundred pieces? Would David have wanted it? I'm a former detective, you know, and I've seen how gory an autopsy can get."

Charlene began to cry. I felt like a grenade had been rammed down my throat.

"Then after all that butchery," Lou continued, "what if you find no negligence? How would you feel then?"

"David would never allow this kind of invasion," I said, choked up.

After a minute of sniffling, Charlene composed herself and walked back into the kitchen. Uncle Mike saw her and said, "The undertaker already picked up the body but—"

"Forget all that legal stuff," said Charlene tersely. "I've changed my mind."

My head eased into decompression, flooded with relief. *Maybe I've been misjudging Charlene. She's not all bad. Maybe she loved my brother more than I thought.*

So much had happened so fast that I felt adrift in chaos. The jangling phone punctured my reverie. It was my wife in Connecticut, returning my call, and I took it in the bedroom. Rina's rich voice reached out to me like arms pulling a drowning sailor from a tumultuous sea. I rarely cry, but I felt tears wetting my cheeks as I told her about David's death.

"I'm flying right down," Rina said. "I'll phone the kids—we'll all be with you." Her tone caressed me, cradled me. I was no longer alone.

Charlene was right. It was a big funeral. The spacious chapel was full ten minutes ahead of time.

We viewed the body when we arrived earlier. An open casket isn't customary in the Jewish religion, but Charlene insisted. She solemnly placed a large red hibiscus blossom on David's chest, and then became hysterical. It took five minutes to calm her.

*What an act,* I thought bitterly. *Charlene thrives on melodrama.* But her grief was real—she was ripped apart by the loss of her meal ticket. I'm being too bitter. Maybe she did love the guy.

When I gazed down at my brother's face, I saw the peace he so desperately sought all his life. I dabbed my eyes with a handkerchief before a tear could escape. Even though I lived a thousand miles away, we never felt far apart. Now it was like a big hole torn in my chest. A vital part of me was missing.

Lou Bianca described how David poured his life into battling for the disabled. Establishing reserved parking places. Setting up subsidized taxi service. Fighting for accessible entrances. It was moving, but I felt he would never stop. I rose to my feet and spoke from the heart—what my brother meant to me. We put David to rest beside our mother and father. No more crutches or wheelchairs. He was free.

The next day, after so many had stopped over to pay respects, the house was quiet. The ghost of David hovered in every room.

Rina cleared the drained glasses, stacking them on a tray. She still has that athletic verve to her movements. Guess I didn't expect to have a wife look so attractive at 60.

"When are you due back?" I asked.

"I've arranged coverage for this week. I want to be with you." Rina teaches psychology and counsels several clients.

Our eyes met and embraced. *God, how I love that woman!*

I gathered the encrusted paper plates, and walked into the kitchen. Charlene looked up and said, "I've made an appointment for us to see Stone and Wertheim at three o'clock."

"Huh?" I said. "What for?"

"Stone drew up David's will. I want him to tell me exactly what I'm entitled to, okay?" Her voice carried a confrontational edge.

"Look, Charlene, I no longer follow the tradition of sitting around all week long to mourn my brother's death. But can't this wait a few days out of respect for the dead?"

"I have to know where I stand," she muttered. "If you won't go, I'll go by myself."

I could see this was going to be a bad day. I reluctantly headed for the den. "Okay, I'll go get David's will."

In a minute I was back in the kitchen, frantic. The will was missing from David's folder! But then Charlene showed me she had a copy. That was odd. David told me she didn't know he had disinherited her when she left him. Did this mean she also knows about Abe's trust?

We were ushered into a dimly lit, hickory-paneled conference room. Benjamin Stone could have been the stereotypical attorney—rotund shape, graying temples and grave visage. He flipped through the pages of the will and said, "David called me at the time, very upset. He asked me to recommend a divorce attorney, and said he was changing his will."

"We reconciled six months ago," Charlene said brusquely. "Did David make a new will after this one?"

"Not that I'm aware of," Stone said. "But under Florida law, you are entitled to one-third of his estate as his widow, regardless of what the will says."

"My brother left no financial assets," I interjected. "There's the home they now occupy, with the deed listing David, Charlene and Uncle Abe. Does that mean Charlene inherits one third of David's share?"

"I worked on that deed." Stone consulted his file. "But the way the title is worded, Charlene and the uncle now own it jointly, as survivors."

"Jointly?" I found that hard to accept. David's will specifically left the house to Uncle Abe.

"Yes," he responded. "And when one of the two dies, title goes to the survivor."

As that sank in, I felt sick. Uncle Abe is 87. Charlene shouldn't have long to wait for the other half.

I felt sicker learning that the lift-equipped Ford van and the house's furniture go to Charlene too, even though Abe's money paid for it all. Florida law overruled whatever David intended in his will. Guaranteed protection for the wife, I guess.

Charlene wasn't satisfied. "What are you going to do for *me*, Martin? I'm left a poor widow. And I'm a sick woman, okay? What will you do for me?"

I flinched under this direct onslaught. "Look—we don't have to take up Mr. Stone's time for this—"

"I've got to know." She was insistent. "I can't go on with things up in the air."

"Charlene," I said, "I understand your problem. When Uncle Abe comes home from the hospital, I'll discuss it with him. He'll surely need the kind of care he's been getting from you and David. I can't do it from up north. I'll let you know."

As we were being ushered out, I had the chilly feeling that there would be trouble. Big trouble.

Rina and I found Uncle Abe sitting up in bed, looking remarkably well after a bout of congestive heart failure. He smiled and patted down several solitary hairs on his bald pate.

"Uncle Abe," I said, holding his hand, "We're here to take you home from the hospital. But I have some sad news for you."

Abe's pale gray eyes fixed on me innocently, and I wondered if I could go on without choking up. "You won't find David when you get home. He's had an accident." I spoke slowly. "We've lost David. He's dead."

At first I thought it hadn't penetrated. Then Abe's face darkened and his lids closed. Rina put her arm lovingly around Abe. "Yes, it's a terrible loss. A terrible loss for all of us."

He gazed at her, eyes clouded with anguish. "I know," he said, voice breaking.

But knowing isn't feeling. I tried to coax his feelings out, but he wouldn't talk. As we took him out he looked crushed and bewildered. He and David had been 'The Odd Couple' for twenty-five years. When David married Charlene, he felt lost. David's death was the second of three shocks that would propel him into senility.


The next morning I walked into Uncle Abe's room and sat next to him. He put down the newspaper and looked at me.

"How do you feel?" I asked.

His gray eyes twinkled. "With my hands," he answered and held out both arms, wiggling his fingers at me.

His sense of humor was back. A good sign.

"Look, Uncle Abe, we must make a plan for the future. If you would come to live with us, you'd make me and Rina very happy."

Abe shook his head sadly. "I'd like that, but it's too cold for me up north. I'm used to Florida."

"Charlene wants you continue in this house, and she'll care for things just as when David was here."

His eyes flickered with fear. He clenched and unclenched his hands, but stayed silent.

"Is there a problem with Charlene?" I probed gently. "The door is closed. You can tell me."

After a pause he said, "She yells at me."

"Does she mistreat you?"

"She yells at me."

"You have another choice," I said. "We can set up an apartment just for you someplace in town. I'm sure Hattie would cook and clean just as she does now." Hattie was the housekeeper who came in daily.

Abe was silent. But I knew his preference.


I took Rina by the hand. "We're going for a walk."

"In this heat?" she objected. "I'd love to, but it's noon, and only mad dogs and Englishmen—"

18

"A walk," I said firmly, pulling her to the door. "We've got important things to talk about."

The Florida sun blazed down on the deserted streets of this Spanish stucco suburb. Rina and I had a habit of moving at a brisk pace, heat or no heat. A slight breeze tickled her auburn hair. Frequent palm trees provided fortunate islands of shade.

"Time for the big decision," I said. "To Charlene—or not to Charlene."

She grinned. "Isn't there a song about that?"

"This is serious business, Rina. As you know, Charlene wants to manage Abe's care after we return home. Abe doesn't want Charlene. I think he's afraid of her." And I told Rina about the alternative of Hattie and the separate apartment.

"Of course our first concern is for Uncle Abe to feel safe. But can Charlene really get by on her own? After all, she's still our sister-in-law."

"I can't cry for her. She won't exactly be destitute once she sells David's lift-equipped van and gets half the proceeds from selling this house."

Rina's eyes looked pained. She argued that losing David had been a catastrophe for Charlene, leaving her rudderless. We owed her more than casting her adrift.

"Maybe you're misjudging Charlene," said Rina. "Remember how she slept in the hospital chair for three nights when David had surgery? Didn't you tell me that she refused the money she could've won in a malpractice suit when it came to cutting David's body up? Think of the love and pleasure she brought your brother. Shouldn't you give her a chance now—when she needs it most?"

My emotions skidded and I felt irritated. How could Rina defend Charlene after she had almost wrecked our family? Not what I expected when I took Rina out for a walk and talk.

But then I heard David's voice softly reasoning with me. Was I being spiteful, vengeful? I thought about it. What would David do in my place?

"Okay, I promise to keep an open mind when we explore Abe's situation with Charlene tomorrow. And if Abe goes to his own place, maybe Charlene should get some widow support."

The next morning I saw Abe come out of the bathroom in his robe, followed by Charlene's friend Alice clad in a blood-red bikini. "I just gave Uncle Abe his bath," she announced as if she had fed the seals at the zoo.

I gazed at her enticing curves and felt vaguely uncomfortable. I pictured her leaning over and washing down Abe's bare body, her ample breasts straining to burst free from the skimpy covering.

19

"Does he give you any trouble?" I asked.

"Oh," she said lightly, "he's the original dirty old man."

*Ah, so. That's another routine we'd better scratch in the future,* I thought grimly, turning into the living room.

Suddenly Charlene tore out of her room, eyes burning black coals. "You killed my husband!" she screamed at me. "You killed my husband! I'm all alone!"

Shock rooted me to the spot. Rina and Alice came running, and Rina tried to calm her. "All this has been too much for you, Charlene. You know Martin would never have done anything to hurt David."

Charlene burst into tears, then drew herself up and glared at me. "You waited ten minutes before calling the nurse. Alice told me. Then it was too late."

Speechless, I looked at Alice for a denial. She just shrugged and said, "You told me you did all kinds of things after David started to choke."

"Damn it! Let's get this straight. I told you that I pulled him up and pounded his back. That took all of five seconds. Then I ran for the nurse."

As if tapped by a magic wand, Charlene changed from hellion to humble in a flash. "I'm sorry," she murmured. "Let's have some coffee."

My guts were straining to explode when my inner 'Not Now' grabbed me. Life sometimes can be like a balloon, blown up till it's on the verge of bursting. Suddenly the air hisses out. The balloon flips and gyrates through space almost too fast for the eye to follow. Then you see it on the ground, limp and sad. Very sad.

We sat around the kitchen table, empty cups stained with brown grains. A noisy fly swooped down to attack a crumb near my hand, and I waved it off.

"What about it?" demanded Charlene. She clipped the words like annoying drops from a faulty faucet.

I glanced at Rina. She had suggested I use a therapist's technique for avoiding a direct answer. "Suppose you tell me what you would need for managing the household and caring for Uncle Abe."

Charlene detailed her modest desires. $1,500 monthly for the supermarket. Plus all the bills to be paid: mortgage, taxes, utilities, medical costs. Plus the cook-housekeeper. Plus her car payments and gasoline, in addition to the van. Plus $200 weekly spending money for herself.

"Is that all?" I asked. It sounded to me like $6,000 a month of Abe's money, and barely enough to buy the Brooklyn Bridge.

"There may be some things I left out," she said. "I'll let you know."

I drummed my fingers on the table. "Isn't $1,500 a lot for marketing?

There's only the two of you."

"Not these days," answered Charlene without blinking. "I clip every coupon to save as much as I can."

Charlene wasn't asking to care for Uncle Abe. She was asking for a golden sinecure. I pondered how to lower the boom.

"Well?" demanded Charlene. Imperious. Cold.

I stared down at the table. "The answer is 'no'."

"What do you mean—no?" asked Charlene, eyebrows upended.

"We're just not interested in your proposition," I said.

Alice got into the act. "What's your counter offer?"

So they think we're in negotiation. But I wasn't playing. "We won't need Charlene to care for Uncle Abe. He won't be living here."

Their chins dropped and I continued, "Since a big house like this isn't needed any longer, it can be sold. You're entitled to half the proceeds, Charlene—about $15,000 after the mortgage is covered. You can also sell the van, so all together you'll have a decent nest egg."

There was a long silence while this sank in. I was prepared to offset the disappointment with a stipend for the widow, but I waited for my sister-in-law's reaction.

Charlene's hate-filled eyes drilled into me. *If looks could kill,* I thought, *call the funeral home to pick up the body.* But no artillery thundered. Charlene and Alice jumped up and took their contained fury into the bedroom.

That left me uneasy. Was the cobra coiling up behind that door, fangs unsheathed, flexing to strike? I felt my old stomach ulcer throb.

Ten minutes later Charlene stormed out and confronted me. "I want you and Rina out of my house!" she commanded. "Abe stays here!"

I raised my voice. "This is Uncle Abe's house as much as yours in the eyes of the law, and he wants me here. He's *my* uncle—not yours!"

She was unfazed. "If you are not out of here in the next thirty minutes, my rotten, scheming brother-in-law, I'll get the police to throw you out. I'm the grieving widow, and you're making passes at me!" She smiled thinly. "I have a witness, okay?"

I saw Alice in the background and felt a small chill. Throwing Charlene a look of poisonous contempt, I turned on my heel. I found Rina talking to Abe in his room, and rattled off what had happened.

"Let's move fast," I said to Rina, closing the door to keep from being overheard. "While I pack our things, throw Abe's clothes in this suitcase. We're taking him with us."

"You're on," she said. No argument.

Rina and I were just shutting the suitcases when Charlene marched over. "Time to go," she ordered.

"You're five minutes early," I retorted. "But we're leaving anyway. Rina's flying home, but I'm staying in town to clean up this mess."

"I won't let you take Abe," she warned, seeing him start to walk out with us.

"He wants to go to the airport to see Rina off," I said. "I can bring him back here later."

*I can, lady. But I won't.*

Charlene took Abe's arm and urged him to visit David's grave with her instead, but he shook her off.

We walked out the front door, and I could feel Charlene's glare drilling into our backs.

As Abe and I bade farewell to Rina at the plane, she kissed me hard and said, "I have complete confidence in you, Martin. But please. Don't ever turn your back when Charlene's around."

Seated in my rented New Yorker afterwards, I said, "Uncle Abe, you don't want to go back to Charlene, do you? Okay, so let's go to a hotel and live it up like a couple of carefree bachelors while I find you a beautiful apartment."

Abe beamed like a newly paroled prisoner, and I drove us to the Royal Poinciana Hotel. After a lighthearted dinner, I dialed Charlene.

It was her uncle's voice. When I asked for Charlene, he ignored it and barked, "Where is Abe? What have you done with him?"

"He's fine," I said evenly. "He doesn't want to return to Charlene. I just wanted her to know."

"You can't kidnap him!" yelled Mike. "We've notified the police at the airport to pick you up!"

"Abe is *my* uncle!" I barked back. *"Go to hell!"*

And I slammed down the phone.

"I thought you said they were due here at 4 p.m." Rina and I were sitting in the law offices of Weiss & Weiss, speaking to Barry Weiss.

"They're only twelve minutes late," said Barry as his phone rang. When he hung up, he said with a weary look, "They're delayed. Won't be here till five."

"I want to get this straight," I said. "What exactly did Charlene's lawyer tell you?"

Barry ran his fingers through his sandy hair and sighed. "They're coming here to discuss what we asked for: your uncle's cat, his TV set, and the rest of his clothes. And we need Charlene's agreement to put the house up for sale immediately."

"Did she agree to do it? I thought we hired lawyers to get answers." I was taking my irritation out on Barry.

He ignored it. Popping a hard candy in his mouth, he stood up. He looked muscular for a lawyer, but I suppose some lawyers find time to pump iron. "Let me show you to our conference room. I have work I must finish before five."

He ushered us down the hall. I wondered why Charlene insisted that Rina be here with me and said, "I smell something un-kosher about this meeting."

The conference room had a vaulted ceiling. Three walls were paneled in burnished oak, and the fourth was glass.

I watched stiffly as our opposition marched in. A highly agitated Charlene, looking like a ghost had just tapped her on the shoulder. Thomas Johnson, Charlene's attorney, a matchstick figure with an undertaker countenance. Alice, wearing an I-know-something-you-don't expression. And Uncle Mike, beaming with some happy secret. My sixth sense began to flicker.

Barry opened by outlining the reasons we had come together, and asked Johnson if that was his understanding. "More or less," replied the funereal voice. "The rest of Abe Bloom's clothes are in this carton. We're even returning the family photo album."

"How is my uncle?" asked Charlene.

"You mean *my* uncle," I said.

Rina said, "Abe is fine. What about returning his cat?"

The phone rang outside. Barry said, "Excuse me. I've been waiting for an important call."

Uncle Mike turned to me. "You must be rich, flying back and forth at a moment's notice." I realized that he thought I took Abe up to Connecticut and flew back for this meeting.

Mike said, "We think you're very rich. We think you're worth ten million bucks."

This was too ridiculous. I kept quiet. But my sixth sense shifted into high gear.

When Barry returned, he asked Johnson, "Is your client ready to sign an agreement for selling the house she now owns jointly with Martin's uncle, with a 50/50 split in the net proceeds?"

Mike suddenly got up and said, "I forgot to put money in the parking meter." Barry followed, explaining, "The office is closed after 5, so I've got to unlock the door."

These penny-ante interruptions were shredding my patience. *Let's get this over with.*

In a moment Barry was back and repeated the question. Johnson pursed his lips and said solemnly, "My client feels she has not been treated fairly by her brother-in-law."

"In what way?"

Johnson made a tent of his fingers. "My client is a poor, sick widow," he droned. "She insists on getting what she is entitled to."

"Can you be more specific?"

Mike came back in, and I was surprised to see him followed by a short stranger who walked directly up to me. "You Martin Richman?" he said, more a statement than a question.

"Yes—who are you?"

He thrust a sheaf of papers into my hand and turned to my wife. "Are you Rina Richman?"

She nodded, puzzled. He dropped similar papers in her lap and silently strode out.

Seeing legalisms, I passed my packet to Barry. He took one look and yelled, "What the hell! You've been served! Right here in my office!" He turned to Johnson. *"You dirty bastard!"*

I saw it all now. We were set up. Mike didn't need to feed the parking meter. We were being sued!

I looked up and saw the glee on the faces of my opponents, set off by the expressionless mask of Johnson.

As Barry skimmed the pages of our problem, he growled furiously at Johnson, "I'm going to bring you up before the Board for this dirty trick!"

Like the dark side of the moon, my world had suddenly revolved to a face I had never seen. It was only three weeks since I landed at Tampa International Airport to find David and Abe in the hospital, to watch my brother dying in my arms, to experience a volcanic eruption with my sister-in-law. I had been making these family visits for forty years. I had no idea that this trip would turn my life into a corkscrew.

Barry turned a grim face toward us. "They're suing you both on five counts. A total of nine and a half million dollars!"

I looked up at the ceiling. "I don't know whether to laugh or cry," I muttered. The cliche said it all.

# CHAPTER II
# SYMPATHY AND SURRENDER

### *David—3 years earlier*

As the years press on, I find myself fighting off emptiness. Abe can't fill it. Martin doesn't come often enough. I've usually kept myself too busy to feel lonely. But today I'm meandering through a winter forest, trees bare of leaves, an endless path.

I'm thinking of Lydia again. The only woman I've loved. We could have been together now. But no—she wanted me too fiercely. Exclusively. Overwhelmingly.

I dug out the story I finished writing yesterday and read it over critically. *My Own Galatea*—the name fits so well. I decided it was the best thing I've written so far. But why is it that I'm never satisfied? I picked up my pencil and went through it one more time.

\* \* \*

### *MY OWN GALATEA*

*I stood in the doorway of my rooming house, watching the snow sifting down from a bottomless sky.*

*Funny thing about snowflakes. Each one flutters so aimlessly until it nears the ground. Then it makes a quick frantic dance before it quietly nuzzles against its friends on the sidewalk.*

*How lonely I was!*

*Cars squished their way past, headlights probing. People were hurrying by too, each with friends or out to see friends. So I began to walk too. But I had no place to go, nobody to see.*

*Angry with myself and the world, I turned sharply and began to cross the street. The sudden screeching of brakes made me jump back. The driver screamed, "Look where you're going, Stupid!"*

*As the car picked up speed again, I heard the woman inside say, "Don't yell at him, Dear. Can't you see he's a cripple?"*

*A pretty girl touched my arm. "Some people are awful. May I help you across the street?"*

*"Oh ... no, thank you," I said shyly. As I crossed, I sensed she was right behind me. She paused on the other side as I turned to face her. My tongue choked as I said, "Good-bye, Miss." With a flicker of a smile, she left.*

*Large snowflakes whirled around my head. What girl would be interested in me—the way I move, the way I look? They just pity me. I started walking, my right foot scraping the ground with each step. I had to go someplace—anyplace.*

*I spoke to God: "Why? Why me? Why anybody? Why all this unhappiness in the world?"*

*But God didn't answer. He never does ... at least to me. Maybe he's too busy. Maybe there is no God anymore.*

*Up this street. Left. Right. Then left again. My feet seemed to be following the same crazy zigzags that my brain was meandering along.*

*There was the park entrance. Good. I was tired of walking straight streets. I needed the twisting paths of the park to match my crooked leg and my twisted mind.*

*That's when I saw her. I stopped. I stared. She was walking toward me. I moved to give her room on the path, but she came to face me and her smile was as warm as a bun right from the oven.*

*"Hello, Drolly," she said softly.*

*I was paralyzed with shock. This strange person knew my "special" name—the one I used only when talking to myself!*

*She laughed merrily, sounding like tiny bells. "You look so surprised, Drolly. Yet you always wanted me to come."*

*She took my hand and led me to a covered pavilion. There we sat without words, her fingers holding mine very tightly. As if I would leave—why, her nearness tingled my every nerve, pounded my blood, made my brain soar.*

*I guess that's why I don't know exactly how she looked or what we talked about in all that time. But what I do remember is enough.*

*Her body was all long, smooth curves flowing continuously into each other. Every motion she made was music, part of an Unfinished Symphony, with her soft, husky voice the accompaniment. Her hair—there were stray snow-petals clinging to the jet black curls—how I longed to stroke the shiny silkiness. Suddenly I did, and she didn't seem to mind.*

*Her eyes were the strangest of all, changing color with her moods. First they were green mixed with tawny yellow ... like a cat's eyes full of secrets. Then sometimes they would be a deep, distant blue ... and I knew her thoughts were far away. Then suddenly they would turn purplish red—like a flickering flame—tearing my heart apart.*

26

*How beautiful she was! Just to think of her is pain.*

*When she leaned over and kissed me, it was too much. I finally opened my eyes, and she was gone. Gone!*

*But somehow I wasn't unhappy anymore. I wouldn't be lonely anymore. She was now part of my life.*

*I struggled up the stairs and let myself into my room. Without turning on the light, I sank into my easy chair, lit my pipe, and re-lived the unbelievable.*

*Much later, that other person who lives in my mind intruded as I filled a second pipe-ful. "Listen, Drolly," it said crassly, "that was only a vision you saw tonight."*

*I grinned. "And what a vision!"*

*"But it was only a phantom, my boy!" it insisted.*

*"Now look...." I objected.*

*"Just a dream image. You reached for it so hard in your mind that you felt it as true—but it's only in your mind."*

*My heart constricted below Poe's pendulum as the sharpness swung deliberately toward my chest.*

*The other voice was merciless. "That girl was not real at all, Drolly. There is no girl!"*

*I could only wish that razor's edge would lower quickly to slice my heart in shreds.*

*"But wait!" I cried out into the darkness. "She was real! She was real to me!"*

*My thoughts were tumbling over each other. "She's my own Galatea! Remember the Greek legend about a sculptor named Pygmalion who made a statue of a woman so beautiful that he fell in love with it? He prayed to the gods to give the statue life so he could love her and she could love him. "Galatea" was her name.*

*"And isn't there a modern tale of a man plucking a girl from the street and molding her speech and personality to where he falls in love with the result? That story,* Pygmalion, *was eventually made into the musical* My Fair Lady."

*I felt delirious with triumph. "Then why can't I create* my own Galatea? *Don't I need her? Don't I love her? How can I live without her?"*

*My other voice was still. It had nothing to say.*

*That's why I wait here now, by dawn's early light, full of happy anticipation. As soon as it is night again, when all is quiet and peaceful, I shall go out into the park to greet her.*

*I know I shall see her again soon.*

\* \* \*

"Every time I come into your room these days, you're on the telephone," complained Uncle Abe.

"Sorry," I said, hanging up. "What's the problem?" And I lay back on my bed to rest. I was feeling my age.

"I only wanted to ask: would you like chicken or chopped steak for dinner tonight?"

I smiled. This man is in his eighties, still pretty active, and still caring for me as if I were a child. "You decide. Whatever you make for dinner—I'll like."

He persisted. "But which do you like better?"

"Uncle Abe, I've told you that the cook should always make the decision." I gestured as if to tip my hat to him. "And you're the best cook around."

Abe sat down next to me on the bed, and I noticed how his shoulders sagged.

"Are you feeling tired, Uncle Abe? I'll get into my wheelchair and we can go out to eat."

Abe stared at the wall. "That's not it." He looked down at the floor. "I think you're getting in too deep with this 'Help' business."

I pushed myself upright and put my hand on his shoulder. "I guess I am spending too much time on 'Help Line' these days. I didn't mean to neglect you."

"I'm just worried that when you get too involved in these volunteer activities you'll start giving away what little money you have left."

"'Help Line' is not that kind of organization. All I do is help people who have problems and nobody to turn to," I said reassuringly. "Why don't we talk about *you*, Uncle Abe? What did you do today?"

"Me?" Abe chuckled dryly. "My day is like every other day. I've seen the things I've wanted to see. I've done the things I've wanted to do." He paused and said roguishly, "By this time, I've even felt the women I've wanted to feel."

I grinned and tried another tack. "I didn't get to look at the *New York Times* today. Anything interesting happening in the world?"

He shrugged. "Same old story. The Israelis and the Palestinians are still at each other's throats. In Africa, millions are suffering and dying in wars the people don't even know what for."

This shook loose one of his old memories. "There once was a war that made me a year younger than I really am." He smiled. "It was back in Austria when the first World War had exploded. They were drafting at seventeen, and I didn't see why I should risk my life to preserve the Hapsburg Empire."

"All these years and you never told us this story?"

"So I befriended an underpaid civil servant, who changed my birth date from 1900 to 1901 in the official records just before my seventeenth birthday. And before the Army could get me, my American visa came through. The Statue of Liberty greeted me and then the United States entered the war."

"That was lucky."

His face grew sad. "My friends weren't so lucky. And what did they die for? The war to end all wars?"

*Wars. For centuries, millennia. People put on uniforms and slaughtered strangers. Nothing personal. Just a different nationality, race, religion. Too bad about the women and children who got in the way.*

Abe had another point. "Then along comes Hitler, only twenty-five years later, and he wipes out the family I left behind, along with six million other Jews. If war is wrong, what do you do about a Hitler? Are there good wars and bad wars?"

*It's a complicated world. Demagogues thirsting for power still twist minds with hatred, mesmerize them into killing for a single word: "justice." Yet if they point the gun at you, don't you have to kill before you are killed?*

"I think," I said, "the answer is in stopping the Hitlers before they get so strong that when the guns point at you it becomes a really bad war."

Abe's dinner was great, as usual. And the phone was ringing again. "Just checking in," came Martin's cheery voice. "How are things down south?"

"Hot and humid," I said. "Uncle Abe and I are floating with the tides of life."

There was a click on the line as Rina joined the conversation. "Hi, David. What's this new thing you're into?"

"'Help Line'. It's a crisis intervention service started here recently. People with emotional problems phone in and counselors listen and talk to them. We give them a friendly ear and make them feel better."

"Sounds interesting," said Rina. "But what skills do your volunteers have for doing this kind of 'instant therapy'?"

I sensed the concern in her voice. The amateur competing with the professional. "They teach us," I said. "Counselors attend three training sessions before the first case is referred. If the problem sounds serious, we urge the caller to visit a professional therapist."

My brother asked, "What kinds of cases have you handled?"

29

I searched my mind. "A woman depressed about finding a job after her husband died. A teenager upset about her parents fighting over a divorce settlement. A father worried how to handle his son who's hooked on drugs. I have a list of referral agencies. But the most important thing is holding their hands and being a good listener."

Rina's voice still sounded concerned. "But doesn't that type of service sometimes involve suicide-prone individuals? Isn't that risky if you're not a professional in the field?"

"I had a woman last week who mentioned killing herself. I made her see there was at least one person who cared. I got her to promise me she would spend thirty minutes re-thinking and making a list of the positives in her life. My next step was to contact the 'Help Line' therapist to follow up."

Martin wasn't satisfied. "How do you avoid kooks from pestering you? Once they have your phone number, they can talk you to death with nonsense. They can even track down where you live and make your life unbearable."

"Can't happen," I said. "'Help Line' operators never reveal a counselor's number or location to a client."

Martin was hearty in his approval. Rina had a cautionary comment: "Just so long as you remember the therapist's cardinal rule, David. If you get too emotionally involved with clients, you can't really help them."

Helping others really does important things for me. I realized that I had to get involved in the world again. "You're both right," I said. "But I just can't be a spectator in life."

I had been resting my eyes in a prone position on my bed, and must have drifted into sleep. So I don't know how long the phone rang before I silenced it. "David Richman? This is 'Help Line'. Please call Charlene ... her number is 973-0419. Call her immediately. She sounded desperate!"

"Right away!" I said, and dialed the number.

"Hello, is this Charlene?" I asked in a soft, warm tone. "This is David from 'Help Line'. I understand you have a problem. It often feels better to talk. Can you tell me about it?"

"Hello, David," the high, querulous voice replied. "I'm down in the dumps. Way down. Life is just too shitty and I can't take it anymore, okay? Why go on living?"

"I'm sorry you're feeling so low," I said sympathetically. "What's happened to make you feel that way?"

"My husband beat me again when he came home last night," she wailed. "Drunk again. First he manhandled me, and then he slugged me so hard that I fell over a chair and couldn't get up." She sobbed bitterly.

30

"That's terrible, Charlene," I soothed. "You say he's beaten you before this?"

"Many times. And I can't talk to Carlos—he's always angry, always yelling. I don't know what to do."

Another case of wife abuse. We can't imagine how many wives are assaulted by their husbands.

"There are always things to try, Charlene. What if you stayed with relatives or friends for a while? Maybe your absence would make him realize he can't treat you that way?"

"Nobody has room for me. Besides—you don't know Carlos' hot Latin temper. He would come after me and beat me silly."

"You could go to the police."

"Hmpf. They can't protect me twenty-four hours a day."

I paused. If only there was a battered women's group in the area to help this tortured soul. I racked my brains for what to say next.

"I can imagine how you must feel. Does he hit your children too?"

There was a pause. "We have no children. My husband is sixty-four years old."

"Oh. How old are you, Charlene?"

Another pause. "I'm thirty-eight."

I digested this. "Charlene—you're still young ... in the prime of life. Why don't you simply leave him and build your own future? You can have many happy times ahead of you."

Her voice had the depressed tone of the condemned. "Where would I go? Where would I get the money to live on?"

"Look, Charlene," I talked upbeat, "you could get yourself a job and rent a furnished room or apartment. Your husband wouldn't know where you are to annoy you. Then later, you could get a divorce and find yourself the right man. You're still young."

She began to sob again. "I can't work for a living. I'm disabled, okay?"

"Disabled? How?"

"I've got a bad heart. Also a diabetic condition, okay? I have to take a shot every morning." More tears. "I get checks from the government. But I couldn't live on my own with only three hundred dollars a month."

My heart warmed toward her. She was a fellow traveler in a world that takes a healthy body for granted, a world that looks upon us with defensive pity, a world that says it wants to help—but makes it so hard for us to help ourselves.

"Charlene," I said, "I may understand you better than you know. You see, I'm disabled myself. So I have a real feeling for what you're going through."

31

"You do?"

"One thing we disabled people must never do is give up hope. There must be a silver lining hiding in all those dark clouds." I tried to give my voice a nurturing feeling, skipping over the wires to pat her shoulder, to hold her hands.

I guess I reached her. Her sobbing subsided.

"You're so good to talk to, David. You're so understanding. You make me feel so much better."

"But I want to hear you say that you won't give up, that you'll stop thinking about doing away with yourself."

After a moment she said, "I'm really not a quitter, David. I know I've got to find some way out of my problem." She had now calmed down after the emotional storm.

"Just remember," I said, putting starch in my voice, "there *are* people in this world who care about you, Charlene. I'm going to give you the number of an agency in Tampa to help you. You simply can't continue to suffer beatings from your husband."

She was so effusive in her thanks that I had difficulty in closing our conversation.

"I'm going out to do a little shopping," said Abe.

When I wheeled out of the bathroom ten minutes later, I heard the phone ringing insistently. I pushed hard to reach it in time. I thought of Charlene being in such a state that failure to catch me might even trigger her suicide.

Charlene's troubled voice was higher pitched than usual. "Hello, David. I appreciate your giving me your phone number. It's devastating every time I call 'Help Line' and they insist on referring me to some nincompoop who doesn't know my case and asks the silliest questions."

"We're not supposed to give out our numbers," I said, "but in your case I didn't see any harm."

"Then why can't I come to your place and talk to you in person? There's nothing like the personal touch, okay? You would help me much more that way, David."

"No, Charlene. It's against the rules." I was firm. "Now tell me—how did you make out at that agency?"

She sniffed. "I went for the appointment. But they couldn't help me."

Charlene had a habit of talking that way. She wouldn't give the details unless you asked. So I asked.

"They put my name on their waiting list. They're very busy, okay?"

"Did you tell them your husband beats you often?"

"Of course. They gave me sympathy. But I need to be rescued, okay?"
I digested this.

"I tried your advice last night," Charlene said. "Carlos wasn't drunk when he came home, so I fixed him a fancy dinner of what he likes best. Afterwards I told him how his beatings were driving me to suicide."

"What did he say to that?"

"He just got mad and slapped my face." She sniffled. "He said I didn't have the nerve to do myself in."

But what if she does? Would a man who beats his wife feel guilty? Probably not.

I thought hard. "Charlene, if he keeps beating you, it seems to me that you'll have to make a break with him sooner or later."

"But he warned me that if I walked out on him, he would move heaven and earth to find me, and beat me to a bloody pulp!"

I tried to reassure her. "I'm sure you could get a court order which would put him in deep trouble if he came near you once you filed for a divorce."

"But David, even if I did...." Her voice was drenched with desperation, "where could I go? I don't have enough money to pay rent and buy groceries and medicines."

I searched for an answer. "You mentioned having a good friend. Couldn't she let you move in with her temporarily?"

"Alice is a wonderful person and she'd do anything for me, okay? But Alice has two kids plus a live-in boyfriend." I heard her start to cry. "I just can't face Carlos coming home tonight and slamming me around. It's Friday and he always gets soused after collecting his paycheck." She was spurting out phrases between sobs.

I had run out of ideas, so I fell back to being gentle and comforting. "Look, Charlene—there must be an answer to your problem. Let's think about it and talk some more tomorrow."

"I don't see any way out." Her voice had a ring of finality to it. And her phone clicked off.

I stared out my window and became aware of perspiration dripping from my forehead. A bit frantic, I tried to remember if I had ever felt this way before. I picked up the phone and dialed her number.

"Charlene—I'm worried about you. I wanted to remind you that you promised not to do anything rash without talking to me." My voice turned soft and warm. "You know that I care what happens to you—don't you? And that I will do everything in my power to help you?"

"I know," she said and let the silence build between us. "But talking isn't enough."

33

Abe was looking wan and listless. I tried again to persuade him that it's time to slow down. But he refused to see that a little help in the house wouldn't undermine his indispensability.

"I'll think about it," he said, and rolled the vacuum cleaner out of my room.

I went back to revising my short story. Just as I was transferring from my wheelchair to the bed for some rest, the doorbell chimed like a flutist practicing the first few notes.

"Who can that be just before lunch?" wondered Abe, as he walked by my door to respond. A moment later he poked his head back into my room. "It's a young woman who says she knows you."

"What's her name? I'm not expecting anyone and I feel like taking a nap."

"She didn't say," said Abe, "but would you turn away a pretty lady at your door?" He stepped aside to let her into my room.

I was busy straightening the folds of my bedding when a powerful orange blossom fragrance enveloped me. I looked up at the stranger standing before me, and I found her staring directly into my eyes.

"Hello David," she said earnestly. "I'm Charlene."

I froze as I recognized the voice of my suicide-prone phone pal. I fought to control my surprise and upset at seeing her appear in my home.

"What are you doing here? How did you get my address?" I challenged her harshly.

"That's my little secret, David," she said coyly. "'Help Line' wouldn't give it out. I tried and tried."

I studied her and saw an attractive woman in her thirties. She had a cupid-doll face which didn't really match her spreading bulk. She must weigh 250 pounds, I thought, amazed that such a small voice could come from such a big woman.

I shifted uncomfortably in the bed, wishing I were still in my wheelchair, where I wouldn't feel at such a psychological disadvantage.

"You know you're not supposed to be here, Charlene," I said firmly. "It's an unbreakable rule. Sure I'm anxious to help you. But you must leave right away and speak to me only by phone. Please go."

Her shoulders sagged and her face collapsed into pathetic furrows. "I have no place to go, okay?" She let out a heart-tugging sob. "He hit me so hard last night that I thought my jaw was broken. And then he forced me to—to do all kinds of horrible things … worse than ever before."

She took out a handkerchief and tears gushed down her face. "This time I just can't go back, David."

There was a long silence as we stared at one another. I became aware of flaming red hair setting off her sharp features: pert, upturned nose, cupid-bow crimson lips and jet black eyes heavily accented in blue mascara. In spite of her girth, I felt a disturbing attraction which I pushed out of my mind.

"Look, Charlene," I said. "You're carrying a very serious problem on your shoulders and I do want to help you. But you can't stay here. I'll phone around. There must be some organization that can put you up until you can get on your own feet. Were you involved with any church?"

She looked at me forlornly. "No. My father was Catholic and my mother was Jewish. But I never paid any attention to religion."

I pulled over the Yellow Pages and began to thumb through. Charlene walked over to a chair uninvited and sat down. That's when Abe stuck his head in the door and said, "Don't get started on the telephone, David. I've got lunch all ready and there's plenty. If your friend can join us, I'll set an extra plate."

I closed the phone book. A decision had just been made for me, even if Abe wasn't aware of it. What could I do?

It was a light lunch: salmon patties and salad. Charlene had somehow transformed herself into a light-hearted, effervescent companion, her cares evaporated. She charmed Abe with questions which were thinly disguised compliments. And she surprised me by facets of her personality she hadn't revealed before, particularly her rapid-fire speech pattern.

"Youcan'timaginehowfantasticitfeelstositwithnormalpeopleatanormal mealandnotfeelafraidokay?"

At times, Charlene seemed to be speaking in a foreign tongue. She would accelerate a sentence as if she couldn't wait for the period at the end, so that the small words got run over in the process. Abe and I found ourselves asking her frequently to repeat, and I finally implored her to speak more slowly.

Charlene insisted on serving the coffee. After she set down her empty coffee cup, she patted the napkin around her mouth with a contented sigh. "You may consider this an ordinary lunch, gentlemen. But I haven't felt so marvelously treated in years."

"I'm glad to see how much this has uplifted your mood," I said.

"You know," Charlene said, "I felt like a disaster when I got on the bus this morning. I fumbled all over my pocketbook and couldn't seem to find the right change. Then this skinny black woman reached right through me to toss her coins in. Okay, but she didn't have to whomp me so hard on the backside that I almost fell on top of the driver!"

"Can you slow down?" asked Abe. "My old ears can't listen as fast as you talk."

"Sure," she continued. "Black or no—I couldn't let her get away with that, okay? I told her off with big red-letter words. I just didn't care if she or one of her fuzzy-haired brothers might pull a knife on me."

An uncomfortable silence settled in. I was irritated by the racial slurs, as I'm sure Abe was. But I hesitated about chiding Charlene while she was riding her emotional high.

Charlene continued unconcernedly. Then I noticed, as she unreeled other personal experiences, that her logic seemed to take kangaroo jumps, often in unexpected directions. Disconcerting. But exciting to listen to.

"Time to get back to work," I said, wheeling myself back to my room. Doggedly, I ran through a round of discouraging phone calls as she sat quietly nearby, again a deflated personality wearing an orphan's expression. Saturday afternoon was not a good time to find people in.

I blocked the mouthpiece as I asked her, "Can you handle a part-time job?"

"Sure," she answered plaintively. "But I never know when my heart starts to act up, or my diabetes gets me hyper. Bosses hate it when they can't depend on you on a regular basis."

I hung up wearily. "Some of these organizations would arrange to put you up temporarily. But they want assurance that you can get on your own feet again. Otherwise they consider you a case for government welfare."

"I can't get welfare when I already get disability payments."

"There's got to be an answer," I said, picking up the phone again. "Let me call some politicians and other people I know."

Charlene jumped up and said she would help Abe with the dishes. She filled the doorway, but her bulk was minimized by her quick, fluid movements, propelled by frenetic energy.

Two hours later, I had exhausted the phone and myself. I was sweating in spite of the air-conditioning, and felt vastly irritated by my lack of progress. All I had was a string of vague 'maybes.' Even my 'Help Line' people were of no help. (Naturally, I didn't tell them Charlene had made a personal confrontation with her counselor in his own home.)

I was down, but Charlene was up. She waltzed gaily into my room, Abe following close behind. "David," she cried excitedly, "guess what? That master chef, Abe Bloom, has graciously allowed me to cook the dinner tonight. I've challenged him to a cooking contest. And you are to be the judge!"

I felt I was slipping into quicksand and was about to torpedo the plan. Then I saw Abe's beaming face—the look of a man who has been exposed to a delightful new experience. I just couldn't prick that bubble, any more than put the lid on Charlene's effervescence. "She really is a good cook," said Abe, with a mixture of surprise and admiration. "And now she's washing the dishes. Some change for me."

"Yes, but she's not supposed to be here. It's against the 'Help Line' rules. She'll have to leave, and we can't allow her to come anymore."

Abe rubbed his chin. "She told me how her husband keeps beating her up, and that she has no place to go. Can't you bend the rules a little and let her stay here tonight?"

Before I could put my foot down, Charlene flounced into the dining room carrying two dishes of ice cream smothered with fruit salad, chocolate syrup and whipped cream, topped with a maraschino cherry. "My iceberg dessert concoction," she announced with fanfare.

Abe accepted his portion with unconcealed delight. "I always forget to serve anything on the ice cream. But—where's your dish, Charlene?"

"Don't worry, Uncle Abe," she said, heading for the kitchen. She was back in a moment with a clone dessert, except that hers had a higher mound of whipped cream. "You didn't think I would pass this up, did you?" She punched her spoon into the goo and shoveled it into her mouth in rapid strokes.

I stared at her. "When you have diabetes, Charlene, is it a good idea for you to be eating such a rich dessert?"

She didn't miss a beat. "What I eat doesn't affect my diabetes. What sends my level up is aggravation, okay?"

I was becoming accustomed to Charlene's habit of tossing out a tremulous 'okay?' in a plea for approval. Charlene had again followed her own convoluted logic. I felt vaguely uncomfortable about my ability to help this woman.

Charlene licked her lips and turned. "Uncle Abe, how old are you?"

"What makes you think I'm old?" joshed Abe, aiming the cherry at his mouth as he parodied the facial expression of an eager child.

I grinned. "We gave Uncle Abe an eightieth birthday party five years ago."

Charlene stopped her loaded spoon in midair "Eighty-five! You gotta be kidding." She took a hard look at Abe. "And you and David live here by yourselves, with you doing all the shopping and cooking and everything?"

"It's a great life, if you don't weaken," said Abe, using a favorite expression.

Charlene fed her face another monster spoonful and said, "I just can't believe you care for David and run the whole shebang here at your age,

Uncle Abe. Tell me, how did you learn to cook so well?"

Abe pushed his plate away, half eaten. "You see, I never married. So I learned in self-defense."

"Never married?" said Charlene. "A handsome devil like you!"

"Why should I settle on one woman," asked Abe blandly, "and deprive all the others?"

Charlene turned to me as she scooped up another iceberg in her spoon. "What a great sense of humor Uncle Abe has! And what about you, David? Ever been married?"

"I'm still waiting for my true love to come rolling along in her wheelchair," I said with mock seriousness.

Charlene stopped her spoon in midair as if transfixed by an arrow. She slowly returned it to her bowl and began collecting the other dishes. Her voice descended to a flat plane. "I'm waiting for my true love too," she said.

Abe poked his head into my room. "It was nice of you to invite Charlene to stay here overnight. She's all set. The bed in the guestroom was already made up, and I gave her towels. But we have no pajamas big enough. The only robe I could find for her was the one your father used long ago. And she's so big that it barely goes around her."

"She certainly is a big woman," I agreed. "And yet she's light on her feet. What do you think of her, Uncle Abe?"

He winked. "She's the cat's meow."

"I'm not talking about her looks."

"She has a jolly personality," said Abe at the doorway. "She just shouldn't speak so fast."

Charlene pushed him out of the way to step into my room. "What are you two bachelors saying about me behind my back?"

I noticed that her robe sash was tied, but the robe itself couldn't quite make the circumference, leaving a tantalizing inch gap in the middle.

I pulled my gaze away quickly. "You should have a peaceful night's sleep tonight, Charlene. This is one night your husband can't abuse you. Then tomorrow I'll steer you to the one source I think may have something for you."

Charlene turned and gave Abe a kiss on his bald pate. "That's for being such a good boy, Uncle Abe," she cooed brightly. "Good night."

Then she strode over to my bed and placed a light kiss on my lips before I knew what was happening. "And you, David," she said, "saved my life!"

I'm up late every night. My habit is to read till about two a.m. before feeling sleepy enough to turn off the bed lamp.

It was an hour after the house grew quiet that I became aware of a scratching noise at my bedroom door.

"May I come in?" the whispered female voice asked.

I hesitated. "Come on in," I hissed back.

Charlene held her hand over her eyes to block the glare as she entered, creating an even wider reveal in her borrowed robe. "I'm sorry to disturb you, David, but I noticed a light under your door so I knew you weren't asleep."

I tore my eyes away from the gap and up to her face. "That's all right, Charlene. What's the problem?"

She approached the bed. "I've tossed and turned, and I just can't sleep. I'm worried and frightened, okay? Do I really have a future?"

She sniffled and bowed her head. "There I go again—burdening you with my troubles. In the middle of the night, yet."

My voice tried to massage her pain. "I can imagine how you're feeling, Charlene. But you don't realize what a capable person you really are. You make a very good appearance. And you have lots of energy. All you need is more confidence in yourself. I'm sure you can make it."

She was quiet for a moment, and then began to sob. She sank down on my bed with her face in her hands, her shoulders giving spasmodic little jerks.

I put my arm on her shoulder to comfort her. "Charlene, don't worry. It will be all right. You can free yourself from that man starting tomorrow. I know you can do it."

"Oh David," she said, tears flowing as she lifted her face. "You're such an understanding person. You're so kind. Not like my father. He was a Spaniard, and he hated me for being a female. He wanted sons, and my mother gave him only a daughter. He never forgave her, and he always hated me."

"I'm sure your father didn't actually *hate* you...."

"He did, he did. He would take his strap to me all the time—even after I got out of high school. That's why I ran away from home."

This woman had a history of being abused by men. No wonder she was so demolished by wife beating.

"That must have been rough."

She let out a big sob. "I've had so many rough things happen to me in this life. Terrible things. It has never worked out for me, okay? And now being out all night. Carlos will go wild. When he finds me, he'll beat me bloody. I'm so scared."

39

I began to stroke her shoulder. "Listen to me, Charlene. Things *will* work out better for you this time. You'll see. Don't be afraid."

Silence and more sobbing.

Then she emitted a deep moan. "I *am* afraid," she wailed frantically. And with a surprisingly quick movement, she twisted out of her robe and slid under the covers next to me. She thrust her big naked shivering body up against mine and cried out, "Hold me! I must have someone hold me tight. *Please.*"

Someone else was writing my new story.

# CHAPTER III
# SERENDIPITY

## *Charlene—One Day Later*

A woman's gotta look her best, and I needed my best right now. I fussed with my lipstick. I fussed with my hair. Then I popped out of the bathroom and gave David a lingering kiss. "Don't miss me too much, Honey," I said.

"Where are you going, Charlene?"

"While my husband's out working, I'll pack up my clothes. Be back in a couple of hours, okay?"

I just couldn't wait to tell Alice about David. It all happened just as I planned. Even better. I can't believe it was so easy. Po' little ole me finally got a break.

Alice was already waiting at our favorite greasy spoon, the *Alamo*. She and I been close since we were kids. *Simpático*, and how. We've both been banged around by rotten men all our lives.

"I knew you couldn't talk when you called me," she said excitedly. "So give!"

I slid into the booth and pursed my lips in anticipation. "I have finally latched on to the golden cow."

"For real?" She was dying to hear the dirt.

"You should see his house. The living room has this barn-like Spanish ceiling with polished mahogany planks. Big lily-white circular couch. Fancy Oriental rug covering the floor. Twelve-foot chandelier. Marble fireplace. Like Hollywood, okay?"

Alice whistled.

"You walk through that and you're in their 'Florida Room.' Jalousied windows all around. It's a place just to relax in. They don't really need it. The dining room's got built-in shelves filled with fancy Chinese gimcracks. You look out on their backyard and see the waving palm trees and those gorgeous hibiscus bushes, okay?"

"You got me salivating," said Alice. "But stop holding out. How did you work it?"

"Shit, it was easy. You know how down I was. I was scraping bottom and it showed. I didn't have to act, okay? David pitied me, and I pushed it for all it was worth."

"Cut the crap. Give with the details."

"Don't rush me." I was enjoying this. "At first David insisted I had to leave. The rules of 'Help Line', okay? But he's got an old geezer living with him. David's got a soft spot for Uncle Abe, and I played up to him. So he was on my side in getting David to let me sleep over in their guestroom. 'Just for the night,' okay?"

"This is getting better and better."

"By the time I got to bed, I was feeling no pain. But I couldn't sleep. What if I couldn't stay? What if David found a place to take me in to protect me from my husband? What if he pushed me out his door and I had to go back to getting my head bashed in again, okay? I tossed and turned. I kept sliding deeper into a hole. I started thinkin' about suicide again, okay?

"Then I thought, *Fuck it! I can't leave this place. I've got to do something!*"

"Yes…?" Alice was breathless.

"So I walked into David's room. He was still up reading. He saw how red my eyes were. I cried some more, and he comforted me. First time I ever got close to a man like that, okay? So caring."

"Yeah. So…? So…?"

"Christ! Don't rush me!" Sometimes Alice is too much. Couldn't she tell how important this was to me? I calmed myself down. "It was a very tender moment. Like you see in the soaps. So I slipped in under the covers to be comforted."

"To be *comforted*?" repeated Alice with a horselaugh

"Can't you just listen without farting?" I hissed at her. "Something like this never happened to me before! I thought all men were gorillas, vampires sucking between our legs, okay? But David is something special."

Alice looked skeptical. "You mean you didn't—"

"Oh, sure. I comforted him right back. I wanted him to know that I loved him, so I went crazy with passion. I wanted to show him I was as important to him as he was to me."

Alice was now getting the message. She stared at me seriously. "You mean —I never thought you could fall in love after all you've been through."

"There's always a first time," I said, vaguely aware that I was also trying to convince myself.

"Well," she murmured, "if you're going to love somebody, it's a good idea to pick somebody who's loaded."

I smiled. "Not only is David loaded, but he's a sheep. A sweet softie. I know how to handle him, okay? I'm sure I can get him to marry me."

"What about Carlos?" Alice was worried about my husband.

"David will help me get the divorce. No problem."

"But David's a cripple!" cried Alice. "What kind of sex can you have with a cripple—and an old man to boot?"

I smirked. "You'd be surprised. This guy's been saving it up for so many years that he erupts like a volcano. All I have to do is wiggle. And sex with a cripple is kinky!"

Alice's eyes were popping. "You've got to tell me all about it!"

I picked up the luncheon menu. "After we order, okay? I'm starving. But I owe you one for tracking down David's address from his phone number. Lucky for me you work for the phone company."

The radio started to play a real oldie: "The Darktown Strutters' Ball." I pulled Uncle Abe up from his chair and said, "C'mon, let's you and me dance."

"I'm too old, Charlene," he pleaded, holding back.

I guffawed. "You're never too old to have fun." I took one arm and put it on my hip. I grabbed his right hand. And then we were whirling around the living room to the lively beat. Abe was breathless, but doing just fine.

"Plenty of piss and vinegar left in the old boy, eh?" I smiled at Uncle Abe. He was flattered, but I noticed a shadow in his eyes. Gotta watch my language around this family. Uncle Abe tells off-color jokes, but he likes his women to be angels.

Then I noticed David in his wheelchair by the fireplace. His eyes were pleased as punch, getting his kicks from watching us trip around. It was like he had transported himself into Uncle Abe's body.

I showed off with more shimmy. The trumpet was really hot, even if the music was ancient. I was enjoying myself as much as anybody. It's been a long time, baby.

Uncle Abe was doing great, for an old fart. I wondered if he was a dirty old man. This was a good time to test. As we danced, I wriggled my big breasts into his chest. And I pressed my body into him. But he didn't feel me up. A gentleman, no less.

The music ended with the horn staking off into space. "Wunderbar!" huffed Abe, leaning on my arm as I led him back to his easy chair. "Thank you, Charlene."

"I knew you had it in you, Uncle Abe," I said. "You just needed somebody to bring it out."

I turned my attention to David, who was sitting there beaming at us. "Can

I get you anything, David? A cold drink? Some grapes? I want to do something for you too, okay?"

He smiled at me. "You're quite a woman, Charlene. Only yesterday you were on the verge of tossing your life away—you were so depressed. Now you've got bells on your toes."

I stared down at the carpet and my head moved slowly from side to side. "I forgot what it is to be light-hearted … till now. I didn't think I could laugh again until I came into this house, okay? David, you and Uncle Abe are like magicians. I feel like I've wandered into a fairy tale."

It seemed like my voice was weaving a spell. Nobody was saying anything.

"But the monster is still waiting out there," I added. "Who is there to slay him and save the maiden?"

David inched his wheelchair up to me and looked into my eyes. "I think it's time we seriously figured out how you can get a divorce," he said.

"I'd like you both to meet my old friend, Alice," I said. "Alice, this is David. And this is Uncle Abe."

Don't know why I was so formal. Alice shook hands with each one, saying she had heard such nice things about them. "Maybe you don't realize it," she said, "but you've saved Charlene's life."

They poo-poo'ed this, but I backed Alice up. "If it wasn't for you guys, I wouldn't be standing here today," I said firmly. "But is anybody hungry? With Uncle Abe's permission, I've cooked up a Hungarian goulash with all the trimmings, okay? This is going to be a dinner to remember!"

As we arranged ourselves around the dining room table, I started with a fancy appetizer. It made a big hit. Alice was telling them about herself. "I'm the original working mother. Husband deserted me when my kids were toddlers. I've been slaving away ever since, and just barely making it."

I served the soup: mushroom barley. I didn't mention it came out of a can. Too many compliments for me to admit it.

The goulash was my own special concoction. I got the recipe from a crazy Hungarian I once picked up in a bar who claimed he had 51% gypsy blood. But I mellowed down his concoction over the years, dropping this and adding that. Now it's original Charlene.

They all loved it.

I brought out the coffee and my favorite dessert: strawberry ice cream swimming in chocolate syrup and crowned with whipped cream. Not the best thing in the world for my figure. But it topped off the evening for my audience.

"Charlene tells me that you're helping her get a divorce," said Alice. "I saw how her husband abused her, and I'm happy to be a witness."

"A marriage shouldn't be a prison where people are tortured," said David. "My lawyer said that this divorce should go quickly."

"But Carlos has that hot Latin temper," said Alice. "What if he comes here to beat Charlene up and force her to drop the suit?"

David smiled. "He won't try it. My lawyer got a court order that will throw him in jail if he comes anywhere near Charlene before the hearing."

"He doesn't know where I am," I said. "If he did, that sonofabitch would still come after me."

This house is a mess. Not the usual mess. I mean: for people who are rich, they shouldn't be living like this.

Take the living room drapes, for example. Fancy-schmancy, but they've begun to unravel at the edges. No wonder. They're at least twenty-five years old.

This place is crying for a woman's touch. Nothing's been done since David's mother died a long time ago. And I just love decorating a home.

"Uncle Abe," I said one day, "Tell me if I'm getting too personal. But are you folks running out of money?"

"What makes you ask that question?"

I took him by the hand and showed him the drapes.

"I never noticed," he said sheepishly.

As we walked into David's room, he switched off his electric shaver. I described the fraying drapes. "I know a place where we can get a 50% discount on custom-made draperies. Uncle Abe thinks it's a good idea for us to drive over there this afternoon. What do you think?"

Later on they both agreed to replacing the towels and the bed linens. Curtains in the bedrooms came next. And at a second-hand shop I found a gorgeous Spanish mahogany sideboard that was perfect for the living room so I could toss out the shitty old piece in the corner.

That jalousied Florida Room was like an old grandfather clock: nice to look at but of no use. Why not eat our breakfast and lunch there, I asked. The Spanish tile floor was one step down from the rest of the house, so I brought in a contractor to raise it and make the room wheelchair accessible.

I was now driving the van most of the time. The driveway alongside the house was so narrow that it was tough for me with my big ole carcass to get out when David needed room on the other side. So we had a front section of the lawn paved.

I was now cooking all the meals, with Abe's help. He was jolly—a real

45

kidder and fun, for an old guy. We would do the food shopping together. He'd have funny stories to tell about his old days in the food business. He and I would make the beds and do the cleaning. But I wanted to make myself indispensable, so I soon talked him into letting me do those chores.

David and I were moving closer together. We would have long talks, mostly about me and the problems in my life. The things he's most interested in, I just don't dig. Who cares about the government's budget deficit and what happens in Mesopotamia? Who cares if the universe is expanding? Not my cup of tea. He reads, and I watch TV.

But the thing we're both excited about is helping the disabled. We've decided to start a new organization called Disabled Voters of Florida to put pressure on the politicians for the rights of the disabled. My idea.

Everything has been shaping up like a dream.

"How about us all going out to dinner to celebrate?" I called out after hanging up the phone.

"Celebrate what?" asked Abe, sitting at the foot of David's bed.

I was wearing a big smile. "That was your lawyer, David. My divorce is final. I'm free!"

I got a kiss and a hug all around. They shared my excitement as if I were already part of the family. Well, as Abe was fond of saying: it won't be long now.

I put on my best dress. I took extra pains with my mouth, my eyes, my hair. I had to look real good. I was coming down the home stretch.

We boarded the van and set off for our favorite restaurant, *The Breakers*. They offer an early-bird special: a complete dinner with a choice of three great entrees. At the unbelievable price of only $6.95. "It hardly pays to cook and do the dishes," Abe said when I introduced them to the place. So we've made a habit of going there Sundays.

Tonight was a bonus. Naturally we ordered champagne. "A toast," said David, raising his glass, "to Charlene's new life. May it be as delightful as these bubbles, and as satisfying as this champagne tastes."

"I like that," I said as we clinked glasses and sipped.

"In my salad days," said Abe, "I once met a woman who was bubbly. But she didn't turn out to be satisfying."

"You're a fine one to judge, Uncle Abe," kidded David. "Look at all those women you went out with, and you were never satisfied."

That was my cue. "It's not easy to find the right partner. Many people never do even though they marry."

"But it's never too late," said David lightly. I sure hope he meant that.

46

It was late when we got back. Abe said he was tired, and went right to bed. David said he felt like doing some reading. He's always reading. So I went into the kitchen and brought back his favorite drink, warm milk with honey.

He put down his book with a smile. I said, "I've been on a cloud all evening. Till we got home. Suddenly it's a dark cloud."

His smile switched to a puzzled frown. "I don't see why, Charlene."

I sat down next to him. "I owe you so much, David. You've given me new life. But now that I'm free to do what I want to, I'm afraid of the future, okay? The world looks scary out there."

David took my hand in his. "Sure, it feels new and strange, Charlene. But for the first time you have nothing to fear. You are now the master of your future."

"I can't keep sponging on you and Uncle Abe. And I don't see how I can make it on my own."

"Charlene, you're very good at giving massages. You can take that course you mentioned and become a masseuse." David was being his kind, comforting self. "Meanwhile, you're not sponging. You cook. You clean. You please Uncle Abe. And—" his eyes twinkled, "you make things mighty pleasant for me."

"I'm glad you said that, David. I was beginning to feel that you take me for granted." I let my head droop. "No woman likes to feel she's just a mistress."

He was quick to reassure me that he thought too much of me for that.

"David," my voice became intense, "I'm happy to be your mistress. You're fabulous in bed. You send fireworks up my spine. But it's more than that. You're so easy to talk to. You're so considerate. I've never met a man like you. You're the top banana."

David's temper suddenly erupted. *"Don't use that expression!"* he barked.

I reared back, startled. What weird hot button had I pressed? It was the first time I ever saw him get mad. And I could tell he was really burned.

"I'm sorry," I murmured. "Did I say something wrong?"

He frowned. "Someone else called me that, years ago." He turned his face away. "It brought back a memory I'd rather forget."

Then he apologized. He said I was very important to him. He said lots of things to make me feel better. But never once did he mention the one word I was dying to hear. Love.

He didn't love me. Yet. I still had a ways to go.

That night I made furious love to him.

I was straightening up the living room the next day when the phone rang. I heard David pick up and say, "Oh, hello, Martin."

He speaks with his brother from Connecticut at least once a week. They have really long conversations. Often what they talk about is over my head.

Sometimes his brother's wife gets on the line. And they always bring Abe in to talk about the family. That's what makes me mad. They're all so lovey-dovey. I'm just a fucking outsider.

This anger yanked at my intestines all day. But I stifled my feelings. After dinner, when I shuffled into David's room, he asked me what was wrong.

"Nothing, okay?"

"I can tell when there's something on your mind. You know you can let it out with me, Charlene."

I thought about how to put it. "We've been together for two months, David. Isn't that right?"

"Yes. Seems longer than that."

"And in all that time, you haven't mentioned me to your brother, Martin. Isn't that right?"

David showed surprise. "I guess that's so."

I waited for that to sink in. "Why?"

He thought about it and shrugged his shoulders. "I don't know. It just never came up."

"In other words, I'm not important, okay? What shall we call me—Miss Nobody?"

"Now you know that's not so, Charlene," he said, beckoning me to sit next to him on the bed. But I stood my ground.

"What else can I think, David? You never mentioned me once in all this time to your brother and his wife. If you took a puppy or a kitten into the house, you would tell him about it!"

"You're right." He rubbed his forehead and his eyes looked distressed. "You'll be number one the next time I speak to Martin."

"What will you say? 'I've picked up a mistress lately who's great in bed? She also does the cooking and cleaning?'"

David's face was pained. "Charlene, you know that's not the way I feel about you!"

"No. I *don't* know, okay? Maybe it's time you said how you *do* feel about me!"

"We've talked about that many times, Charlene. You're just upset this evening. Come sit by me and we'll clear this up."

I wouldn't buy his soothing. "Did you ever tell me you cared for me, David?"

"Well, of course I care for you. I don't have to say it in words. I show it."

"Like you care for a puppy or a kitten who's homeless and forlorn?"

"Oh, come on, Charlene! You know that's not what I mean."

"Well, what do you mean? Do you care for me a little or a lot?"

"I care for you a lot."

"Do you care for me enough to miss me if I'm away from you?"

"Yes, I'd miss you."

"Would you miss me very much?"

"Yes, I'd miss you very much."

"And do you like me enough to want me to stay on as your lover? To take care of you? To work together for the cause we believe in? To have fun and be partners in what life brings?"

David nodded in reassurance.

I rushed to his side and flung my arms around him. I kissed him hard and stared in his eyes. "Does that add up to a proposal of marriage?"

I didn't wait for his answer. "I *love* you, David. You're the only man I've ever loved. I love you fiercely, and I'll never let you go."

I hugged him tightly. "I'm deliriously happy," I said. And I was.

David slept late. I had breakfast with Abe, and prepared a tray for David. I kept peeking into the bedroom till it was time to bring in the tray.

"'Morning, Sweetheart," I sang cheerfully. "Sleep okay?"

He looked at me. "I couldn't seem to wake up."

I laughed. "I don't want to ever wake up. This dream is good enough for me."

He gave a small cough. "Now about last night—"

An icicle touched my heart. "David! You haven't changed your mind about me?"

"No ... it's not that." He was having trouble finding the words. "It's ... it's that it all happened so fast. I'm trying to sort out my own feelings. I'm trying to understand what all this means...."

"But you know that I love you deeply, don't you?"

"Yes, I know."

"And you know that you don't want me to leave you, that you want me to stay around and share your life?"

He was thinking hard. "Yes, I do," he said slowly.

"Well? Then what's the problem?"

He was slow to answer. "Charlene, I'm almost twice your age, and getting older."

"So what? I prefer older men. They're more settled. And smarter, okay?"

"I'm a paraplegic."

"I'm one of the disabled, too, so I understand you. And I want to take care of you, Sweetie, okay?"

He gave a long sigh. "There's one other important thing. Uncle Abe has been taking care of me for many years. He's a father to me. I wouldn't do a thing to hurt him."

"He's a doll," I said. "I wouldn't hurt him either."

"I'm not sure you understand. Uncle Abe and I have been together too long to be separated. You and I can't get married unless you agree that he continues to live with us, and be cared for just as you care for me."

"Of course," I said.

"I want to be sure you understand this clearly."

"I know," I said, slapping my thigh with glee. "You mean that I'm marrying the both of you!"

David rolled into the living room and guided his wheelchair next to Uncle Abe, who looked up from his newspaper with a smile.

"How's our Uncle Abie feeling this afternoon?" I said brightly, coming up alongside David.

Abe put down the paper and pulled his old gag. "With my hands," he said, clasping and unclasping his fingers.

David said, "You like Charlene, don't you, Uncle Abe?"

"Of course. She's very likeable."

"Wouldn't it be nice if she didn't leave us to go off on her own? Would you like to see her stay on with us?"

"That would be very nice. She's a good cook. She takes good care of the house. And she's a lot of fun."

David took my hand in his. "Uncle Abe, Charlene and I have decided to get married!"

It took a few moments for this news to sink in. Abe first looked perplexed. His face contorted. Then he put on a pleasant expression and said, "What a surprise! Congratulations."

He got up from the easy chair and kissed me on the cheek. He put his arm on David's shoulder and squeezed. Then he took his newspaper and went to his room.

David and I looked at one another. "Old people find change hard to take," said David. "Once he gets used to the idea, he'll be fine."

"Hello, Martin? It's David. I have some very special news. Ask Rina to get on."

"Hi David. Rina here. What's up?"

David paused. "I—I'm getting married."

"Married! That's some surprise!" cried Martin. "Congratulations! Who's the lucky girl?"

"I'd like you to meet Charlene. Charlene, this is my brother and his wife."

"Hi Martin. Hi Rina. I'm dying to meet you both."

"Wish we were down there so we could hug you," said Rina. "When is the engagement party?"

"We've already started planning the wedding," I said. "The date is Sunday, December 26. Is that okay with you?"

"That's less than a month off," said Martin in a surprised tone.

"I thought it would make it easier for the out-of-town folks," I said, "since it's holiday time."

"That's very thoughtful," Rina said. "Perhaps we can come down a few days before the wedding to help."

"We won't need it," I said. "But you're more than welcome to come down early, okay?"

"Say," said Martin excitedly. "It's just hitting me what a great occasion this is: My brother David is getting married!"

"Finally," said David.

"After all these years," said Rina, "you finally got lucky!"

# CHAPTER IV
# SIMCHA

## *Martin—One Month Later*

As the jet engines warmed up, the flight attendants went through their ritual about oxygen masks and nearest emergency exits. I fastened my seat belt and said to Rina, "Just like old times … flying down to Florida again."

She buckled her belt. "But this time, Martin, we're going for a happy occasion, a *simcha*."

"I love weddings." I took Rina's hand in mine.

"Remember ours? Your father and uncles standing up to harmonize as a barbershop quartet. My cousin calling square dances. The whole mob of two hundred people whirling around as the band played the hora."

"I remember that you kissed me so hard and long at the ceremony that your father had to yank at your sleeve," laughed Rina.

I turned serious. "I only hope that David's marriage turns out as well, or even half as well, as ours.

"You're having doubts before we even meet Charlene?"

"Look—Charlene's half his age. And it's so odd that David never even mentioned her to us before announcing their marriage. That's not like my brother."

"At David's age, he's entitled to make a quick decision."

The plane was now taxiing to the runway. A flight attendant was offering pillows, and Rina took one.

I sighed. Rina was right, of course. David and I have been very close. If he picked a new partner in life, she's got to be okay.

"Frankly," Rina said, "I'm more concerned about how Uncle Abe is taking this. He and David have had such interdependence over so many years. A deep, symbiotic relationship. Now along comes an outsider to take over Abe's functions. He'll begin to feel useless."

I argued the point. "At 85, Abe isn't up to keeping house like he used to. David told me that marrying Charlene means they both would be cared for."

Rina frowned and said archly, "As a feminist, I don't care for the idea of choosing marriage in order to gain a housekeeper."

"You know that's not what David meant."

"My concern," said Rina, "isn't over Abe's physical needs. It's his psyche."

Our 747 lifted upwards in a roaring take-off.

I eased my rented white Buick Century through the traffic at Tampa airport and headed for Sarasota along the route I had followed for so many years.

It was another glorious tropical day. Larger-than-life cottonball clouds filled a Renoir-blue sky. Palm fronds stirred lazily in the ocean breezes. As we crossed the bridge, Rina admired the cobalt water gold-flecked by the sun. I drove up the familiar street, and there was the aqua-tinted stucco house my parents bought forty years ago, with the giant cactus standing sentinel beside the door.

I remember how overjoyed they were when they moved in. Never before had they had enough money to consider a house. We occupied so many different apartments in so many different locations that my mother called us "modern gypsies".

The door opened and there was Charlene greeting us. We exchanged kisses, and I barely concealed my astonishment. Charlene was big—huge for a woman. I suppose she topped 250 pounds. Yet she had a small face with petite good looks, and was light on her feet.

She was surprising in other ways. She had a machine-gun way of spitting out sentences. I couldn't tell whether she was slurring words or simply skipping some. We usually caught the general meaning, but sometimes had to ask her to repeat.

This paled in the air of excitement as we all chatted happily about the forthcoming nuptials. "Scott will be flying in from Denver, and Annabel from Minneapolis," I announced. "Our children are very anxious to meet their new Aunt Charlene."

"Will there be a big crowd at the wedding?" asked Rina.

"We're expecting about a hundred and fifty," said Charlene.

"Really?" I said. "You must have a big family, Charlene. We have only about a dozen coming from our side."

Charlene smiled. "I have only Uncle Mike, Aunt Millie and a handful of cousins. But David has a carload of friends. People he's worked with in his handicapped activities from all over, okay? Mayor Gomez of Tampa and Mayor Rogers of Sarasota will be there to say a few words."

I looked around the living room. "This place looks different. Aha! New drapes. And some new furniture, too."

"Looks like the woman's touch," said Rina, smiling.

Something wasn't quite right. I looked around. It was the empty dining room shelves. "What happened to the Chinese artifacts?" I asked.

Charlene shrugged. "I'm in the middle of decorating. Some things are up in the air."

Rina said, "Martin brought those statuettes and vases home from China during World War II. If you decide against them, Charlene, please let us know. Martin's mother said he should have them once they're no longer wanted here."

"Say—where's Uncle Abe?" I asked.

David looked downcast. "I should have told you earlier. He's in the hospital."

"In the hospital?" I cried. "What's wrong?"

"It's not serious," said David. "He became disoriented, and the doctor felt he should be brought in for testing and observation."

Rina asked how it happened. David said Abe had a fall and hit his head. The doctor checked the small swelling and said there was no problem.

Charlene chimed in, "But there was. I woke up during the night and found the front door open, with Uncle Abe gone. We located him wandering the streets and he didn't know who he was. This happened a second time, okay? That's why he's getting a full checkup."

"Can we visit him today?" I asked quickly.

"I knew you'd want to," said David. "Just bring the bags in from your car to the guestroom. We'll all go together in my van."


Abe, looking wan and somber in the hospital bed, came alive as he saw us. His embrace was longer than usual. I asked, "Uncle Abe, how are they treating you here?"

"It's not a treat," he said with his wry humor. "They charge plenty."

Rina sat down on the edge of his bed, took his hand and held his eyes in hers. "How are you, Uncle Abe?" He evaded her direct gaze. "How should I be, with all those pretty nurses traipsing in and out of my room?"

"Charlene and I will be getting married in two days," David said. "A big wedding. The doctor said there's no reason why you can't be there for the festivities."

Abe's face became a mask. "I can't go," he said.

Rina was right. There's a real problem here.

"Not go to David's wedding?" I said. "Why not? The doctor says you're well."

"I just don't feel up to it."

"Scott and Annabel will be here," I said. "The Mayor of Tampa and the

Mayor of Sarasota are coming. You won't want to miss it."

Charlene sidled up to Abe's bedside. "Uncle Abie and I are old buddies, aren't we?" She rubbed his bald pate playfully. "You won't let us down, will you?"

He just stared ahead without expression.

We all tried to change the mood, but how do you keep a one-way conversation going?

Serving dinner that evening, Charlene outdid herself. It took no effort for Rina and me to pile on the compliments. Charlene was warm, vivacious. But we were surprised to find her shrill and brassy at times.

"Did David tell you we've formed a new organization?" asked Charlene in her rapid-fire way of speaking. "It's the Disabled Voters of Florida. All power to the handicapped! We'll show them politicians they've got to listen to us—or we'll put their *calzones* in a wringer! Come spring, we'll start a voter registration campaign. At every supermarket, okay? Not just for disabled people. Everybody'll be talking about the Disabled Voters of Florida!

"Then we'll kick off the big event," she rushed on earnestly. "A fund raiser for Governor Lawson, okay? Running for re-election. We wanna get in under his underwear and scratch his back. Then when we need him, he'll scratch ours!"

It was embarrassing. Rina had to interrupt a few times to ask Charlene to repeat. So did I. Charlene had no particular accent, but she seemed to avoid the pause after most sentences. I figured it was just a question of getting used to her clipped manner of speaking.

"Don't you need lots of rich contacts to run a hundred-dollar-a-plate affair?" I asked.

"That's not for us. We're gonna put on an ole'-fashioned barbecue. Right here in our own backyard, okay? A fund raiser for the common man. We can handle five hundred people at ten bucks a head!"

"Good idea," said Rina. "But can you raise much after paying for the food and stuff?"

"Charlene has that figured out, too," said David admiringly.

"Our expenses will be...." Charlene's voice rose to a shrill, "*zilch!* I personally put the bee on the merchants around here. 'We're giving a party for the governor! Cough up some hot dogs! I need fifty pounds of hamburger meat! Fifty cases of soda! Paper plates! Napkins! C'mon—it's for our governor!'"

Her enthusiasm was infectious. I touched glances with Rina. No question

… this Charlene sounded like an express train on a single-minded track, smoke belching and whistle screeching as she roared to an unstoppable destination. We began to sense what attracted David so strongly as to choose marriage so late in life.

While the women attacked the dishes, I followed David to his room. I said, "Your Charlene is really something. Full of surprises. Talented in many ways. I'm glad you're bringing her into the family, David. But do you think we can get her to slow down a little when she speaks?"

David smiled. "I know. I keep after her, but she's a hyper personality. I'm getting used to it."

I suppose I will too. "Tell me, David, how does it feel after all these years, to think of yourself as being married?"

"I'll know after the smoke clears, Martin. It's all happening much too fast. I never expected to find someone who loves me, at my age, and makes my sap rise."

I asked him if he had thought about protecting Charlene financially, and he hadn't. "If you predecease Uncle Abe, she'd have very little. Maybe you could suggest that Abe set up a trust fund for Charlene, to start after you're gone."

David agreed, and told me how pleased he was that Rina and I would care for Abe during their honeymoon. "He'll be okay. After all, he's very fond of Charlene. He jokes with her all the time, and she likes him a lot."

I had to make Rina's point. "One thing I wish you'd watch for, David. Abe's prime reason for living, at a deeper level, has been to care for you. Charlene is now here, very willing and very capable. I hope Abe won't begin to feel useless."

It was the night before the wedding. The arrangements were complete, and we took David and Charlene out to dinner for a pre-celebration. I ordered champagne, but Charlene was bubbly even before it came to our table.

"I still can't believe this is happening to me," she cried. "A husband like David! And such a wonderful family. I'm dying to meet your two kids!"

"You may not be as lucky as you think," teased Rina. "Just wait till you get to know us better."

"Charlene never had much of a family life," said David. "No brothers or sisters. Her father was a cold Spaniard who never forgave her for not being the son he wanted. And her mother died when she was thirteen."

"That's rough," I said. "But we can help make up for it. I feel there should be no such thing as an 'in-law.' I hope, Charlene, you'll soon begin to think of me as the brother you never had."

She smiled enigmatically. "That would be something."

As the waiter filled Charlene's champagne glass, a passerby jostled his elbow and soiled the tablecloth. Charlene pulled back sharply and lashed out, "You stupid bastard! You'll ruin my dress!"

"It wasn't his fault," said Rina, quickly stemming the spill with her napkin.

To clear the air, I raised my glass. "May I propose a toast? Here's to tomorrow's newlyweds—may their love and their lives sparkle as does this delightful champagne!"

We all clinked glasses above our smiles and drained them of the wine.

Charlene's mood switched to high. "Say, did you hear the one about the rich guy and the champagne bath?" She didn't wait for an answer. "Well, they had just finished a fancy banquet and this rich guy corners one of those sweet young things with baby blue eyes and two big boobs. 'Look,' he says to her, 'I'll give you $10,000 if you'll take a bath in my bathtub using the finest French champagne. You'll have the key and I promise not to look, okay?'"

The rest of us displayed the uneasy anticipation engendered by an off-color joke.

Charlene rolled on. "She took the dough and locked herself in his bathroom. Leaving her time to undress, the rich joe goes to his bedroom, where he has a peephole in the bathroom wall, okay? He chuckles and licks his lips, imagining the titillating titties, the captivating curves, the virginal vagina. He carefully places his eye to the peephole. And what does he see? He sees a big blue eye staring back at him!"

The punchline of the story brings forth a loud guffaw from Charlene herself, causing heads to turn in the restaurant. The three of us smiled politely.

"My language didn't offend you, did it?" she asked. "After all, we're all adults."

There were reassuring murmurs. The night before the wedding was a time to be indulgent.

I checked my watch. "We'll have to leave for the airport in the next fifteen minutes to pick up Scott and Annabel."

"No problem," said Charlene, jumping up. "I've had all the coffee I want. Ready, Davy sweetheart?"

Rina and I deserted our coffee when we saw Charlene wheeling David out. We gave each other amused grins over the unnecessary haste and rushed after them. I almost forgot to sign the check.

Charlene nosed the van out of the underground garage and headed for the airport. Suddenly she jammed on the brakes as a white Datsun 280Z cut her off.

"God damn you, fucker!" she burst out, but the car had already zoomed so far ahead that the comment only vented her feelings. Her crude language was an intruder on our family mores—I'd have to get used to it.

Arriving at the airport, we soon saw the smiling faces of our children. As I loaded their luggage, I noticed Charlene was politely cordial to Scott, but she made a big fuss over Annabel.

"You are the first and only niece I've ever had," she crooned, hugging Annabel tightly. "What do you do?"

"I'm studying zoology."

"Well, I'll be a monkey's uncle!" responded Charlene, completely unaware of the pun. "Now Annabel, I'm staying at the hotel tonight. The nervous bride, you know. How would you like to bunk in with me? I need somebody to hold my hand."

Annabel was momentarily taken aback by the unexpected familiarity. "Sure. Glad to."

Scott, ever the brash young man, had to have the last word. "Zoologists have all the fun!"


The next morning I drove the van. We left early, and David wheeled himself into the room where the reception was to start. Then Rina, Scott and I doubled back to the hospital. We wanted to make one more stab at persuading Uncle Abe to come.

He was sitting up in bed, looking fit and reading the newspaper. "Look who we brought you, Uncle Abe—" I announced gaily. "Scott!"

Abe's face broke into a big smile as Scott embraced him. "It was only yesterday," said Abe, "that I carried you into the ocean waves."

"You'd have a little trouble doing it now, Uncle Abe," said my strapping son. "But you look healthy enough to try it. So hurry up and get dressed. We have a wedding to catch today.!"

Abe stiffened, then his shoulders slumped. "I know. I'm sorry. I can't go with you."

Rina sat on the side of his bed, took his hand and asked softly, "Why can't you, Uncle Abe?"

"I'm just not up to it."

"We're asking you to reconsider," I pressed. "It's such a special *simcha*. It will mean so much to David ... and to all of us."

He didn't respond. He just stared.

Rina made one last try. "Uncle Abe, I think I understand. It's hard for you, after so many years of just you and David. But just think. If you miss this wedding, you may be sorry later. How about it?"

We finally left him staring at the opposite wall.

The crowd in the reception room seemed bigger than the one hundred fifty mentioned by Charlene. But they soon seated themselves facing the traditional *chupah*, a flower-bedecked blue-and-gold canopy suspended from four poles.

The rabbi was first up front, a short, thin man with a small goatee. The wedding procession followed, with David rolling past the seated guests in his motorized wheelchair. Charlene looked radiant in the fluffy white gown, a veil framing her pretty face. She was escorted by her Uncle Mike, whose huge bulk helped put Charlene's large figure into a lesser perspective.

After the rabbi intoned a brief version of the customary blessings in Hebrew, Mayor Gomez of Tampa and Mayor Rogers of Sarasota were introduced and spoke effusively of David's dedicated efforts on behalf of the disabled, describing Charlene as his chief assistant.

The rabbi quickly moved on to the ring ceremony, concluding with the blessing over a glass of wine, from which David and Charlene each took a sip.

Then came the traditional climax of Jewish weddings, when the groom stamps his foot on the wineglass in memory of the destruction of the Temple in Jerusalem 2,000 years ago. I handed David the contraption I had put together: a length of 2x4 attached to a flat 12" square of plywood. David's arm brought this down on the glass to create a resounding crash. The audience broke into applause as Charlene leaned down to exchange kisses with her new husband.

It was a joyful affair. David threaded his wheelchair through the throngs of well-wishers, exchanging greetings and quips, an ecstatic Charlene at his side. The band played the "Golden Oldies" of the Big Band era. The bandleader's wife, in a tight-fitting gold lamé gown, belted out songs in Barbra Streisand style. And when they played a waltz, Charlene grabbed David's wheelchair and twirled him around the dance floor by tugging this way and that.

Following old Jewish custom, Charlene was then seated on a chair and lifted up in the air by her burly uncle and three other men, who danced her around to the audience's wild applause. Spurred on by this, the four males struggled to lift David and his 250-pound wheelchair up in the air. Two other husky men rushed forward to help, and soon the bridegroom was being exhibited on high to the delighted howls of the wedding party.

We were formally introduced to Charlene's cousins and her Uncle Mike and Aunt Millie. He was a bear of a man, with a handshake like a steel trap. "What business you in?" he asked.

"I work for Clifton, the plumbing manufacturer. I'm their Marketing Manager."

He peered at me. "Marketing, eh? You must make a bundle."

As the last of the guests were straggling out, Charlene surprised us. She came to our table with David and said, "Before we take off on our honeymoon, we're stopping over at the hospital to see Uncle Abe and say good-bye."

"That's so thoughtful," I said. "We'll follow you over there as soon as I finalize things with the banquet manager."

When Rina and I arrived with Scott and Annabel, Charlene had already set up banks of wedding flowers at the foot of Abe's bed and was reeling off the highlights of the affair in her whirlwind diction. Uncle Abe was sitting up, but his eyes reflected only a polite interest. Perhaps he was having trouble understanding much of Charlene's cascading monologue. David sat in his wheelchair with a happy grin.

Then Charlene uncovered a huge slice of wedding cake she had brought. "I saved this just for you, Uncle Abe," she said brightly. "David and I must leave on our honeymoon now, okay? But I want you to pretend you were at our wedding as you dig your fork into this cake. And *enjoy!*"

All over but the shouting.

"What did you think of the feature article in yesterday's paper about the wedding?" Rina asked.

"I loved the headline: 'PAIR UNITED BY ROMANCE AND MISSION,'" I said.

Rina smiled. "I liked David saying he was just beginning to live. Here he is at 69, and he's not letting life pass him by."

"Listen to this last quote," I said. "It really sums up David's personality: 'I'd like to walk along the ocean shore, kicking my feet in the surf. I'd like to go dancing. I can't. But there are things that make life worthwhile. Like helping other people. And now I have a partner to help me do more.'"

Uncle Abe came into the room and wished us all good night. "I think he's pretty much back to normal," said Rina after he left.

"But he's not the old Uncle Abe I remember," I said. "Making jokes. Kidding around."

"He's just getting over his depression," she said. "He told me that if

Charlene will make David happy, he'll be happy.

"Do you think Charlene will make David happy? She's so different from David, you know."

Rina defended Charlene. "All the excitement made her hyper. And remember … some of the happiest marriages are between opposites.

I thought aloud about my brother Herman, who also married a woman very different from him, and regretted it. Rina capped it off. "Men frequently marry the image of their mothers. The problem with your brothers seems to be that the women they end up with have your mother's worst qualities without Mom's redeeming good ones."

That was too perceptive for comfort.

# CHAPTER V
# DIVISION

## *Martin—Two Months Later*

The phone was ringing insistently. "I'll get it!" I called to Rina.

"Hi, Charlene. How's everything going with the young lovers?"

The voice at the other end was frantic. "Martin! I'm calling from Carmel Hospital. We just brought David in. They're getting ready to operate!"

"My God! What happened?"

Charlene tried to control her jingling speech. "He's been having trouble passing water. The pain in his groin was bad all night. And this morning he was burning with fever. It's his bladder."

"That's bad. But it doesn't sound life-threatening," I soothed.

"They have to give him anesthesia!" she cried. "At his age, he may not come out of it!"

My knuckles turned white around the phone. "I'm flying down on the next plane. Try not to worry, Charlene. He'll come out of it fine."

Five hours later I was striding into the lobby of Carmel Hospital. Only two months ago we were here at Uncle Abe's bedside, urging him to come to the wedding. Now I was riding up in the elevator not knowing whether my brother was still alive.

Charlene saw me as the doors opened and rushed over. I embraced her and her head fell on my shoulder sobbing with joy. "He's all right! My Davy came through it all right!"

"Thank God!" My throbbing headache eased off.

Charlene led me over to the bench. "The surgeon came out fifteen minutes ago. He removed three stones from David's bladder, okay? The fever was so high that David stopped breathing during the operation and we almost lost him!"

"This all happened so fast."

"Naw, stones take a long time to develop. David has been getting lazy and putting it off when he has to pee."

"Well, when you're in a wheelchair—"

"No excuse," she interrupted, and took an envelope out of her pocketbook. "Just look at the size of these stones the doctor handed me."

I stared at the objects in her palm and gave a low whistle. Two were the size of cranberries, another as big as an olive .

"They won't allow visitors for two more hours," she said. "Maybe you'll buy me lunch downstairs?"

The shiny bright cafeteria was ablaze with sunshine from the big windows and awash with white uniforms. As we carried our trays to a table, Charlene said, "I once wanted to be a nurse. To help people, okay?"

"Oh," I said, taking a seat. "Did you take courses, Charlene?"

"I took practical nurse training. But people don't appreciate what you do for them."

I took a bite of my tuna fish salad sandwich. "What kind of work have you done?"

"All kinds. Receptionist. Filing. I filed nails too—as a manicurist, okay? Even short order cook."

"You're a good cook even when it's not so short," I joked.

She waded into her hamburger, loaded with pickles and relish. "Can you keep a secret?"

"Sure, as long as it's not illegal or fattening."

"I'm going to become an undercover agent."

I smiled and went along with the gag. "You're going to act in a play?"

"Sort of. It won't be hard for me to act the part because I speak Spanish. My father was from Spain, you know."

It felt like she wasn't kidding. "Sounds fascinating. What's it all about, Charlene?"

"Well, my diabetes was acting up a couple of weeks ago and I went into one of those clinics in Tampa run by Hispanic doctors. Being on Disability, I'm covered by Medicaid, okay? And I noticed that the bill they wanted me to sign was inflated with health problems I didn't have."

"Oh?" I said. "I understand, but could you speak a little slower?"

She made another excavation into the hamburger and reduced her speech from a gallop to a trot. "Them bastards were ripping off the government— probably millions a year. I know—'cause I asked a Hispanic patient on the way out and she told me the same thing happens each time she goes to that clinic, okay?"

Now Charlene had my full attention. "So what did you do?"

"I went straight down to the Tampa F.B.I. office and reported it. And I told them I'm ready to be their undercover agent. I'll go back in that clinic and collect all the evidence they need."

What a nervy woman my brother married. "Have they called you?"

"I'm sure they will." She dabbed her napkin at the corner of her mouth. "I want to see them doctor bastards nailed to the wall, okay?"

"Undercover work could be dangerous."

"Can't scare me."

I went back to my sandwich, feeling a new appreciation for this brash lady who was now part of our family. What other unexpected depth would surface?

That reminded me of the other person in our family. "Say, how did Uncle Abe react when the ambulance came for David?"

Charlene knitted her brows. "We've been having problems."

"What sort of problems?"

She chewed on her bottom lip. "Well, David doesn't like to worry you with what he calls 'little things.' But I don't think they're so little, okay?"

"Has he begun wandering in the streets again?"

"No. I had an inside lock installed and he can't get out all by himself anymore. He just acts peculiar at times."

Now I was puzzled. "Why not give me some examples?"

She polished off her hamburger. "Well, he imagines things. People in the air. Hallucinations, like. Sometimes, when you talk to him, he's in another world, okay?"

"Maybe he's getting a little senile." I sipped my coffee. "After all, he's eighty-six already."

"And showing it," she said. "I've been finding puddles in the hall outside the bathroom. He doesn't always make it in time, okay?"

I didn't know what to think. Was this Abe's unconscious protest against the intruder in the family?

"Maybe it's just a phase."

"Maybe," she said. "I hope so."


I walked into Uncle Abe's room. "David's coming home from the hospital today. Charlene and I are leaving to pick him up."

"I'm glad. I was worried."

I sat next to him. "I'm very impressed with Charlene. For the first three days, she wouldn't leave David's bedside. She slept on the visitor's chair in his room."

"She seems very devoted to him."

"How does she treat you?"

"She's okay," he replied, picking up his newspaper.

"I see Charlene has hired a full-time housekeeper. So now you don't have to shop or clean or cook anymore. Doesn't that make life easier for you?"

His silence gave me the answer I didn't want to hear.

Charlene came in and said, "Time for us to bring our David home." She walked over to Uncle Abe, playfully rubbed his bald pate and kissed it. "And how's our Uncle Abie today?"

He didn't answer that one either.

After we got David comfortable, Charlene went to consult with the housekeeper about preparing dinner.

I sat down on David's bed and told him how much I admired Charlene's deep commitment to his recovery. "I've really gotten to know her this past week. I didn't appreciate her better qualities before this. And I'm catching on to the way she speaks."

"I'm so glad you like each other," said David. "Charlene is something special. She's got the Disabled Voters of Florida organized and ready for voter registration next month."

"Sure is capable and efficient." I paused. "That's why I was wondering why a sleep-in housekeeper was hired."

"It's just temporary," said David. "We took her on a month ago when Uncle Abe became difficult to handle."

I asked for details and got the same hallucination and incontinence story I heard from Charlene. Why hadn't David told me about this before? Puzzling.

Charlene came in with an armload of clean, folded laundry. "How do you two find so much to gab about?" she asked.

"We don't see each other that often," said David. "And we have the whole world to catch up on."

Charlene began putting the clothes away in the drawers. "What we need is a bigger house."

I chuckled. "Many people would give their eyeteeth for a house of this size. Especially that living room with its cathedral ceiling."

"It's this bedroom that's too small for David and me," she said.

I looked around. I hadn't noticed before. The room was small for two when one used a wheelchair.

She slammed the drawer shut. "But the worst problem is the bathroom. You ought to see David take a bath, okay? His muscles are too weak to lift himself from the tub. We had to rig up a wood platform across the tub."

I examined the bathroom. She was right. No way could it be enlarged.

When I returned, Charlene said, "I spent a day looking at houses two weeks ago. There's a real beaut two blocks from the beach. It has a stall shower so David can soap and rinse right in his wheelchair. And the money you get for this house should cover most of what they're asking."

I turned to David. "Sounds like you need something like that. Have you given any thought to a new house?"

David shrugged and said, "I guess we'll need it one of these days."

"I'd better sound out Dora about selling this one as soon as I get home," I said. Turning to Charlene, I explained that our mother had left this house to Herman and me, with a life estate for David and Abe, so Herman's half now belongs to his widow, Dora.

"Dora?" asked Charlene, puzzled. "I didn't see her at the wedding."

"She hasn't spoken to me or David since our brother Herman died years ago—don't know why. I need to get her okay to put the house up for sale before you sign a contract for the new one. Empty houses get vandalized."

An agitated look filled Charlene's eyes. "I thought this house belonged to David," she said, and her eyes turned hooded. "You mean that if David hadn't made it, I'd have no house to live in now?"

David said, "You don't have to worry, Charlene. I told you Abe is setting up a trust fund which will give you an annual income after he and I die. You can find yourself a very nice apartment."

"I like a house," she said, and walked from the room.

Uncle Abe came in and I explained how the house was getting difficult for David to live in. "What we'd like to know, Uncle Abe, is how you feel about the idea of living in a different house, a bigger one?"

Abe thought about it. Then he said, "I don't like changes. But to make life easier for David, we have to do what's necessary."

Charlene stuck her head in the door. "Haven't you talked yourself out yet, Martin? Dinner's ready!"

"You look troubled," said Rina, looking up from setting the table for dinner.

I had just finished speaking to David on the phone. "Yes—I'm *very* upset," I said.

Rina came over and put her hand on my shoulder. "What's wrong? Is it about Uncle Abe?"

"No." I slumped. "They've just bought a new house."

"Good. You told me they needed one."

"You don't understand. The problem starts with Dora. She hates me. She won't agree to sell the old house without making a lot of trouble."

·Rina sat next to me and took my hand. "You're not telling me what's really eating you."

"David knew this. Yet he rushed to buy, dumping an empty house in my lap."

Rina waited, knowing there was more. I muttered, "What's *really* bugging me is that David sounded like another person when we spoke ... like he had put an ocean between us."

*"David?"* Rina was incredulous.

I was becoming more and more depressed as I spoke. "After David told me they had signed the papers for their new house, he said, 'As for our life estate in the old house, Abe and I will sign over our interest for $20,000.'"

"I'm trying to understand...."

"I was completely stunned," I said. "The amount of money isn't important. It's that David had never spoken to me in that cold, mercenary tone before. I felt as if Charlene were speaking through David's voice."

"Martin," said Rina, "you'll have to accept that your relationship with David must change. He has a wife. She's his partner now—not you."

I rested my chin on my hand. "Yes, I know. But I think there's more to it. I sensed something just before I left Sarasota—a change in Charlene's attitude. I think she's becoming uncomfortable with my closeness to David. She may be building a wall to divide us."

# CHAPTER VI
# SEVERANCE

## *David—Two months later*

I powered my wheelchair into the kitchen, where Charlene was unpacking the groceries. She seemed upset over something.

"Look, Hattie," she said sharply to our aproned housekeeper, who was fixing dinner. "I expect you to do *everything* I tell you. And that includes folding up the chairs around the pool, okay?"

Hattie was unruffled. "I hear you," she said, slicing away at a large carrot.

"Charlene," I said, "can we talk?"

She looked over at Hattie and cried, "Haven't I told you to use the knife with the black handle for cutting carrots?" She strode over, yanked open a drawer and pointed. Hattie reached in for the other knife without a word, but her body language told a different story.

"And then finish putting these things away," snapped Charlene. I turned my wheelchair around and we went into my study.

"What's eating you today, Charlene? You've been happy as a lark since we moved into this new house. Till now. Did you forget to take your insulin injection this morning?"

"Naw. It's that people everywhere are incompetent, okay? I had to wait forever on the checkout line because the stupid woman packed the bags like she was on overtime. When I stopped for gas, the lousy kid there overfilled the tank and left a gas stain on the rear fender."

I reached for her hand. "Why let yourself get so annoyed over these little things, Charlene? Didn't your doctor say that getting upset is bad for your diabetes?"

"What did you want to talk to me about?"

I paused, wondering if the mood was wrong to bring it up. "I was thinking about what you said this morning," I began. "Why were you so insistent that I don't tell Martin and Rina about Abe?"

Charlene's face took on an expression I knew too well. There were some subjects which would sizzle if she spoke what was on her mind.

"I don't see," her lips were tight, "why you have to go running to them every time something happens down here."

"I think they should know about Abe."

She stared at me, unyielding. "Go ahead. Tell them your uncle has Alzheimer's, okay? But don't you tell them he's been taken to the hospital!"

The phone suddenly shrilled and I picked up the receiver. Both Martin and Rina were on the line. Charlene deposited herself in the easy chair and sat glaring like a cat as I mentioned how Abe seemed to be getting increasingly senile. That he had memory lapses and hallucinations. That he has been overmedicating himself, so that Charlene had to lock up the containers and dole pills out herself. They asked questions, but I avoided the mention of hospitalization. "Yes, we've had a specialist examine him," I said. "The diagnosis is Alzheimer's. Charlene feels Abe would be better taken care of in a nursing home."

"Hold the line for a moment," said Martin.

Ten seconds later he was back on. "Rina and I would like to come down tomorrow. Is that all right with you both?"

We picked them up at Tampa airport in our van as usual. But nothing else was as usual. Charlene's welcome was matter-of-fact—not warm, as on past visits. Martin's handclasp lacked the usual familiarity.

Of course I had to tell them that Uncle Abe was in the hospital, and they were shook up. When they came into Abe's room and saw him trussed up in a straitjacket, they looked thunderstruck.

"He's asleep right now," I whispered. "Let's go out in the hall and I'll explain."

I dreaded what I had to say, but there was no holding back anymore. "You see," I said, "Abe has gotten worse. He would eat lunch and say it was breakfast. He would talk as if he just moved here from New York. Then the night before last, Abe suddenly flew into a frenzy. He attacked Charlene, grabbing her by the breasts. She had to fight him off and hold him down."

Martin and Rina were in a state of shock.

"I know," I added. "I found it hard to believe when Charlene told me. We phoned the psychiatrist, and he sent an ambulance. Abe can't really be blamed. Doctor Brown said it's Alzheimer's Disease."

"But why a straitjacket?" implored Rina.

"When the ambulance arrived, Abe resisted," said Charlene. "He just wouldn't go with the medics, okay?"

Martin gave me an agonized look. "Why didn't you call and tell us?"

"It's so hard to talk about such things over the phone," I said. A lame excuse, but I simply didn't know what else to say.

When we took Uncle Abe home two days later, he was subdued. He spoke only when spoken to. While his memory had some weak spots, I was relieved that he showed no irrationality.

After he went in for his nap, I said, "He seems to be much better. Maybe it was just a temporary lapse."

"Hell," said Charlene, "you wouldn't call it a lapse if somebody became violent and grabbed *you!* Who knows when he'll have the next 'lapse', and what he might do."

Rina interjected. "In my professional opinion, Abe is not dangerous. Otherwise, they wouldn't have allowed him to come home so soon."

"Say," said Charlene, hopping up as if injected with adrenalin, "you haven't even seen our new house yet. Let me give you the two-bit tour!"

Martin and Rina murmured the anticipated compliments over the spaciousness of the rooms. They admired my study, adorned with a new computer. And they ooh'ed and aah'ed over the fancy pool out in the back.

"Now this is Uncle Abe's room, with his own TV set," announced Charlene. She opened the door and put her fingers to her lips so we wouldn't wake Abe. Closing the door, she added, "By the way, Dr. Brown wants to see Abe this afternoon at 4, okay?"

"How about Rina and me taking him to the appointment?" asked Martin.

"Yes," added Rina. "My speaking with Dr. Brown might give us a clearer picture."

Charlene held out the keys to the van. "Be my guest."

Charlene was visiting Alice when they returned. This gave me the chance for a private talk with Martin and Rina.

After Uncle Abe retired to his room to watch Phil Donahue, I asked, "What did Dr. Brown have to say?"

There was an awkward silence as Rina and Martin looked at each other. "Who recommended Dr. Brown to you, David?" asked Rina.

"Charlene got him from somewhere—I don't know. Why?

Rina chose her words carefully. "I have never before encountered such an unprofessional approach in a psychiatrist. He sat behind his desk and asked Uncle Abe only three questions: 'How do you feel now?' Abe said, 'Fine.' 'Do you remember what happened to you?' Abe answered, 'Yes.' 'Do you think it will happen again?' Abe replied, 'I hope not.'"

My surprise was tinged with disbelief. "That's all Dr. Brown said?"

"We were just as stunned as you when he announced the appointment was over," said Martin. "So I took Abe out and left Rina to ask the questions."

Rina gazed at me. "I explained my professional background, but got very

70

abbreviated and unsatisfactory answers. For example, I asked him what Abe's symptoms were which indicated an Alzheimer's diagnosis. 'He hears and sees things which aren't there,' said Brown. 'And he couldn't say what day it was or who the President is.'

"When I asked Dr. Brown what bizarre behavior did he observe, his answer was, 'I was told of his behavior by the family.' In other words, he didn't observe any problem personally. That's slim evidence for a diagnosis like Alzheimer's.

"So I asked the doctor about the extent of the brain deterioration shown on the CAT Scan. His answer was: 'I don't recall.' And he sounded like the interview should have been over five minutes ago."

Rina shook her head. "I couldn't believe any doctor would give an answer like that, and not check his records."

Frowning, I said, "Charlene told me Dr. Brown is the top man around in geriatrics."

"He has lots of framed certificates hanging," said Rina. "But my own conversations and observations of Uncle Abe are that he is too rational too often for a sweeping conclusion such as Alzheimer's."

"What bothers me," said Martin thoughtfully, "is that it fits right into Charlene's urging that Abe be put into a nursing home. And I don't like the idea of his being stuck away on the shelf like a worn-out toy."

As I had feared, this visit was turning out to be one of underlying tensions. And the worst was still to come.

Martin came into my den. "Rina is having a chat with Uncle Abe, so this is a good time for a private talk," he said.

I looked up at him. "I'm glad. I have the feeling that things aren't quite right between us, and I don't know why."

"Yes," he said, his eyes thoughtful. "You've changed. Our relationship just isn't the same."

"I don't see why you say that, Martin. I'm married, but I feel the same way toward you. Why do you say I've changed?"

"Your marriage was a complete surprise. This new house was a complete surprise. We used to talk about our plans."

Martin's hands were in his lap but they weren't still. The fingers opened and closed. How can I make him understand that I have a new partner? That he's the same brother but can't expect to be in on my decisions?

I pointed to the end table. "May I have some water?" He poured, and I took a sip.

"Sometimes things just happen fast," I said. "And I don't have much time

71

left. I want to please Charlene. She's much happier now because she finally has a home of her own. Including her name on the deed represents a strong sense of security for her, after such a rough life."

Martin said he understood.

"None of this changes how much we think of each other," I said. "We're still kernels in the same walnut."

Martin pursed his lips. "I was hurt when you told me I should buy out your interests in the old house—the one Mom left in her will. You and I have never talked money that way before."

I rushed to explain. "I was merely quoting our lawyer. He said that based on life expectancy tables, $10,000 each would be fair value."

"You're missing my point. I don't care whether it was $10,000 or $100,000. You just didn't sound like the David I know."

This was getting sticky. "Let's forget about the money. Abe and I will simply sign off our interests right now." I wanted to clear the air.

Martin stared at me. "You still don't get it, David. Of course you and Abe need to be compensated from the sale proceeds. It's the way you spoke to me. It sounded like someone else speaking *through* you."

"All I know is that I feel just as close to you as ever," I persisted.

Martin turned his face away. "Well, that house still remains our joint problem. I drove over this morning to check, and found somebody had broken in through a rear window. With an empty house, there's bound to be more vandalism."

I made a mental note to have that window fixed.

"Since Dora didn't answer my letters about putting the house up for sale, I phoned her. She said she has to think about it. When I pointed out the vandalism problem, she screamed, 'Don't you try to rush me,' and hung up. So since selling the house may take forever, we'd better do something else."

This was getting complicated. I asked what he'd suggest.

"How about phoning a real estate agent to rent the house out for a year? You and Abe keep the proceeds. You still have a life interest."

"A fine idea," I said, lifting the receiver and starting to dial.

I wish I had an idea on how to smooth things over between Martin and me.


I was happy that Charlene didn't slip into one of her moods during their visit. While she no longer showed any warmth, she was pleasant.

Until the end.

Martin casually asked Charlene, "By the way, what ever happened with the F.B.I.?"

"The F.B.I.?" Charlene was startled.

"You know, when you were upset with the medical clinic rip-off and told me you wanted to volunteer to help the F.B.I. I was wondering if you ever got involved."

"That's my business!" she snapped.

I couldn't understand why Charlene was so abrupt and secretive. Especially since she did something worth bragging about. Charlene had gone undercover to collect evidence for the F.B.I. on the Medicaid rip-off racket involving the Cuban community. Who knows what might have happened to her if she had been exposed before the arrests were made. She'd been telling all her friends about it. So why did she stonewall Martin?

Rina came into the living room carrying her suitcase after bidding Abe good-bye. "His outlook is much better," she said. "We certainly haven't seen any bizarre behavior during our visit."

"But when a person has Alzheimer's, you never know," said Charlene in an ominous tone.

"I'm not convinced that diagnosis is correct," said Rina.

Charlene stiffened. "Are you saying that I made up all those crazy things? Abe thought he was in New York, okay? He pissed in the hall. *He grabbed me by the tits!*"

Rina attempted to mollify her. "That's not what I meant, Charlene! I was only saying that right now Abe seems all right."

Charlene jumped up from the sofa and ran into her bedroom. She was back in a moment with a squarish carton, which she plunked down in front of Rina.

"Here!" Charlene's voice was booming. "Take these back! You said you wanted 'em. Now you got 'em!"

Astonished, Rina opened the carton and saw the lacquered vase on top which Martin had brought to our parents from China. The carton was packed with other Chinese art objects.

Rina turned to Charlene. "You're taking what I said the wrong way," she cried. "When you were redecorating the old house, I mentioned that if you didn't want them, we'd take them back." Her voice turned urgent. "But please —please display them in your new home."

"You demanded 'em!" growled Charlene. "So take 'em away!" And she spun around and stalked out.

Stunned silence. I tried desperately to think of something to cushion the reverberating shock waves.

"Looks like we have no choice," said Rina. "Let's find places for them in Connecticut."

Just then we heard the taxi's horn outside, summoning Rina. Even that raucous tone seemed sad.

I had a long talk with Charlene about it in our bedroom. She wouldn't give an inch, and accused me of always taking their side of an argument.

"But there was no argument," I tried to point out. "It was a simple misunderstanding. Rina only meant that you shouldn't discard any of the Chinese stuff which has sentimental value to Martin."

"Do you really believe that? You heard her call me a liar about Abe's nutty behavior! She's a schemer, that one! She's using all her psychology to put me in the wrong, okay?"

I could be talking to the Great Wall of China. Charlene was off on her own wild carousel of furious self-justification.

She's right and the world's wrong.

Sometimes she gets upset even when I string along with her:

*Charlene:* Whenever you say that, I want to slap your face.

*Me:* Why? I said, "You're right." I didn't disagree.

*Charlene:* You don't mean it. You're just running away from what we're discussing, okay? And you do it all the time. You try to shut me up that way.

*Me:* But I wasn't arguing with you—

*Charlene:* I wish you would fight. Then maybe we'd get somewhere.

She was giving me miserable choices: conflict or peace at her price.

As Martin was about to leave the next day, I felt so embarrassed that I didn't know how to say it.

"Something is on your mind—I can tell," he said. "Come on, let's get it out in the open."

"Look," I said. "When you visit us next time, maybe it would be best if you came alone. You know, without Rina."

Martin stared at me. "Without Rina?"

"Yes," I said, eyes downcast. "It would help things go smoother."

"I'll tell her," he said. Then he turned abruptly and walked out.

The governor was coming.

Charlene was wild with excitement. "The governor of the state of Florida is coming to our house!" Charlene had just gotten the confirmation on the phone, and she was prancing around like a stallion confronted by a mare. She ran to Abe, pulled him up from his chair and whirled him around in a two-step. Then she dashed to my wheelchair and planted a noisy kiss on my lips.

It was a red feather in her cap. Months ago she had issued the invitation in the name of the Disabled Voters of Florida, offering to run a fund raiser for Governor Lawson's re-election. A string of follow-up phone calls had left her hanging in the air. Now Governor Lawson himself had called to apologize for the delay and to provide a gracious acceptance.

Suddenly she stopped short and cried, "That gives me only two weeks to do everything! Shit! We'll have a mob! I've got to roll like an express train. Alice's gotta pitch in with both hands. Better call her first thing!"

I watched my dynamo swing into action. In rapid succession she called the managers of two supermarkets, four liquor stores, three delicatessens, two bakeries, a pizza parlor and a party goods store. "Whaddya mean?" she barked into the receiver. "The governor of our state is making a special trip here to talk to the people in Sarasota on September 12th—and all you can give is a lousy two cases of beer? Hell—there'll be at least two hundred people here at my house. I'm putting on a gigantic spread, okay? Will you ever have another chance to be part of a big shindig like this?"

On September 12 she had twenty cases of beer, delivered from each of four stores. The folding tables in our backyard were loaded with cold cuts, cheeses and a variety of goodies. A dozen large pizza pies were being sliced, and steaming hot dogs were piling up on the grills borrowed for the occasion.

"Do you really expect two hundred people?" I asked her that morning as we finished dressing.

"More," she said confidently.

"Where will we fit them all?" I asked. But she didn't have time to answer. She had run herself ragged publicizing our fund raiser, and people began streaming into our house an hour beforehand. A black limousine with the governor's security detail rolled into the driveway and the blue-serged crew snooped around every corner.

Then a school bus drew up and disgorged the high school band, which arranged itself on the front lawn to welcome the governor. They had to share the grass with a troop of Boy Scouts, flags unfurled, which acted as an honor guard. I shook my heard in admiration. Charlene didn't believe in half measures.

By the time Governor Lawson arrived, we were bulging at the seams with wall-to-wall people, both inside and outside the house. The band struck up a bravely strident marching song, and the Boy Scouts lined up as the official reception committee.

While I waited with Charlene at the door, two burly state policemen cleared the way with great difficulty. The popular 6'2" governor stood out above the crowd as they engulfed him behind his escort. He waved and shook hands on every side, his handsome face sporting a beaming smile.

Governor Lawson greeted Charlene and me effusively, and Charlene was floating. We then introduced Uncle Abe as "our octogenarian uncle, going on one hundred and twenty."

"Now look here," said the governor as he shook Abe's hand, "how come you look so young? And why won't you share the Fountain of Youth with the rest of us in this here state?"

I could tell this was a real highlight in Abe's life—just as it was for Charlene.

Governor Lawson stood up on a wooden crate in our backyard and skillfully elevated the crowd's mood with a folksy story that ended with a high-tech punch line, earning hearty laughter from his well-tanked audience.

Then he said, "I won't ask you all to vote for me this fall. I won't—'cause I can tell you will! But we gotta do something about those people out there who simply aren't as smart as you folks. So I want you all to go out and carry my message wherever you go—to make this state even better than it has been these past four years."

He paused for effect. "I wish that were enough, my friends. But what if it isn't? What if 'Old Curly Head' were to beat me this fall? Now, I'm not one to disparage anyone who has the misfortune to be bald. Matter of fact, I think my opponent has a wonderful head of skin. I'm referring to his record in the state legislature—it's enough to curl your hair!"

He had the crowd rocking, and he continued. "We just can't take any chances this fall. And so, my friends, I need each and every one of you to dig into your pockets this afternoon. Give me the funds I need to finish the job I started in this state. If you do, you'll be able to stand up four years from now —proud that you helped make it happen."

As the governor drove off, we passed the hat—actually, we passed around a half dozen derby-shaped party hats. And while everybody seemed in a giving mood, the final take was only about three thousand dollars.

"But that's all clear!" said Charlene excitedly. "No expenses, okay? Governor Lawson's sure to be impressed when I send him the money."

I thought of the huge fat cat checks that a governor is accustomed to see in campaign contributions, and wasn't so sure.

But Charlene's euphoria was infectious. She had accomplished this almost single-handedly. This was her moment of triumph.

"Maybe he'll be impressed enough to do something for me in return later on," said Charlene with a faraway look.

Two months later, Martin was back for a weekend visit. It was part of a business trip, so the issue of Rina didn't surface at first. He was especially anxious about Uncle Abe.

"He's better," I said happily, "now that he's becoming accustomed to our new home here. He likes going into our backyard pool on hot days."

"You let him go into the pool by himself?"

"Not at his age. Hattie's got a grandson—a strong young man of 18. Jimmy helps me take a shower. And he comes over to help Abe into the pool and keep watch while Abe bobs up and down in the shallow end."

Charlene's huge bulk came breezing through the front door and she called out, "Is anybody hungry? I'm starving!"

"Dinner's ready for the table," boomed Hattie.

Charlene rushed over with a big hug and kiss for me before giving Martin a polite peck on the cheek.

As Martin and I unfolded our napkins in the dining alcove, Charlene was rattling off the little anecdotes of her day. The putrid little man who tried to rub up against her in the elevator. The old lady with the silly hat who stepped off the curb without looking and was almost knocked down by her car. The furtive black man who tried to sell her a gold chain "which the bastard probably stole just minutes before."

The casual stereotype made me wince. Yet Charlene is such an exciting person to have around. She brings the whole world to my doorstep.

"People are just a pain in the ass," she concluded.

I've been trying to get Charlene to stop using the coarse language of the streets. She tries to avoid it when I'm around, but old habits die slowly.

"Where's Uncle Abe?" she cried, and in a moment she was in his room, making a big fuss to get him to the table.

"How do you like my Abie?" she chortled, rubbing his bald pate as he seated himself. "I just bought him that handsome blue Lauren shirt, okay? Take a look in his closet. I got him a whole new sporty wardrobe so he can dazzle women again."

"It's a great life," said Abe, "if you don't weaken."

Abe was smiling pleasantly, enjoying all the attention. Charlene has been spending much of her time with him lately, and it's sure been paying off. He no longer seems depressed.

Martin chatted with Abe all evening in Abe's room, and escorted him into the pool for a relaxed morning interlude. Then, while Abe was napping, Martin interrupted me at my computer.

"Except for some memory loss, he seems pretty normal to me," confided Martin. "But there's one thing that bothers me. When I mentioned that incident of the Chinese art objects, he was aware of what happened—that Charlene had turned them back to us."

"Yes?" I said, wishing I could avoid this tender subject.

"But when I tried to point out what Rina had said and how Charlene had taken it the wrong way, Abe surprised me with, 'If Charlene heard her say it, then she must have said it.'"

Martin looked so crestfallen that I said, "I wonder where he got that from? I never discussed the incident with him."

"Then it must have been Charlene," he said thoughtfully. "What gets me is that, after all the years he's known Rina, he believes *Charlene*."

There must be other things we could talk about. "How is Rina?" I ventured.

"Keeping busy," he said, his jaws tense.

"Martin, I feel badly about what I said when you left us last time. About Rina, I mean. Charlene somehow is convinced that Rina doesn't like her. And I thought it would be better for things to simmer down before Rina visited again."

It didn't help. Martin just looked grim.

My brother and I had never had this kind of problem before. No matter what blows the world dealt us, we two bared our scars to one another, bonding to ease the pain. I saw that same grim expression on Martin's face that he wore forty years ago, when he was fired from his first job. Our family had depended on his wages, since my father was unemployed right then and Herman had been drafted.

*"How can I face Pop and Mom?" he sobbed on my shoulder.*

*"You'll get another job. It's no sin to be let go."*

*"But I did it to myself. I was fired for trying to start a union. The pay was so pitiful."*

*"Isn't it against the law to fire for union activity?"*

*"Sure. The union organizer wants me to file a complaint. But he admits the case can take months for reinstatement. I want to get back at those bastards, but how does the family eat in the meantime?"*

We talked it through. The family managed to get by. Martin and I connected, and this connection grew ever closer through the years.

Now I tried to figure out how to put my delicate question. I adopted the tone we used in our confidential talks. "Has Rina had any difficulty with incontinence, Martin?"

His eyebrows shot up. "Incontinence? What makes you ask that question?"

"Well," I said hesitantly, "after your last visit, Charlene found Rina's bedsheet wet and smelling from urine."

Martin looked flabbergasted, and I was immediately sorry I'd brought it up.

"David, David," he said, shaking his head. "Even if Rina wet the sheet, is she the kind of person who would leave a urine-drenched sheet on a bed? Would *I* leave a room that way?"

I was overcome with embarrassment.

Martin bore in. "One more thing. Charlene couldn't know which bed each of us slept in. So if she found urine-smelling sheets, how did she know it was Rina—and not me?"

He fixed me with his eyes and added, "Think about it, David. You wouldn't have mentioned this unless you believed what Charlene told you." He paused. "Maybe you believe her about the Chinese things, too."

That wasn't so, but my protests sounded hollow.

Later that day, Martin commented, "I notice that Charlene and Uncle Abe seem to be hitting it off nicely these days. Does that mean Charlene has stopped talking about a nursing home for him?"

I hesitated. "Well, no. You see, Charlene won't have much time to care for him now that she has a beauty parlor to run."

Martin turned to me, eyes wide. "Charlene now runs a beauty parlor? That's interesting. How did this happen?"

"Well, she wants to be independent. And I admire that. So when a beauty parlor near here came up for sale two weeks ago, I bought it."

I could see Martin trying to react unemotionally in absorbing this news. "Does Charlene have any beauty parlor experience?"

"Well, no. But she took over all the personnel there. All she has to do is manage the operation."

"I see," said Martin. But I could see that he didn't really see.

Martin was now getting ready to go home, and I was feeling depressed. There was an invisible wall developing between us, growing thicker all the time. I didn't want this to happen. But we both seemed to be riding an uncontrollable stream, with the currents dividing.

There are important problems I wish I could talk over with him. Charlene gets so hot-headed over little things, like that knife incident with Hattie. And so emotional that I can't reason with her, like the Chinese artifacts. Yet she's so vital and exciting that she's giving me new reasons for enjoying life.

So instead I stuck to the mundane. "Anything happening with Dora and the old house?"

"Dead silence," said Martin. "She simply won't answer me. So an idea hit me. I arranged to have the house appraised. The value was estimated at $80,000. And I wrote Dora with a simple proposition. I'll buy out her share for $40,000 so it can be sold. Or, if she feels the house is worth more, she can buy out my share for the same amount."

"Sounds fair."

"We'll see." Martin turned and asked, "What's happening about the rental of the house?"

"We finally have a tenant. But he's insisting on so many repairs that the rent he pays may not even cover the expenses."

"Look at the bright side," said Martin. "With a tenant, we avoid vandals."

"I am looking at the bright side," I said. "Charlene is helping Uncle Abe get back to normal. Abe likes and trusts her. He told me yesterday that he looks upon her as a daughter. He even changed his will to put her in."

A shadow passed over Martin's face. "He looks upon Charlene as a daughter now? That's interesting. I wonder how he looks on Rina now? Or me?

"I think you're jumping to conclusions—"

"Know what *I* think?" he said, picking up his suitcase. "I think we're being locked out of your lives."

That hurt.

# CHAPTER VII
# CUTTING LOOSE

*Charlene—Two months later*

They're driving me crazy. Martin and Rina, always interfering in our lives. And their freeloading brats, who drop in on us to vacation and party in Florida. More likely, they come to spy on me.

"I'm heading out to the shop, Honey," I called out to David as I grabbed my purse.

He called me back, so I made a fast U-turn. "Charlene," he said, "I was up late last night doing the books. Our beauty salon is going deeper in the red each month. What can we do?"

"Stop fussing yourself. Every business takes time to build, okay?"

"But I thought you said it was a profitable operation when you bought it. Your receipts are running behind your costs. If you can't increase income, can you cut some expenses?"

I blew my stack. "Wassamatter, you think I don't know how to run the shop? It's your brother Martin, isn't it? Why is he poking his nose in my business? Or maybe it's his wife, the sly one. Shit, they keep you on the phone every week for hours."

David always defends them and I'm sick of it. He's my husband. Love, honor and obey. Not remote control from 1,200 miles away. I let David have a mouthful of what I thought and stomped out.

Alice was minding the store as usual. I hired her after the phone company cut staff and her unemployment pay ran out. "Business been good today," she said.

"About time. It's been stinkeroo all month. David tried to puncture me about it this morning."

"The Connecticut connection again?"

"They better keep their putrid paws out of my business and let a poor girl earn a living, okay?"

I settled down to do the nails of this floozy who just had her hair done. I don't know if she is a floozy but she sure looks like one.

By the end of the day I had done three nail jobs, between making appointments and managing the place. Alice had done four, and all the beauticians were busy. I counted the take and wished we could do this every day.

Back home Hattie had dinner ready and I was starved. David rolled up to the table, but where was Abe? Christ, he was snoring in his room!

"What the fuck's the matter with you, Hattie?" I yelled. "You're supposed to have him up a half hour ahead of eating time."

"I did wake him, Mrs. Richman. He musta just rolled over after I left."

I shook him and he moaned. So I jabbed him with a sharp elbow. This got his attention and he lifted himself up, bleary-eyed. "You got all day to sleep," I said. "Now you're late for dinner."

While Abe was washing his hands, I told David about this great nursing home the frowzy floozy lady mentioned. She visits her father there. It's clean as a whistle. Run by nuns, and everyone knows how efficient they are. I said I'd phone tomorrow to get the details.

"I don't like nursing homes," said Uncle Abe, now sitting at the table.

"You'll be happier there," I said, helping myself to a chicken breast. "You'll have people your own age to talk to, okay?"

"A nursing home is not for me," he said stubbornly, as Hattie filled his plate.

I raised my voice. "Don't shut your mind. You're old and weak. You can't expect us to wait on you hand and foot all day long."

That took away his tongue. Now I'll have to work on David. All the money in the family was Uncle Abe's, of course. But David has half, since the bank accounts, C.D.s and stocks are in joint names. Once we get Abe into a nursing home, we can switch everything over to David. And me jointly, of course.

I thought I had it made. David was coming around to the idea that Uncle Abe would be better off in a nursing home, and that he's just resisting change. But then David pulled the plug on my beauty salon.

"I'm afraid this can't go on, Charlene," he said to me one evening.

I glared at him because I knew what was coming. He had been harping on the subject for weeks. Each time, I'd get so upset that he'd give up. So this time I got even more strung out. I even screamed at him, "You're taking orders from that fucking couple up north! They're not your wife—I am!"

This time he didn't back down. He told me he ran an ad and had a buyer. He said he was taking a loss on the salon now to avoid worse operating losses later. But I didn't believe that. I knew who was really behind my amputation.

I carried on plenty. For three solid days I made life miserable for him. And for Abe. "You won't let me make a living! I'm married to you for a whole year but I've got nothing! And you want me to stay a nothing!" Finally, to make peace, he added my name to the bank accounts. A bunch of C.D.s were up for renewal, and he added my name to his and Abe's. Nice to own some big money. I've been sucking up to men all my life. Time for a change, baby.

But I was going nuts with nothing to do. I sent away for tips on running a business out of your home. That gave me my first money-making idea. Then Alice came along with our second big idea: KALL GIRLS. It'll be an on-site manicure service for busy executives.

Suddenly I heard we're being invaded again. First Scott. Then Annabel, coming here for vacation. Do Martin's kids think this is a fucking hotel?

Martin thinks this is *his* hotel. He's in and out all the time. Next time he comes I'll make sure he won't feel so welcome. If only his plane would crash, it would solve my problem.

I'm feeling so frazzled that I need a vacation myself. Get away from it all. Maybe I should take a cruise in the Caribbean. David can't go; most ships aren't wheelchair accessible. But Martin's not going to stop *me* from cruising.

Maybe when I'm away I can figure some way to stop him from interfering in our lives. Don't know how much longer I can stand being strung along like a fucking marionette.

# CHAPTER VIII
# DELIVERANCE

## *Martin—Three Months Later*

Our daughter Annabel was heading to Sarasota to visit David and Uncle Abe. This pleased me no end. How many young people would sacrifice precious vacation time to visit elderly relatives? But I wondered whether Charlene's negative attitude toward our family would leave Annabel feeling unwelcome.

Rina and I were raking leaves on a perfect autumn day. The cool breezes caressed our clothes. "Rina, what have we ever done to Charlene to make her dislike us?" I wondered. "She's so cold to us. I think she's building walls because she sees us blocking her plans."

Rina absently plucked dead leaves from a fading daylily. "What plans?"

"Look, Charlene knows by now that David has hardly any assets of his own. She's certainly got her eye on Uncle Abe's money."

"But didn't David tell you that Uncle Abe changed his will to include Charlene?"

"Yes, but she still keeps pushing to get Abe into a nursing home. She probably doesn't realize how fast his money would disappear that way. My point is: we're the only ones standing in her way if she's out to get rid of Uncle Abe. From my last visit, I'd say she seems to have them both wrapped around her pinkie."

Rina let out a sigh and said, "It's hard for me to believe that our David would put Abe in a nursing home against his will."

"David's seventy years old. With a wife who is strong-willed. And manipulative. But Uncle Abe has always hated nursing homes. And he can afford to pay for care."

It was our fortieth anniversary. Both kids had called this morning, sending well-wishes. As we dressed to go out to dinner, the doorbell rang. When we opened it, who was on our front porch but Annabel and Scott, suitcases in hand! A happy confusion of hugs, laughter and surprised delight ensued. "We've been plotting this for 3 months," grinned Scott. "We just couldn't let this anniversary pass without sharing it with you."

"Besides," piped up Annabel conspiratorially, "your anniversary fell on a Friday, so it was easy to come in over a weekend." Boy, those kids sure know how to make our hearts glow!

As we wielded our chopsticks in the Hunan Wok, I asked Annabel about her visit to Sarasota. "I'm glad I went," she said. "I spent most of my time with Uncle Abe, and I could see how much this meant to him. He got such a kick out of tossing the beach ball into the pool so I could dive in and bring it back."

"What about David?"

"Oh, Uncle David's fine. And it's always fun talking to him."

I could tell from Annabel's tone that there was more to the story. "What's bothering you, Annabel?"

"Well," she said, "it's not like it used to be. My flight was delayed, so I didn't arrive in Tampa till 11 p.m. But instead of picking me up, Charlene told me to stay at a motel overnight. I didn't figure that cost in my budget."

Annabel, on her first job out of college, was with an activist community group which had more ideals than funds. I had offered to pay for her fare to Florida, but her independence rejected my money. So the motel was not a casual expense.

"Then later on," added Annabel, "Charlene accused me of showing up there without advance notice. I was stunned. I had phoned her a week earlier, but she sounded like I was lying."

"How did Charlene act toward you?" asked Rina.

"Cold. I don't understand it. She was so warm around their wedding, so I can't see why she would dislike me now."

"I had the same experience with Charlene when I visited there a month ago," Scott interjected. "Her attitude toward me was Siberian."

So I filled the kids in on the problems of our last visit. The scene with the Chinese art objects. The accusation of urine-smelling bed sheets. Charlene's pressure to put Abe into a nursing home.

"I believe that David is being fed lies about all of us," I said. "Charlene is trying to isolate us from David and Abe so she can control their money. And she seems to be succeeding."

I slapped my chopsticks down on the plate. "But I won't surrender. David and Abe mean too much to me. I'm going to pay a little visit to Sarasota every month or two."

Scott looked at me quizzically. "Did you retire early because of them, Dad?"

"No, I'd been planning to resign from the rat race for some time. This is just the catalyst. I want to do volunteer work and play some serious tennis.

And," my tone turned jovial, "I'll be glad to let your mother support me."

"But what can you do about the situation down there?" asked Annabel.

I thought for a moment. "I think I can block Charlene's moves to unload Abe into a nursing home. You two can help. Let's maintain the lifeline with frequent phone calls and letters. And all of us should visit often, even if Charlene makes it unpleasant."

I stared at Scott and Annabel. "I insist on paying your fares."

They were with me! Eagerly! I summed up our battle plan. "Charlene is trying to undermine the family relationships we have built up over all these years. We've got to fight her in the only way we can: with love and caring. We won't give up."

I had lots of trepidation when next I flew down to Florida. David had been lukewarm when I told him of my plan to visit. It isn't easy to fight a battle from a thousand miles away.

David and Abe seemed glad to see me. Charlene was cool in her greeting, but just as flouncy and gregarious as ever. She was all agog over her new ideas for making money.

"People get rich fast in the mail-order business," she said as we sat drinking coffee. "Last month I saw this ad on how to make a thousand dollars a week working out of your home, okay? So I sent in my ten bucks."

I held my tongue, wondering what was coming.

"What a rip-off!" she cried. "All I got back was two sheets of mimeographed instructions about how to develop a mailing list and how to become an agent for companies who print mail-order catalogs and ship the merchandise for you."

I looked at her questioningly. "So?"

"So that gave me my idea," she said brightly. "Why don't I do the same thing, okay?"

I could see that David was eating this up. He was entranced by her strident, braggadocio approach. Abe was stimulated, too. He asked, "Do what?"

"I sell two pages of information for ten bucks. They cost me all of thirty-seven cents, including postage, okay? I sell a thousand a week and I make nine hundred and seventy bucks!"

I couldn't resist probing further. "How will you get a thousand people each week to order this?"

"Well, *I* did—didn't I? There are a million suckers out there dying to get rich right from their home. I'm going to run my little ads in Spanish, in the Spanish-language newspaper. I know those people, okay? I can't miss!"

"Is that legal?" I asked.

Charlene snorted as she tossed her head. "What the hell's wrong with it? I send 'em what I promise—don't I? A sucker is born every minute!"

While we digested this, Charlene finished off her huge slice of chocolate layer cake and tossed something white in front of me. "How d'you like my new card?" I picked it up and read:

### KALL GIRLS
*Manicures for busy executives*
*executed in your office or home*

Below that was Charlene's name, address and phone number.

"You're offering manicures by direct mail?" I asked facetiously.

"That's a *different* business," cried Charlene in a contemptuous tone. "KALL GIRLS is what me and Alice are running. We save executives time by prettying up their nails wherever they are, okay?"

If ever there was a time for me to practice discretion, this was it. I clamped my mouth shut. Charlene patted away a crumb on her lips with her napkin. "I'm heading over to Alice's house now. We're having a conference on launching our new enterprise."

When Uncle Abe went in for a nap, David and I headed for his study.

"Have you heard from Dora about buying out her half of the old house?" asked David.

"No response. She won't answer any of my letters. I'm proceeding with my lawyer's suggestion for a 'partition' action against her."

David looked shocked. "You're going to sue your own sister-in-law?"

I grinned. "Not really. My lawyer will serve Dora with a notice requiring that she state her reasons for refusing to sell her share . If she can't present a valid reason, the court can force the sale. This is a case of two partners in a property disagreement." David shook his head sadly.

I ventured to ask David how he felt about Charlene's 'Kall Girls' venture. He thought it would work. "Businessmen today must be well groomed. And they don't have time to make a special trip to have their nails done."

I sat down on a chair facing David. "The idea is good. But that name: 'Kall Girls.' Isn't that highly suggestive for a service where women are summoned to an office or home?"

A roguish grin played in the corner of David's mouth. "I think it's amusing."

"How about 'provocative?'" I pressed. "Isn't it possible that some customers may think it's a cover for providing more intimate services than manicures, and may get rough about it?"

"Oh, you don't know Charlene. She can handle any man. So can Alice."

I thought I'd better drop that subject and asked about Charlene's mail-order business. "It may be legal—but how ethical is it to take money from Hispanic people who are gullible?"

He looked thoughtful. "Well, she sends them the information she promises."

I let out a long breath. I didn't recognize my highly ethical brother. I wished he hadn't answered my question at all.

After an awkward pause, he asked me to read the story he finished writing yesterday.

"I have one other question," I said. "How does Charlene have time for all these other businesses if she's running a beauty parlor?"

David didn't answer at first. Then he said, "I sold the beauty parlor. It was running at a loss, and it turned out to be the wrong thing for Charlene."

In the old days, David and I would have had a heart-to-heart talk about this. I knew he needed someone to provide a soft shoulder for his problems. So I waited without speaking. It was his move. But he didn't make it.

I began to read the story he had written, but I couldn't keep my mind on it. I set it down. "David, let's talk about Uncle Abe. He doesn't look good to me, and his speech is slurred again."

David conceded that Abe had taken a turn for the worse. "Charlene feels he'd be better off in a nursing home. All the nursing homes in the area have waiting lists. But Charlene has a contact at one to get Abe in without delay."

My mind heard alarm bells ringing. "Better off in a nursing home?"

"Yes. St. Agatha's is kept very clean, and he would have people his age to talk to."

I tried to choose my words carefully. "You said, 'St. Agatha's.' Is it a Catholic place with a cross in each room?"

"Why … yes. But it's very well run. And the nuns are very caring."

I stared at him. "I'm shocked, David. You know Uncle Abe. With his fundamental Jewish background, can you believe he'd be comfortable in a room with a cross on the wall? And being cared for by nuns?"

David's eyes fell.

"Look," I said slowly, bringing my forefingers up to my lips. "I've heard of a neurologist in Tampa who specializes in geriatrics. My internist says Dr. Klein has a national reputation. I'd like to take Uncle Abe to see him. Let's get another opinion."

"Hi!" I called out from the front hall. "We're back." I helped Uncle Abe off with his jacket and he lay down on his bed to rest. "My knees hurt," he said.

I went into the bathroom and brought back a bottle of rubbing alcohol. Rolling up his pants, I gently massaged around his knees. He sighed in satisfaction.

"How are you and Charlene getting along?" I asked.

"We get along. How is Rina?"

"Don't change the subject," I said. "Are there any problems?"

"Why should there be problems? So long as David is happy."

"I've been talking with David. He feels that Rina shouldn't come here to visit."

Abe nodded. "It's better that way. Because of her."

"You mean Charlene?"

He didn't answer.

I found David in his study; Charlene was out. David asked, "What's the story? What did your Dr. Klein say?"

"He's a very impressive guy," I said. "Thoughtful. Probing. I told him what I knew of Abe's case. He gave Abe a complete physical examination. Then he asked him a hundred questions, starting with his childhood."

"And...?"

I rubbed my nose. "Dr. Klein felt the probability of Alzheimer's is slim. 'Some senility with memory loss is quite normal at his age,' the doctor said, 'along with some incontinence.' Dr. Klein questioned the strong medications which are prescribed for Abe, saying that heavy dosage could cause slurring of speech and lead to disorientation."

"Did you ask his opinion of a nursing home?"

"Dr. Klein felt Abe is rational enough to make his own decisions, even though he is timid about asserting his wishes."

David looked surprised. "That contradicts what Dr. Brown said."

"David, isn't the important thing how Abe seems to you and to me? I just don't see him as ready to be shoved into a nursing home. He washes and dresses himself. He gets around on his own two feet. You have Hattie here full time to clean up after him as necessary. And we know he hates the idea of a nursing home."

David was silent. But I could tell my points were sinking in. So I pressed my advantage.

"David," I gazed deeply into his eyes, "Abe is my uncle, too. Will you promise me that he will never be put into a nursing home without my consent?"

I was pleased that he didn't hesitate. "Of course. You've got to be in on that decision."

This seemed to be the time to lay it all out on the table. So I said, "I've got to talk to you right from the heart, David. What's happened to the closeness you and I have had over all these years?"

A shadow passed over David's face. "I still feel close to you."

"It's changed. Not that I expect it to be the same now that you're married. But I feel we're drifting apart. Not just me—our family relationships are running into rough waters."

David squirmed in his chair. "I want to hear what's bothering you."

"Number one: my wife is no longer welcome to stay in my brother's home … after a loving relationship going back forty years."

"That's just temporary. Charlene feels Rina looks down on her and dislikes her. Charlene gets emotional about things at times. She'll get over it."

"Number two: Annabel and Scott no longer feel they're welcome here. Annabel says you believe she came down without notifying you in advance. That just isn't so."

"Are you sure? Charlene said Annabel's arrival was completely unexpected."

I shook my head from side to side. "David, David … I get the feeling that we can't defend ourselves. Charlene also told you that Rina urinated on her sheets during our visit. You believed her. She also said Rina demanded the return of those Chinese artifacts, which she didn't. We get the feeling that anything we say or do could be blown up into a major sin by Charlene."

David bent his head, torn by conflicting loyalties. Finally he said, "Charlene does get nervous and high-strung. Frankly, I often find her unreasonable. But I'm working on it."

"You mean you're having some problems yourself?" I struggled to keep eagerness out of my tone.

He stared at the wall. "Well, she's changed from the person I married. Once she takes a dislike to someone, she thinks the worst of them. Little things upset her. She insists on things being done *her* way. But I know she loves me, so I've got to work things out."

Then he added, "In the meantime, maybe it's better that Rina holds off on visiting us."

My hopes crumpled. Charlene still held the upper hand. "I'm trying to understand," I said. "Rina and I have been very close to you for many, many years. A year ago you got married, and it made us all very happy. We did everything we could to make Charlene feel part of our family. I can't understand what went wrong."

90

"Maybe it's something I have to get Charlene to understand," he said in a defensive tone I had never heard him use before. "I'm trying to make a go of it with Charlene. I think she loves me. But my feelings toward you haven't changed."

*If Charlene loves you*, I thought, *shouldn't she be willing to meet you halfway?* I took his hand in mine. "David," I said, "You and Abe are very near and dear to me. I don't want to add to your concerns. Anytime I can be of any help, you can count on my flying down. Just call."

His eyes told me his gratitude. I could tell that I had given him a lot to think about. And I felt a lot better.

David did call three weeks later. He sounded tense, distraught. Charlene was gone. She had left him. For another man.

I was astounded. Rina was incredulous. I grabbed the next plane to Tampa.

Flying down, I struggled to contain my jubilation. Charlene had schemed to undermine our relationship, but she had failed. She lost and left. The family was back together again.

Then I sobered, thinking of my brother. He had tried so hard with Charlene. What a wrench to have her suddenly leave him. And for another man!

My mind reached out to caress the splintered heart of my beloved brother. It was wounded and bleeding. He would need much tender support.

His van was waiting when I walked out of the terminal, and his greeting was as warm as an electric blanket on a cold night. Hattie was behind the wheel, and she was more jovial than I had ever seen her.

"So nice to see you back again so soon, Mr. Richman," she said, "'specially at this time!"

I gave her a big smile, and began to ply David with questions. At first I thought his matter-of-fact responses to being abandoned were the facade he had erected to shield him from desolation. But he was obviously more relieved than shaken up by Charlene's desertion.

"What's Uncle Abe's reaction?"

David grinned. "He's pleased. Charlene had been putting him down lately. He's glad to be rid of her."

"And you, David?" I asked with earnest concern. "How about you?"

He looked at me with a wan face. "I surprised myself. I was angry at first, of course. Then I realized I was feeling relief. She was always exciting to be with. And I'm going to miss that. But she was too hard to live with."

Uncle Abe welcomed me with open arms. "You look better than I've seen you in years," I said. In truth, I was surprised by the new vigor in his movements and the absence of stress lines in his face. Looks like Charlene's departure was turning into a lovely gain all round.

Not completely. After Hattie's scrumptious fried chicken dinner, Abe ambled to his room to watch TV while David rolled out his tragic tale.

It seems that Charlene had been unusually high-strung, so David had bought her a ticket for a Caribbean cruise. "I couldn't go, of course," he said. "Wheelchairs don't fit in their bathrooms."

The ship was back in a week, and David could tell something was impossibly wrong. Charlene had begun to pack instead of unpacking. He confronted her. She flatly informed him that she had fallen in love with somebody else.

"I'm leaving you, David," she told him.

"Who's the man?"

"He's an officer on the ship, okay? We're going to Puerto Rico together."

"I see. Are you planning to come back?"

"Oh, I'll be back tomorrow morning to get the rest of my things. This is all I can take with me now."

David related this as if it were a breakfast conversation between husband and wife.

"Didn't you get excited or upset?" I asked, wide-eyed. "Didn't Charlene say why she fell out of love with you and fell in love with somebody else in just one week?"

David rubbed the stubble on his chin. "Well, when she came back the next day to get her clothes, I asked her. She ranted and raved about you and Rina always interfering in our affairs and breaking up our marriage. She's been on that kick for months, but I thought I had shown her she was being unreasonable."

"It's all so sudden that it's hard to believe. Are you telling me the whole story?"

David's eyes looked around for a way to answer and gave up. "After Charlene left, I found a packet of our bank books missing. The ones where we had added Charlene's name in the past months."

"She cashed them in?" But I already knew the answer.

"I phoned the banks. Charlene had already cleaned out the accounts."

I was afraid to ask the doomsday question. "How much did she take altogether?"

David hesitated. "It looks like over ninety thousand dollars, mostly C.D.s. Plus ten thousand she charged on two credit cards."

I let out a low whistle. Ninety thousand dollars! And David can talk about it without sounding furious ... or even upset.

Then another thought hit me. I had refused to give up on David—and I had won.

But Charlene didn't exactly lose.

# CHAPTER IX
# SURPRISE!

### *David—3 Months Later*

Hattie came in with the breakfast tray and set it next to my bed. Life without Charlene is much simpler. I've reverted to my old habit of staying up till one or two in the morning, and then sleeping late.

"Morning, Hattie. How's everything going?"

"Things just fine this morning, David. Uncle Abe's his old self, jokin' with every sentence." Hearty and bustling, she had the rich contralto voice of a Hazel Scott.

"Is Jimmy coming over this afternoon?" Her grandson stops in twice a week to help me with my bath and does odd jobs around the house.

"Yeah. He be come his usual time—'bout two. If'n there's nothin' else you need, I'll head out to do the marketin' for the week." She grew a big smile, displaying bright white teeth. "Uncle Abe goin' with me. He like to push the cart."

It's remarkable how much Abe has improved since Charlene left. He no longer slurs his speech. He's occasionally incontinent. But he's recovered much of his old *joie de vivre.*

Hattie's a gem. She drives us everywhere in my van. She cares for me and Abe like a mother hen. And Hattie's sister comes in on Sundays to cook and serve, so Hattie can have her day off.

As I finished my breakfast, the phone rang. It was Greta Townsend, my divorce lawyer. "Sorry, but we still haven't located Charlene."

"You tried her uncle Mike and her friend Alice?"

"They both insist they have no idea where she is."

"I don't believe it," I said. "Isn't there some way we can tell when she contacts them?"

"Not unless you authorize me to hire private surveillance. That's costly."

I was becoming irritated. "Look—we've been trying to file divorce papers for months. Are you telling me there is nothing I can do until you find Charlene and serve her? She has a lawyer. Why can't you serve her through him?"

"I'd like to," said Greta. "But Charlene must be served personally. She has a shared title to the house and van. There can't be a property division unless she has the opportunity to contest it.

"I don't understand," I groaned. "She deserted me. Why can't I get a divorce?"

"I feel for you, David. But that's the law here."

Now my other lawyer is on the phone. I seem to be supporting the legal profession these days just to survive.

"David?" It was Barry Weiss of Stone and Wertheim. "They've set a date for the eviction action. April 15th."

"That's three weeks from now!" I cried. "Tobias is already two months behind in his rent!"

Take my advice—never be a landlord. I wouldn't wish it on my worst enemy. Abe and I fell into landlording only because we couldn't sell our old house. My crazy sister-in-law is still blocking it. So we rented it out six months ago.

Tobias and his wife seemed like a nice young couple: warm and friendly. But no sooner were they moved in than he was pestering me to make repairs. Sure, the house needed updating. But we've had repairmen working there almost continuously on items big and small. And there seemed to be no job that could be done to the satisfaction of Tobias.

"I can't speed up the process," said Barry. "The court calendar is crowded. Shall I try to settle with Tobias instead?"

"I wish we could," I moaned. "He claims he's holding back the rent because of a long list of injustices. I've asked him more than once to put them in writing, but he won't. He's paying only five hundred a month, and we've already put out $10,000 in repairs."

"At this rate you'll never qualify as a gouging landlord," kidded Barry.

"I'll see you in court," I said, and hung up.

Hattie stuck her head into the room. "Time to leave for the airport."  ·

Martin now visits frequently, and it's getting to be like a merry-go-round. Every month or two we swing around Tampa International Airport and there's my brother, waiting to be picked up like the golden ring.

I grasped his hand tightly as he entered the van. "Okay, Hattie," he said, seating himself. "Give her the gas." And he sized us up appraisingly. "Looks like bachelorhood these days really agrees with you guys."

"Why isn't Rina here with you?" challenged Abe.

"I'm now retired. But she has to work; I need her to keep supporting me in the style to which I've become accustomed."

Abe smiled, somewhat mollified. "How is Rena?" he asked..

"She still makes a wonderful wife," kidded Martin. "After all these years, I've decided to keep her."

As we gathered round the table for dinner, I filled Martin in on Tobias. "The eviction hearing is tomorrow. He hasn't paid rent for over two months."

"Too bad we can't evict Charlene," said Abe. "They can't find her."

"Do you mean to say," Martin scrunched up his face, "that in four whole months, your lawyer hasn't been able to get to first base in your divorce?"

I nodded hopelessly.

Abe had the last word. "As I said before, marriage is a wonderful institution. But who wants to live in an institution?"

After Uncle Abe went off to bed, Martin came into my den, and it was like old times. We talked about family. We debated the latest theories of why the dinosaurs became extinct. We bemoaned the punitive cycle of welfare, where unwed mothers were raising the next generation of welfare mothers.

"How is it," I pondered aloud, "that Nature is so orderly and rational, while Man is so irrational?"

Martin humphed. "I wouldn't call Nature's cancer cell very rational," he said. "It goes off on a wild rampage, killing its innocent host."

"Maybe that's in the point of view," I argued. "After all, the antelope is innocent—but to a lion, it's only natural to run it down and tear it apart for a juicy meal. And he'll fight other lions for it."

Martin smiled and asked, "How shall we classify Charlene? Is she the cancer cell? Or the lion?"

I preferred to keep the conversation general. "The prime difference between the lion and Man is that Man has options for survival without destroying other human beings."

But Martin kept boring in. "How about those people who had no options? The six million in the Holocaust? The million innocent genocide victims in Cambodia? I might even mention the hopeless millions in our own city ghettos." He humphed again. "Charlene had options. And look at the choices she made."

I let some minutes flow by in silence, but there was no escaping.

Martin asked, "Why do you think Charlene gave up the security of this nice home and marriage for an uncertain future? Did Rina and I get in the way of your lives?"

"That wasn't really it. Charlene got frustrated when she couldn't have her own way. There were big arguments when I wouldn't give in. Especially over

Abe's going into a nursing home."

"Maybe she was seduced—mind as well as body—by that ship's officer?"

"Negative," I said. "If she told me she needed an outside lover, I would have understood. I could live with that. But I can't forgive her taking all that money. She knew it belonged to Uncle Abe—not me."

Martin stared at the opposite wall. "Maybe the world would be better off if money were abolished."

"Many people think money is the answer to all their problems," I said. "Money can bring pleasures in life—but you can't buy lasting satisfaction."

I unlocked the bottom drawer of my desk and handed some documents to Martin. "I want you to have copies of our revised wills. Abe leaves everything to me. And I'm leaving everything to you. Just like before Charlene.

"There's specific wording in my will to completely exclude Charlene," I added. And I waited to see what my brother would say about my Charlene fiasco.

He didn't. That's the wonderful thing about Martin. Not a word of 'I told you so' to rub salt in my wounds. He hasn't even let me see the satisfaction he must be feeling with Charlene no longer around.

That's *simpático*.


Life can be pretty tough for those of us who are disabled. It isn't only that so much of the world is barred to us. It's that most people don't try to understand how it feels to be treated as second-class citizens.

I had phoned the courthouse in advance and was told the building was accessible at the rear. Martin drove me in the van, and Uncle Abe came along because he always enjoys new experiences.

We arrived to find that there were two steps at the rear entrance. Not too bad. Martin pulled my wheelchair up without too much difficulty. But it turned out that the courtroom itself was on the second floor, with no elevator. I looked up at the forbidding row of steep steps and shook my head in disgust. In spite of our winning fight in the state legislature, so prolonged and bitter, even this courthouse had not complied with the state disabilities act of two years ago.

Barry Weiss came into sight and his face fell as we explained the problem. "I'll make a special pleading before the judge," said Barry. "He can hear the case down here just as well."

The lobby was small and crowded, with people having business with the municipal offices clustered on both sides. So they took me out in front of the building, where I could bask in the morning sun and read the novel I had brought along.

A half hour later, Martin came out to bring me up to date. Our case was about midway in the court calendar. Meanwhile, Barry had interceded with the judge to present my problem.

"Judge Flagler is just as insensitive to the disabled as most people," said Martin. "His solution was to send a couple of attendants down to carry you and the wheelchair up the stairs."

I grunted and Martin continued, "I stood up and pleaded that a disabled person feels demeaned to be carried. The judge tried to dismiss the problem by saying our counsel could represent our interests."

"And shut me out?"

"I controlled my temper and asked, 'Your Honor, isn't it a fact that my brother, as a principal in this proceeding, is entitled to be present? And isn't it also a fact that Florida law requires that this court be made accessible to the disabled?'"

I chuckled. "How did he take *that*?"

"He didn't like it at all. Then he muttered that he would hear our case from the front courthouse steps."

I congratulated Martin as a worthy advocate of disabled rights. Then at noon he returned to report that the court calendar was dragging. Uncle Abe and Barry came down the front steps, and we tried out a sandwich shop nearby. As we munched, Martin asked Barry, "What about the 'partition' action to force the sale of the house?"

"We haven't been able to serve your sister-in-law in California," said Barry.

Martin and I exchanged looks. "Do all you lawyers have a conspiracy?" asked Martin facetiously, then quickly added, "What's the specific problem?"

"They've gone to her apartment several times, and she won't open the door. She always asks who it is, and then says: 'Mrs. Richman is not at home.'"

"Why can't they just slip the papers under the door?"

Barry finished his coffee. "These papers must be served in person. And in California, service must be by a deputy sheriff. He won't hang around."

"I can't believe this!" cried Martin. "Are you saying we've got no recourse in a simple matter of serving papers? Is it fair for Dora to retain ownership in a property where *we* must pay the taxes and all the expenses?"

"Oh, we'll get her," said Barry confidently. "I'll arrange for a deputy sheriff to quiz her neighbors. He'll serve her when she goes shopping."

Martin heaved a sad sigh and paid the check.

When we returned to the courthouse, Martin said, "We can't leave you here on the sidewalk, David. The sun is fierce."

But there seemed to be no choice. No trees or other shade in sight. And I certainly didn't want to be sitting in that lobby, my wheelchair jostled on every side by the shifting crowd. So I said, "I'll be all right here. It probably won't be much longer."

But it was. The minutes dragged by, and then the hours. The Florida sun was blazing hotter than any day I remember. I began to feel I was in the Sahara. Martin came out several times to bring me a cold drink and to urge me to come inside. He had attempted to get the judge's attention but was reprimanded for interrupting.

This was getting me out of joint. Here was Justice practicing simple human injustice. My frying out here on the sidewalk was symbolic of the insensitivity suffered by the disabled community all the time.

About four o'clock Martin came rushing out to say the judge was on his way down. I discovered later this was because my brother made a scene in the courtroom and wouldn't be shut up.

Abe and Barry came to the bottom of the steps, followed by Tobias. Judge Flagler appeared at the top landing with a shorthand reporter, and they sat in chairs prepared for them. After cautioning Tobias of the risks he faced as his own attorney, the judge heard Barry's opening argument while mopping his brow every sixty seconds.

Tobias responded by saying he felt justified in holding back rent payments "because of the landlord's refusal to render the quarters habitable." He then began to reel off a whole litany of sufferings, starting with the roof leaking— when I paid $2,200 to have a new roof installed six weeks ago.

"Hold it, hold it," said the judge, raising his arm. "I've heard enough to know this case is too complex to be tried in the time remaining today." He lifted his gavel and suddenly realized he had no place for it to strike. But that didn't faze him. "Case postponed. Check with the clerk for the next open date on the calendar."

As the judicial robes moved out of sight, I saw Martin's face darken with anger.

"Who will judge the judges?" he growled morosely.


Two months have passed. Still no word of Charlene. I find myself thinking of her more and more. Where could she be? Is she still alive? Does she miss me? Do I miss her? Yes and no. I can't say I was ever in love with her. But she was so vivacious, so *exciting*. Put champagne into my daily living.

Of course, life with Charlene was a two-edged sword. The unpredictible could be joy. Or zaniness. The unexpected could be pleasure. Or pain.

Well, yes, I do miss her. The house is too still. I'm lonely. It's great when Martin is here, but he's gone. I feel empty.

I turn to writing more and more. The word processor is my constant companion. I punch up my latest short story and stare at the heading on the screen, "Together Again." Maybe this will be my final draft:

*The house was too silent. It didn't help his numbness.*

*He was accustomed to Martha's chatter during breakfast, but now all he heard was the annoying buzz of a fly coming nearer and nearer, and then the irritating tickle as the fly landed on his forearm and wandered there among the hairs. He brushed it off, getting more and more upset as the fly kept returning and had to be waved off again.*

*He stared at the untouched bowl of cereal before him. "You don't eat enough, John," Martha would warn him for the millionth time. She was a nagger. "You're as thin as a skeleton. Eat this. It's good for you." But the thought of inserting even a spoonful of that oatmeal into his mouth—*

*The fly suddenly landed on his forehead, then crawled over to explore his eyebrows. He slapped at it swiftly in frustration. But it got away, while he smarted.*

*Martha had hated flies. She said they were one of God's mistakes, and she kept a flyswatter handy in every room of the house. He picked up the swatter near him and waited, tensely, for the fly to touch down. It finally settled on a few specks of spilled sugar on the table. It was just beginning to savor the sweetness when he smashed it into a blob.*

*That was what happened to Martha.*

*She didn't see the trailer truck bearing down so swiftly. It rammed into her, ran her below its wheels, smashed her into pulp and bone while he could only watch, horrified, unable to move, until a policeman gently took his arm and led him away.*

*He pulled a paper napkin from its holder, picked up the fly's remains and placed the crumpled napkin on an empty plate. Lighting a match, he watched the paper and its contents burn until only the black ash was left. "Ashes to ashes," he thought, as he remembered the ceremony at the cemetery.*

*"But is death so final?" he asked himself. "Could there be another existence, another plane, where bodies are not needed?"*

*Such vital questions. Where are the answers? Even though Martha had been such an exasperating nagger, he still missed her. With all her faults, she had seeped into him, had subconsciously become a part of him. But now she was gone, and he felt as if part of his body had been sliced away.*

100

*For no apparent reason, a sense of urgency pulled at him. He knew that he had somewhere to go, someone to see. But the where, what and who eluded his brain. He knotted his tie carefully and slipped into his jacket. Martha had always insisted that he "dress up" before going out, and it was easier to go along than to disagree.*

*As he walked toward the door, his feet tangled with the cat, who let out a howl. Concerned, he reached down and tenderly explored whether he had injured the animal. She licked his hand and rubbed up hard against him. He smiled and lifted her into his arms*

*He loved this cat as much as Martha hated it. Maybe Martha disliked the animal because it had been close to him before he met Martha. She blamed everything that she could on the cat.*

*The urgency within him was growing stronger now, so he placed the cat gently in the easy chair. Its claws dug into his jacket as it attempted to cling to him, but he reluctantly disengaged. As he walked out the door, he could feel the cat staring at him with reproachful eyes.*

*He walked through the crowded streets, bemused, letting his feet carry him on his unthinking quest. His arthritis stiffened him more each year, so that he walked with a shorter, somewhat painful gait. But he covered the blocks between his house and the cemetery in a comparatively short time.*

*The cemetery? Why did he want to go there, today, now? Yet here he was, standing at the curb across the street from the entrance, waiting for the traffic light to change.*

*He felt a little hand slide into his, hold on to his fingers, tug at him. He looked down at the child's face, into Martha's eyes. Martha's look? In a child? What could it mean?*

*She was nine or ten, with an impish face and long blond hair, dressed in a green blouse and short yellow skirt. She was looking intently at him and motioning with her other hand. Did she want him to take her across the street? Or was she pointing to someone across the street—*

*Suddenly another hand jerked the child's hand from his, and a tall lady's angry voice hissed at him: "You dirty old man! I should have you arrested!" And then she was gone, dragging the little girl after her through the eddying crowd of people, her voice fading as she continued to admonish the child: "You should know better than to let a strange man touch you! Why, you might—"*

*He tried to put it out of his mind, and looked across the street. A woman was standing there, at the entrance to the cemetery. She looked like Martha. She looked very much like Martha. She WAS Martha!*

*She was now waving to him and smiling. She was looking at him as only*

*Martha could. Now she began moving fast toward him in the same way that Martha did when they met again after a separation, running toward him, oblivious of the traffic speeding both ways and the horns blowing their warnings, and he ws shouting at her to STOP! LOOK OUT! And he was dashing across the street to save her and—*

*'That's when the big truck hit him and smashed him to bits.*

*That's when they were together again.*

It was three o'clock in the morning—much later than I usually stay up. But I wanted to complete the finishing touches on my story. This is one story I was thoroughly pleased with. At last I have something I feel is worthy of sending out for publication.

I heard a noise outside my study window, and the hair on the back of my neck stood on end. There had been no robberies in the neighborhood that I knew of. Doesn't mean we couldn't be the first break-in. With Hattie gone, me in a wheelchair and my 87-year-old uncle asleep, we were as helpless as babes.

As I reached for the phone, a face suddenly appeared in my window, and I was transfixed. It was Charlene!

"David," she called. "Come to the front door and let me in. I must talk to you."

I couldn't believe my eyes and ears. I pinched myself to see if I was dreaming or acting out my fantasies.

"It's really me, Charlene." Her voice was insistent. "Please let me in."

My nerves were beginning to settle back into their accustomed places. I thought I had heard someone at the front door earlier, but dismissed the noise. Now I remembered that I had arranged for the locks to be changed after Charlene left.

"Why?" I hissed at her through the windowpane.

"David, I'm terribly sorry for what I did to you. I made a horrible mistake, okay? Please open the door. I just want to talk."

"Where have you been all this time?"

"I've been wandering. Everywhere. And I've been very sick, okay? You must let me in."

This was too much like a dream. Maybe exploding into a nightmare. "No," I said.

She pleaded through the window with big tears in her eyes. She told me how many agonies she had gone through. How many times she had written to me, and then torn it up because she didn't know how to beg forgiveness. How she had had a mental breakdown because her stupidity had brought her to a dead end. How she was on the verge of taking her life now because she had lost all hope.

Too much of this was familiar stuff, and it strengthened my resolve. "It's too late," I said to the anguished face in the window. "If you have any feelings left for me, you'll let me have my divorce!"

I swung my wheelchair around and clicked off the light as I sailed out of my den, leaving her standing outside in the empty darkness.

The next morning I became dimly aware of more than one female voice outside my bedroom. Who could Hattie have visiting? I opened my sleep-starved eyes to check the time. Only 9 a.m., and their voices were so loud?

With a start I heard Charlene's voice at my doorway. "I thought you'd never wake up, David. I must talk to you."

I dragged myself up on one elbow, drowsiness banished. "What are you doing here, Charlene?" I demanded in a stiff, stern voice. "How did you get in?"

"Please don't be mad, David. I had no place to go last night, okay? I slept in the car. In the driveway. Till Hattie arrived this morning to let me in."

This upset me. "I told you last night that I didn't want you in this house!"

"David, I came to tell you that you can have the divorce, and I want nothing from you. You're just not letting me explain."

That was a surprise. I stared at her. "Why did you duck it all this time? Where were you?"

She came over and sat on my bed, her head hanging low. "I never believed that people can suddenly go crazy ... until it happened to me. I don't know what came over me to leave you. Two weeks later I felt sick about it and wanted to come back, okay? But I was afraid."

"So where did you go?"

"I went wandering all over the Caribbean, trying to forget myself, to escape from my guilt, okay? But I couldn't. I was sick with stabbing head pains. I was a bundle of nerves all the time."

I stared at her. "Where's the money you took?"

She looked away and didn't answer. Finally she murmured, "I'm broke, David. The money's gone. To doctors, mostly. Nervous breakdown. I spent months in a sanitarium in Mexico to put me back on my feet. I went completely out of my mind."

I wondered if I could believe her. She did have the wan, strained look of one who had spent time in a sanitarium. She must have lost fifty pounds, and the lines on her face were etched deeply. She had aged a lot in just six months.

"David, I'm well enough now to work again. And I promise to pay you back—every penny, okay? I know that seems like a lot of money. But I expect a settlement soon in my case against the Ramada Inn, and my lawyer said that should be about $150,000."

I had almost forgotten about that lawsuit. Three months before Charlene left me, we attended a meeting of the Disabled Voters of Southern Florida held at the local Ramada Inn. When Charlene got up to speak at the mike, she tripped and fell with an enormous crash and had to be taken to the hospital. She seemed okay the next day. Yet she claimed negligence on the part of the hotel, and her lawyer cousin initiated a claim for $300,000.

"You won't contest the divorce now?"

"I'll be devastated if you go ahead, but I won't fight it."

"Would you be willing to give up your rights to our van and put me back as the sole owner?

"Yes."

"Would you be ready to sign your rights to this house back to me and Abe? You know it was all Uncle Abe's money, and we added your name to the title only because you said it would give you a feeling of 'security'. Will you sign the house over to us?"

"Yes."

"And do you promise to give Abe back the money you took, and promise not to charge anything on credit cards in the future?"

"Yes, yes. I'll do anything you ask," she said, tears welling up in her eyes. "I know I was wrong, okay?" I began to see Charlene in a new light.

After I had breakfasted and dressed, I called Greta Townsend, my divorce lawyer, and told her tongue-in-cheek, "You couldn't find Charlene for six months, and I have her here now in my house. And she won't run away."

Greta was astounded to hear my story. "Some people become born-again Christians," I told her. "I guess Charlene has become a born-again wife." And I asked Greta to draw up reconciliation papers to cover all the stipulations I had made, and to which Charlene had agreed.

I could barely restrain my joy at this turn of events. In a sense it justified my judgment about Charlene at the beginning. She was basically a good person. She had just gotten off on a wrong path. It wasn't too late.

Then I dialed Martin's number. I just had to tell him how beautifully things were working out.

I described how Charlene was going to make good on all the problems she had caused, but I could tell I wasn't getting through to Martin. I sensed he was overcome by shock and anger. When I finished, he blurted out, "David, you're a chump to believe her!"

I lowered the phone in disappointment. Martin had always been so understanding in the past. How could he say that now—just when I needed him most?

I answered him right from the heart. "Maybe I am," I said. "But you're not the one who has to be lonely in his old age!"

# CHAPTER X
# SWEET MYSTERY OF LIFE

### *Martin—One day later*

I wasted no time in flying down to Sarasota. Hearing that Charlene was back in our lives again was like feeling a black widow spider crawling on the nape of my neck. But as I finished packing, Rina took me by the hand, sat me down, and massaged my emotional trauma.

"I want you to think this through carefully," she said. "You've got to see it and feel it through David's eyes. Remember what he said: 'You're not the one who has to be lonely.'"

I took a deep breath. "You're right. I'm biting my tongue for calling him a 'chump'." I let out a sigh. "But I don't need a crystal ball to see all the heartache he's letting himself in for."

Rina stared through my eyes into my brain. "How much of what you're feeling is because of the misery he's letting *you* in for?"

Touché. Once I recognized that, my anger simmered down and was replaced by concern. Concern for my brother. Concern for my uncle. Concern for the best way to deal with the new face on the situation.

I did some hard thinking on the plane. True, Charlene had hurt us all, stolen money and shattered trust. Part of me was reluctant to forgive her. But did I truly believe, as I thought I did, that a person isn't born evil—but is buffeted, distorted and molded by a critical series of experiences? If so, maybe I had to give Charlene another chance. Should I reach out to help her? Help her re-shape her thinking, her motivations, her behavior patterns? *This is what my brother will be doing. I must give him every possible support.*

So I took a sheet of paper and set down the things that were so special about our family relationships. Maybe these points could help Charlene understand and begin to feel part of the family.

David and Uncle Abe were delighted to see me. Charlene greeted me with wary overenthusiasm. Her face was sallow and I guessed she had lost over fifty pounds. Hattie served dinner, and there was an air of normalcy that I hadn't felt for a very long time.

All through the meal I wondered what the new Charlene was really like. Shouldn't I probe to see if she might reveal her true feelings? After Abe went to his room, I suggested that the three of us have a talk.

I told Charlene that I wanted our relationship to get off to a fresh start. "But just to clear the air, I'd like to ask some frank questions. Please don't answer any that make you feel uncomfortable."

She nodded thoughtfully for me to go ahead.

"First, what prompted you to leave my brother?"

"I thought I had fallen in love with somebody else."

Tears formed in her eyes, and she said through muffled sobs, "I made a terrible mistake, okay?"

"I understand." I kept my voice gentle. "But why did you take the money?"

After a moment she stopped sobbing and said, "It seemed to me that David was criticizing me all the time. I felt he didn't want me around anymore, okay? So I decided to leave. And I felt that, as his wife, I was entitled to some of his money."

"Are you aware that all of the money you took belonged to Uncle Abe?" I tried to keep the accusing tone out of my voice.

"I know. But I just wasn't thinking straight. And I told David that I want to pay it all back. I feel very bad about it, okay?" She started to sob again.

She sounded contrite, sincere. But I had to ask one more question. "Charlene, David tells me you were ill much of the time you were away, and that you spent a long time at a sanitarium in Mexico. What was it called?"

She continued sobbing, and finally said, "I don't remember the name of the place."

"What city was it in or near?" I asked softly.

"I don't remember," she moaned, eyes flooding. "I was mixed up. My life was all cracked up, okay? And I was broke, okay? I just wanted to forget everything that happened and put my life back together."

That told me what I wanted to know. Charlene was still not ready to open up to us. How, in just six months, could she have spent the entire $100,000 she took? How could she have stayed months at a sanitarium without knowing the name of the place when she left? It just didn't add up.

Maybe the real story is: 1) her funds began to run dry; 2) she came back for a meal ticket and to reinstate herself for inheriting the house and Abe's money.

Hold it. Here I am, carrying over my yesterday's attitudes about Charlene into today. That's the same kind of thinking that propelled Charlene into mistrusting us, into mistaking our goodwill as antagonism toward her. In all her yesterdays, her prime experience was that she just couldn't trust anybody.

Another chance. David wanted it. I had to give it a fair try, realizing that Charlene couldn't transform forty years of negative attitude overnight.

Late that evening, after Abe was asleep and David shifted from wheelchair to bed, I took Charlene aside for a heart-to-heart. She certainly had changed. She listened without saying a word. And I had the feeling I was really reaching her.

I started out by saying, "Charlene, I'm ready to forget all the ill feelings which developed between us. I'm anxious, not only for David's sake but for all of us, to give our relationship a fresh start."

My voice was earnest, imploring. I wanted so much for this to work.

"Charlene—I would like to be your brother. Not a brother-in-law. A true brother.

"I suppose this is hard for you to understand and believe. Please try, Charlene. Try very hard. Think of the closeness between David and me. Anytime he has any trouble, he can count on me. He always has someone to tell his troubles to. Even when he hates himself, he knows he has a special person who believes in him and loves him.

"Wouldn't you like to have that yourself, Charlene? Wouldn't you like to have a brother you could feel very close to? Wouldn't you like a soft shoulder you could cry on … someone you could always depend on whenever you needed help?"

I looked into her eyes and saw the desperate yearning there. Tears were forming and dribbling down her face. I had touched a nerve, a vital one.

But wait. This can't last unless I build a strong foundation. I had opened the gate, so I went charging in.

I put my hand on Charlene's shoulder. "I'd like to help you understand what a close family relationship is like," I said, taking out the notes I had written on the plane. Using them to refresh my mind, I spelled out what David and Uncle Abe mean to me:

*1) I feel a deep commitment to David and Uncle Abe. They are family, like my wife and children. This means putting their welfare before my own. And we're anxious to make Charlene feel part of our family.*

*2) The health of David and Abe is extremely important to us. We will jump on a plane whenever necessary to be sure they get the best care. We will not allow anyone to be shuffled off to a nursing home if there's an alternative.*

*3) Also important is our financial commitment. Suppose Charlene had taken ALL of Abe's money. You can be sure Rina and I would immediately offer to support them. Even if that meant my giving up retirement and going back to work.*

*That's the real meaning of family.*

Charlene absorbed all this with rapt attention, eyes wide as if exposed to a new revelation. Was I breaking through? Now the most important thing.

I said softly, "I know you're not used to trusting people, Charlene. And you have good reason not to, I suppose. But maybe this is the one time when you should take the risk.

"Let's start out fresh. I'd like to be your brother, Charlene. Let's work on it together. It can't happen overnight. But it can develop and grow. Charlene—" my voice was insistent, "I can be the brother you never had."

As this sunk in, the dikes of her emotions burst and she threw her arms around me, her large bulk heaving in great sobs. I embraced her warmly, feeling a catharsis sweeping through me as well.

It was a non-sexual climax, an emotional high. It doesn't happen very often in one's life.

Charlene was a new person for the other two days of my visit. David was overjoyed to see how lighthearted and considerate she had become, and wanted to know what magic I had wrought.

My concern now was with Uncle Abe. He was clearly depressed. He spoke only in response to a question. Finally I said, "What's wrong, Uncle Abe?"

"Nothing."

But I knew the answer. He had been buffeted too many times. First the intrusion and takeover by Charlene. Then the uprooting from the house he was used to. Then Charlene's abandoning David and absconding with his money. After all that, she was back again. How much could an 87-year-old man cope with?

"You look younger than you did a year ago," I lied, trying to cheer him up. "You're getting younger all the time."

This usually stimulated a wisecrack, but not this time. So I added jocularly, "Say, how about coming back with me for a visit, Uncle Abe? For a bachelor like you, I may be able to arrange some hot and cold running blondes."

Not even a flicker of response.

I tried another tack. I described my talk with Charlene, how I think she is changing and becoming a caring member of our family, and that this could all work out for the best after all.

I looked at Uncle Abe. He had left me and retreated to a world of his own. I didn't know what else to say or do. Maybe only time could do the healing.

The letter from David two weeks later was very encouraging:

> *Dear Martin and Rina:*
>
> *I wanted you to know how great things are here since Martin's visit. Charlene goes around with a happy face all the time. She's even begun singing to herself, which she never did before. Her attitude toward me is also remarkable. Like we're on a second honeymoon. I can't help being skeptical, but I'm too happy to let it bother me.*
>
> *Uncle Abe has come out of his depression. Charlene is jollying him just as in the days before we got married, and he's responding like the old Abe—you know, making wisecracks.*
>
> *I reminded Charlene of the promises she made when I agreed to take her back. No problem. I'm contacting our lawyer for Charlene to sign over her share of the house.*
>
> *Love,*
> *David*

On my next visit to Sarasota some weeks later, I experienced the surprising change for myself. Charlene was cordial and caring. I thanked her for the charming hand-knitted afghan she had sent up as our anniversary gift.

"I wanted to do something nice for my brother and sister," she said. "Now how would you like to do something for me?"

She picked up a syringe from the kitchen counter and handed it to me. "Jab it right here," and she bared her upper arm. When I hesitated, she said, "Come on, it's only my daily insulin shot."

I winced as I complied. Then I felt a rubbing against my ankle and glanced down. Looking up at me was one of the cutest kittens I'd ever seen. Its coat was reddish-brown, with white setting off the whiskers on its pert face.

It inclined its head to the right and gazed up at me quizzically. I smiled and picked it up. Holding it in one palm, I stroked it gently and scratched behind its ears. It purred contentedly.

"I brought her home ten days ago for Uncle Abe," said Charlene. "Cinnamon has become wonderful company for him."

"What a good idea," I said, stroking some more.

"Wait till you see how carefully Abe fixes her dinner each day, okay? He won't let Hattie do it. He opens the cat food with the electric can opener and scrapes out every scrap into the feeding dish. Cinnamon is friendly to everyone, but she's adopted Uncle Abe as her sweetheart."

I took Cinnamon into Abe's room, where he was watching TV. He smiled as she jumped onto his bed and rubbed against his arm.

"I hear you have a new girlfriend," I said. "Glad to see you haven't lost your touch, you old bachelor."

He grinned at me as he petted Cinnamon. "She's the cat's meow," he said.

I could see that he was back on the happy road. This kitten from Charlene was inspired, and I complimented her again when I returned to the living room.

"As soon as I saw it wandering around outside without a family, I thought of Uncle Abe," said Charlene.

After dinner Abe went to his room to watch his favorite TV program. The three of us moved to David's study and we talked late into the night. Our conversation rambled around things of the heart. Like the importance of love. Charlene said her favorite song was "Sweet Mystery of Life," and she proceeded to sing us some of the words:

*Ah, sweet mystery of life, at last I've found thee,*
*Ah, at last I know the secret of it all...*
*For it's love and love alone the world is seeking,*
*And it's love alone that rules for aye.*

I mentioned seeing a quote by Ralph Waldo Emerson that went something like: "What lies behind and what lies ahead are tiny matters when compared to what lies within." I suggested that maybe the meaning of life is summed up in three words: Love. Trust. Commitment.

The next morning, Hattie served us one of her prodigious breakfasts, which was too much for me. I eat lightly so early—just enough to 'break my fast.'

Charlene kissed each of us and announced, "Sorry to leave you all, but I gotta go off to work, okay?"

She was out the door before I had a chance to ask about her job. So she's working. Happy days.

"Good news," said David, opening the day's mail. "We've collected the back rent on the old house from Tobias the Troublemaker. Here's a certified check for $1,500, covering three months. Now if Dora would only agree to sell the house, we could get rid of Tobias once and for all."

"Sure, but nothing's happening. Except that we get bills from the San

Francisco sheriff's office for 'attempting to serve papers.'"

"In other words, they charge for failure?"

I grinned and changed the subject. "I like the happy way Charlene sailed off for work. She's not doing Kall Girl manicuring again, is she?"

"No, that's behind her. She has a friend in the travel business, who's breaking her in. Charlene has the personality to be a successful travel agent —don't you think? And she's anxious to earn her own way and not be a burden."

Another score for Charlene. I was wrong. People can change. Then I wondered about the promises she made when David took her back, and asked, "Has Charlene given up her title to the van and the house?"

"Not yet, but she will. Hasn't she improved tremendously?" he said, beaming. "She does everything I say. No more arguments. Abe is happy to have her around. He even said last week that he wants her to stay with us always. It's like old times."

That sounded pretty good to me.

# CHAPTER XI
# MARITAL MIGRAINE

### *Martin—Two months later*

My consulting work had kept me from visiting Sarasota for a while. David and Abe greeted me warmly, but I was puzzled by Charlene's reception. I had given her a big kiss and close embrace, but she was matter-of-fact. Had she forgotten the emotional bonding of our last visit? Was she disregarding the warm tone of my letters and phone calls?

When she walked into the bedroom to refurbish her face, I followed her and asked softly, "Charlene, is there anything wrong?"

"Naw." She applied the blazing red lipstick artfully. "Why should there be?"

"I heard you weren't feeling well lately. I was just concerned."

"I'm fine."

"I just hope you're not letting things that happened to you in the past get you down." I put my arm on her shoulder and said compassionately, "You know, Charlene, if you carry your childhood with you, you never become older and wiser."

She shrugged and spoke as if she hadn't heard me. "I stopped in for a bite of lunch, okay? Now I gotta get me back to work." And she was off.

After Hattie served us lunch, I followed Uncle Abe into his bedroom for a talk. He also seemed out of sorts. He sat on his bed and petted Cinnamon, but I couldn't get him to open up.

"You're so quiet, Uncle Abe—is there anything the matter?"

After a minute, he said he had no money left. I reminded him that he had bank C.D.s and stocks, as well as a checking account. He was skeptical. I got the records from David's den and showed him.

"This is the same joint account you've had for years. It has David's name and yours so David can pay the bills without bothering you. Look—your balance is over twenty-five hundred dollars right now. Anytime you need money, you can just write a check and cash it."

"How can I cash it? I don't drive anymore."

"No problem. Just ask Charlene to cash it for you. Or Hattie. In the meantime, here's twenty dollars." And I took a bill from my wallet and placed it in his hands.

I thought I had convinced him. But the next day he asked me if Charlene had taken all his money, and I had to go through the whole routine again

I questioned David about it. "Just before you came down," he said, "Abe asked me how much money Charlene took. I couldn't lie to him. He was shocked to hear it was a hundred thousand dollars. So it's still on his mind."

"Anything wrong with Charlene?" I asked. "She greeted me like I was a wet sheet. And I notice she's put on a lot of weight again. Has her diabetes been acting up?"

"Charlene gives herself an insulin injection every morning," David said, "but she hasn't been well. She's been to several doctors, and none can put their finger on it."

"If she's not up to par, is it a good idea for her to be working?"

David assured me that working was the best thing for her. She was too hyper to sit around. "As a matter of fact," said David, "she decided to handle the house on weekends. So we've cut out Hattie's sister. And I give Charlene two hundred dollars a week for Saturdays and Sundays."

My red flag went up but I let that pass. "What's happened with Charlene's lawsuit, where she expected to get a big settlement for injuries at the Ramada Hotel?"

"Doesn't look good. One of the women at that event is hostile towards Charlene. It turns out she is ready to testify that Charlene was drunk when she tripped. That just isn't true. But some people are spiteful."

After a pause I said, "David, Charlene has been back with you for over three months. I'm sure you don't expect her to pay back the hundred thousand. But have you decided to forget the other promises she made?"

"No, I had Greta, my divorce lawyer, draft up a document where Charlene agrees to sign over the van and the house as the reconciliation. But I've been dissatisfied with the wording. I've just done a revision myself and Charlene has agreed to sign it."

I wondered why an agreement was necessary. Why couldn't Charlene just *do* it?


Charlene breezed through the front door as if her vast bulk didn't conform to the laws of gravity. She immediately flooded us in a torrent of her experiences and frustrations at the travel agency where she worked. Meanwhile, she removed a half gallon of ice cream from the freezer and proceeded to ladle out about a third of the tutti-frutti into a large bowl. Interrupting her rapid-fire delivery just long enough to offer us some, she didn't wait for a reply, and quickly replaced the container in the freezer.

"But what really bugs the shit out of me," Charlene said testily, "are those bastards who use the handicapped parking places without a permit, okay? Everyplace I go—the post office, the supermarket, the cleaners—I find perfectly healthy people taking up the spaces reserved for the disabled."

"Is there a lot of that going on?" I asked.

"Bet your ass," she grunted, starting on the tutti-frutti. "So I ran this off at my office. I'm sticking it on every windshield of every car parked illegally, okay?" She handed us a sheet which read:

*YOU JUST DEPRIVED A DISABLED PERSON OF A PARKING PLACE! A PERSON WHO HAD NO OTHER PLACE TO PARK. SHAME ON YOU!!*
*YOU ALSO BROKE THE LAW! NEXT TIME WE WILL REPORT YOU TO THE POLICE. YOUR CAR WILL BE TOWED AWAY AND YOU WILL BE FINED*
*YOU WILL ALSO GO TO HELL!!!*

"Hey—that's really telling them!" cried David with spontaneous glee. Turning to me he said, "Charlene has been doing a lot for the disabled lately. We've formed a new group—Disabled Citizens of Florida—to make sure the laws are fully enforced."

I was impressed. But as I watched Charlene spoon all that ice cream into her mouth, I couldn't help feeling uneasy. As a diabetic, this gorging could be more than a little threatening to her health. It looked like she had put on most of the weight she had lost before David took her back.

Still, I felt this wasn't the time for me to play big brother. So I finished packing and went to chat with Abe.

He lowered his newspaper as I walked into his room. I peered into his eyes. "How're you feeling, Uncle Abe?"

He gave me the old routine. "With my hands," he said, flexing his fingers in the air.

I tried to engage him in conversation, but he seemed introspective. So I brought him up to date on Scott and Annabel, and his eyes took on some of the old warmth. He was so close to our kids while they were growing up. "They ask about you all the time," I said. "Remember, you were the grandfather they never had."

Suddenly Charlene's ample frame filled the door to Abe's room. I turned to see her glaring at me in a barely controlled rage. "Again!" she grated through clenched teeth. "You're interfering again! Everything was going so smooth before you came down, goddammit!"

I was struck speechless. Charlene disappeared before my brain shifted back into gear. I rushed after her, hoisting up my big question marks, but I was too late. The door to her bedroom slammed and I heard her inside, letting off steam to David.

I turned back to Abe's room and saw that he felt as speared as I did. His eyes were filled with pain.

David came out an hour later and apologized for Charlene's outburst. He had asked her to sign the simplified agreement. She took it the wrong way—blaming me for coming between them, for telling David not to trust her. "She's just over-hyper," he said. "It'll be okay once she settles back to normal."

My taxi was at the door. It was time for me to leave for home.

I just wish I knew what was normal for Charlene.

Back in Connecticut I had a long discussion with Rina. "She promised David the world if he'd take her back. Then after three months, her excuse is that I'm interfering!"

Rina tried to mediate. "Isn't that a matter between husband and wife?"

"Of course. But my brother is so easygoing, and it hurts to see him taken advantage of," I said. "He pays every dollar of Charlene's bills even though she has a job, plus now he's paying her two hundred dollars for weekends. That's the first I've heard of a husband paying a wife a salary."

Rina grinned. "Maybe it's about time men realized that wives work, too, when they fix meals and care for a home. And wives don't even get the minimum wage."

"I hope you're not including me in the male chauvinist brigade, Rina." I knitted my brow. "Actually, what concerns me is my relationship with Charlene. I felt so sure I had gotten through to her. I thought she would reach out for the brother she never had. We felt so close that night. She cried. Was it just an act?"

Rina thought it wasn't. "Psychology teaches us that the past is never over. It flavors our feelings, our thinking. It breathes over every action we take, often unnoticed and often in opposition to what we really want.

"Charlene is terribly insecure," Rina continued. "Her father and her previous husband traumatized her. Her experiences all through her life hardened her against trusting anybody. You probably touched a nerve that night. But can you really expect to soften that encrusted shell with just one small opening?"

True. I could see how difficult it must be for Charlene to trust. Maybe I *was* at fault for interfering between husband and wife. Why did I have to stir things up?

Yet Charlene had made specific promises to achieve the reconciliation with David. The van and the house were bought with Abe's money, giving her no rightful claim. Why hadn't she carried through in the past three months? Why was it even necessary to have a signed agreement instead of just doing what she committed to?

I put my thoughts into words. "What if it's really *Charlene* who can't be trusted?"

Rina gave a small smile. "How will we know unless we keep trying the other alternative?"

That evening I sat down and wrote a warm, brotherly letter to Charlene.

A month later I found myself rushing to the airport. David had phoned to say that Uncle Abe was in the hospital after another incident of disorientation. He addressed Charlene by our mother's name, 'Rose'. He'd lost all bladder and bowel control. And he'd suddenly became so weak that he could barely stand up.

At Tampa airport I grabbed a taxi and went right to the hospital. Uncle Abe recognized me, but that was all. I couldn't get him to respond rationally. His speech was slurred. He seemed groggy and his eyes kept closing into brief naps all through the day.

As I was about to leave for Sarasota, Dr. Brown, the psychiatrist, walked in and checked the clipboard at the bottom of the bed. I accompanied him out of the room and asked for an update.

"Mr. Bloom has had a relapse, but it's not serious," he said crisply. "I have him on sedatives, and he should be better in a few days."

I touched the man's arm as he was turning away. "Doctor," I said, "this came on so suddenly. Is it possible it was caused by my uncle's overmedicating himself? He has done that in the past."

Dr. Brown paused. "It's possible."

I tried to interpret that reply. "I mean—did the tests here show anything?"

Dr. Brown shrugged. "I'll order a check on that," he said, and turned quickly to leave.

I stared at his retreating back and became upset. *That's too late, Doctor. You mean no tests were taken when Abe arrived at the hospital? And you call yourself a psychiatrist?*

Hattie served dinner as I described my conversation with Dr. Brown. David sympathized, but said my concern was unfounded. "Abe can't overdose himself anymore. We keep his medications in the cupboard above the sink, where he can't reach them. Charlene sets out the right pills at each meal and

117

before he goes to bed."

"I just don't understand these ups and downs," I said.

"Martin, we've got to accept the fact that Uncle Abe is now eighty-seven years old. Maybe Charlene's right. Maybe it's time for Abe to be in a nursing home, where he'd have the companionship of people like himself, and where he'd be looked after more closely."

I stared at David. "I hope you don't mean that," I said firmly.

Charlene was strangely quiet during the conversation. I couldn't remember a time when we talked and she didn't deliver her opinion. I wondered what she was thinking.

Uncle Abe came home two days later. His speech was slurred, but he was back in our world. He was weak, but could walk with the help of his cane. He asked about Rina and my kids. He even made a small jest with Hattie. But he was far from the old Abe.

Cinnamon was his constant companion. He no longer set out her food, but he petted her and played with her, using a piece of string. He kept to his own room except for meals.

Charlene's attitude toward me was cool and wary. I had the feeling there was something simmering under the surface that I wouldn't like to see. She made no mention of my solicitous letter.

After she left for work, David told me he had been doing some hard thinking. "Charlene has been giving me a tough time lately," he said. "She flies into a rage over little things. And she expects everything to be done her way."

So Abe wasn't the only one on an emotional roller-coaster. I pursed my lips and asked, "What sort of things?"

"The latest is that she wanted to go on another cruise. I wasn't opposed, but she got mad when I refused to provide the money."

"Aren't you giving her that $200 every week? And isn't she earning money at her job?"

"Not enough," said David quickly. "She keeps putting off going for her travel agent's license, so she gets only part of the commissions."

"I see. So?"

"Charlene's one big weakness is that she doesn't see things through. So I've decided not to let her procrastinate any longer on the house and the van. I've made an appointment to see our lawyer tomorrow for her to sign that paper we spoke about. I'd like you to be with me, Martin."

I was surprised at David's spine-stiffening. It seems that the lines were being drawn. "Of course I'll come. Where is Greta Townsend's office?"

"We'll be using Stone & Wertheim instead," he said. "Greta wanted to dot every 'i' and cross every 't'. I don't want Charlene to feel hemmed in with all that legalistic language."

I just hoped that without all that "legalistic language" the signed agreement would still be legal. But I held my tongue.

That evening after dinner, as I chatted with Abe in his room, all hell broke loose. Like a repeat performance, Charlene came bursting in. She was breathing fire and brimstone.

"Goddam you! I'll fuckin' never sign any paper for you!" she screamed in my face. "All you want is to break up our marriage! That's what you've tried to do ever since you first came down here!"

"Look, I—"

"You and your ass-sucking wife!" She gave me no chance to speak. "Making nicey-nicey while you try to drown me in shit! And your stupid-ass kids coming down here for free meals and vacations in the sun!"

My blood flared hotly and I held my arms rigid to keep from slapping her contorted face. "You'd better not say another word about my wife and kids." My voice was low and menacing as I put my face close to hers and glared into her eyes.

We stood that way for maybe a minute, silently locked in each other's fury. Then she whirled that globular body around and stalked rapidly out. I heard her bedroom door slam, but it could do little to muffle her high-pitched screeching at David, laced liberally with more profanity.

It was still going on when I closed my bedroom door in the vain hope of getting some sleep.

As Abe and I were finishing breakfast the next morning, Charlene marched into the kitchen in her robe. Sullen and silent as a Mayan god, she poured herself coffee and stiffly exited. Soon thereafter David joined us, and Hattie laid out his meal.

"How're you feeling this morning, David?" I ventured.

He grinned weakly. "We are all going to the lawyer at 10:30."

"How did you manage that?" My voice was admiring.

He buttered his toast. "I'm getting tired of Charlene's hysterics. After she ran out of breath, I told her it was lawyer today—or divorce right away."

I gave a low whistle. "David, I never thought you could be a rock where Charlene is concerned. Congratulations!"

David smiled grimly. "I told Charlene when I took her back that it was a trial. She made promises. There comes a time when she has to prove herself."

I turned to look at Uncle Abe. He had heard but obviously didn't get what was going on, so I slowly explained. Then, after David finished eating, we three boarded the van and I drove to Stone and Wertheim's office.

Along the way David said, "After I turned Charlene down on the cruise, she asked Uncle Abe to give her the money."

"Oh? Did he?"

"He told me later that he felt like giving it to her because she had already taken so much—what's a little more?"

My heart skipped a beat. "What happened?"

"When he came to me for the money and found out I had refused her, he told her he couldn't go against my wishes."

We found Charlene already sitting in the hickory-paneled conference room, along with her Uncle Mike. When the portly Benjamin Stone entered, she introduced Mike Fox as her spokesman. What followed was so bizarre that it could have come right out of a soap opera.

"I understand that you are here simply to have a reconciliation agreement signed and notarized," said Stone, looking down. "Is this the document?"

"Actually," said Mike in his smoothest car-dealer tone, "we're meeting here to clear things up. We're all family, and people shouldn't get excited over a few little differences in the family—"

I couldn't help blurting out, "A few little differences—?"

"Look," said Mike soothingly, "Charlene made a big mistake in leaving David. Everybody makes mistakes. She's sorry. She's so sorry, she's mortified. But they love each other. And that's the really important thing—isn't it?"

"What are you suggesting?" David asked.

Mike's voice was oily. "We're all family. We can patch up our differences. Why do we need lawyers and legal papers? Why don't we just go home and work things out?"

There was a pregnant silence, and David said quietly, "Charlene made certain promises to me when she asked me to take her back. I want to know now whether she is prepared to carry out those promises."

Mike jumped to his feet and grew fiery. "What's the matter? Hasn't this poor girl suffered enough? She knows she made the biggest mistake of her life. It's been tormenting her, ruining her health. What do you want—blood?"

Uncharacteristically, David was not to be intimidated. "Charlene promised," he said. "The house and the van were bought with Uncle Abe's money—not mine. I put her name on the titles to please her, as my wife. She must sign them over as she promised."

Charlene didn't say a word. But Mike was ready with an answer. "Okay. She'll sign. But what will you do for her in return?"

David looked puzzled. "What do you mean?"

"You want her to give up something. Okay—what's it worth to you? What will you pay?"

David looked dumbfounded, so I asked, "What do you have in mind?"

"Well, half of the van would be eight thousand dollars and one-third of the house down-payment would be ten thousand. I'd say that eighteen thou would be fair all around." He ended with an owlish grin.

David quickly turned to Charlene. "Is Mike speaking for you on this? Are you asking me and Abe for eighteen thousand dollars?"

Charlene's lips compressed in stubborn defiance, and she nodded agreement.

I couldn't believe what was happening. Charlene, who had begged David to take her back and had made every kind of promise—including paying back the hundred thousand she took—was now asking for eighteen thousand more from her husband. Actually from his uncle's money. And she expected to continue on as his ever-loving wife.

I looked up and saw the thunderstruck expression on Stone's face. He knew Charlene had deserted her husband. He was amazed to hear that David had taken her back. And here she was, brazenly demanding money which doesn't belong to her husband.

"That's a lot of money," said David. "I'll have to think it over."

"Oh sure," said Mike expansively. "Think it over. I'll take Charlene across the street for some coffee. We'll be back in fifteen minutes."

As they walked out, I asked Uncle Abe if he understood what was going on, and I explained. He was aghast at the turn of affairs.

Then I asked David what he wanted to do. He didn't hesitate. "I'll reinstate my divorce suit right away," he said grimly. "I can never trust Charlene again."

It gave me a lift to hear him say that. The triumph of reason over blind emotion. My old David was back.

We started working out a plan. I said to David, "If you mention 'divorce' when they come back, Charlene might disappear again. Why not avoid it till the divorce papers are served?"

Before David could answer, Mike and Charlene walked in and seated themselves. "Well?" asked Mike.

"I'll need more time," said David. "Let's go home."

# CHAPTER XII
# SURVIVOR

### *David—One Month Later*

Life is a comedy interrupted by tragedy. Of course, comedy day after day can get boring. But must there be so many interruptions?

I was waiting in my van with Hattie for Martin to arrive. Tampa airport was crowded, as it usually is on a Friday evening. And I pondered what to do about Charlene.

I haven't changed my mind about the divorce since Martin was down a month ago. But messy it will be. So I asked Martin to come back and help me with the first step.

"There he is," I said to Hattie, and she inched the van forward to where Martin could see us waving. He tossed in his bag and, on the way to Sarasota, talked about the consulting work he'd taken on since his retirement.

"When it comes to marketing," said Martin, "executives at the top think there's a magic bullet. But the answers are always complex. And the biggest problem is that old attitudes die so hard. People pay you for the ideas and advice which they admit are good. And then they don't follow through. What a waste!"

'Back at the house, Martin said, "I see Charlene is out, so I wish you'd explain the delay in filing for divorce. I had a nightmare that you and Abe became increasingly incapacitated while Charlene did nothing to care for you—not even notifying me when you got sick. I flew down to find you in the hospital's intensive care unit. The doctor turned to Charlene—not to me—to make the decision on whether to operate." His voice turned grim. "I had no say."

I winced at the thought! "Well, I don't think the divorce will take that long. I contacted Greta right after that crazy scene at Stone and Wertheim's office. I wanted her to serve papers on Charlene right away. But she told me it was a whole new case."

"But doesn't Florida have no-fault divorces? I don't get it."

I tried to find the right words. "Before Charlene came back, I had a simple case of a wife deserting me for another man. But by accepting her in my home again, I have to establish entirely new grounds. Charlene will fight the divorce tooth and nail. I've got to show why my wife is not entitled to get a piece of me."

Martin shook his head. "You really are in a swamp. How can I help?"

Of course I shouldn't have taken Charlene back. I know that now. But my brother had no "I told you so." Just sympathetic support.

"I have an idea, and I need you to handle it," I continued. "All of Uncle Abe's money was set up in my name as well as his. Bank accounts, C.D.s, stocks, mutual funds. I'd like to see all these assets protected by a trust in his name only."

Martin grinned. "You think that Charlene might manipulate Uncle Abe to sign away his money?"

"It's more than that. I want to be sure that my relationship with Charlene can't hurt Abe. There should be no chance of her getting the rest of his money."

Martin was thinking it through. "Then it should be an irrevocable trust. With a set amount paid to you every month to cover all your expenses."

"Right. Three thousand a month should do it, which will go into our checking account to pay the bills. But in case we need more, the trustee should be authorized to go higher. And I'd like you to be the trustee, Martin."

"Of course. When do you want it set up? And will Uncle Abe agree?"

"The sooner the better. I've already discussed this with Uncle Abe. He says he favors anything that protects against Charlene."

I didn't tell Martin that Abe has been complaining bitterly about Charlene of late. Privately—not in front of her. Now she's demeaning him even when I'm around—treating him like he was in his second childhood. Yesterday she yelled at him, "You're full of shit!" I saw the pain disfigure his face.

Of course I've called her on it. She's quick to promise, fast to forget. She's reverted to peppering all her conversations with foul language. It depresses me, too.

Martin interrupted my reverie. "You say Abe has improved over the past few months. Change in medications?"

"Still at the lower level. And Hattie and I dole them out very carefully."

Martin gazed out the car window and then said, "Before you two supervised Abe's medication, doesn't it seem odd that his condition went up and down without explanation? Wasn't Charlene supervising his pill-taking then? And hasn't Abe been doing remarkably well ... so long as she wasn't controlling his pill intake?"

"It does look suspicious," I admitted. Could Charlene stoop so low as to overdose Uncle Abe? It was hard for me to believe.

123

Charlene was due, and I feared a confrontation. When she heard Martin was flying down for another visit, a major storm had erupted. "Martin is always telling you what to do." "Martin causes all the problems in our marriage." "Martin is only interested in getting his hands on Abe's money."

I was getting fed up with this kind of talk. When she insisted that my brother stay at a hotel, my line in the sand became a stone wall.

Surprise. After a casual hello, Charlene acted as if there had been nothing between them. She simply monopolized the conversation with the frustrations of her day. The dog-doo she stepped in. The stupid cleaners who couldn't find her fuchsia-colored dress. The nail-biting line at the post office because the black clerk "moved like he was picking cotton."

Charlene certainly has a knack of turning minutia into melodrama. Intolerant melodrama.

She poured herself a cup of coffee, attacked a slice of chocolate cake, and spewed a tired stereotype. "Say, didja hear on the news about the woman raped in her car by a black man with a butcher knife while her child was in the backseat? That's why I carry a pistol in my purse. Protection."

One-hundred-eighty-degree turn: "What do you think of my new business idea?" Charlene asked Martin.

He looked puzzled. "What new business?

She gave me a disdainful look. "I thought you told your brother *everything.*"

Wolfing down the last of the cake, she continued, "Have you any idea how many women there are like me in the country? Millions! And we can't find clothes to fit us, okay? Everything is size six to sixteen. Sure there are some sacks on the racks. But we big women want *style*—just like other women. Why should we be second-class citizens, okay?"

"I certainly agree with you on that," said Martin piously.

Charlene hurried on with her machine-gun dialogue. "So anyway, I found a dress manufacturer who specializes in big women's fashions. In the New York garment district. I'm gonna start small, okay? I'll put up racks in our guestroom. I'll bring customers in by appointment. Evenings and weekends, so it won't interfere with my travel agency work, okay? Then I'll expand into a whole chain of Big Belles stores throughout the South."

The phone rang and Charlene answered. "It's Alice," she said. "I'll take it in the bedroom."

I hung up the phone and said, "She's good for an hour once she and Alice get talking."

"Is she serious about selling clothes out of this house? If the guestroom is loaded with clothes racks, there'll be no place for Rina and me."

"I wouldn't worry. Charlene has a rich fantasy life. The other day she was describing how she expected to sell a cruise ship in Miami for five million dollars to a wealthy South American contact for a 10% commission. She still hasn't gotten around to taking the exam for travel agent. She doesn't seem to follow through on anything."

"Does she know you're working on a divorce?"

"If she did, she'd be screaming her head off," I said.

Martin was back from Tampa the next day with news. He'd had a fruitful discussion with Charles Jacoby, the lawyer recommended by Greta Townsend as specializing in estates and trusts. Martin had one question for me. "What should happen to the remainder in the trust after you and Uncle Abe are gone?"

"Simple," I said. "Any balance goes to you, Martin ... or to your family if you're not around."

Two days later, Martin and Abe returned with copies of the completed document, entitled the *Abraham Bloom Trust.*

"Some project," commented Uncle Abe. "They sent Martin out of the room and brought in a secretary to be the witness. Then they read it to me one paragraph at a time. This lawyer kept asking me if I understood it, and did I have any questions. He did this over and over again after each paragraph. Then I had to initial each of the six pages, and sign all three copies. What a job! It took the whole morning!"

Martin smiled. "Jacobs was thorough. Since I briefed him about the Charlene problem, he wanted to be on solid ground if the trust is ever challenged."

As I finished reading the document, Martin said, "Now I have to take Uncle Abe around to the stockbroker and to the banks to transfer Abe's assets to the trust. The total value will be about $350,000. Which gives you and Abe about ten years at the payout rate of three thousand a month."

I grinned. "Well, Abe and I have already passed the biblical age of three-score and ten, so I don't think we'll run short."

Just then the front door opened and Charlene sailed in. I quickly slipped my copy of the trust under a magazine, and Martin folded his into his pocket.

"What are you guys plotting?" she called out breezily. She entered the study carrying a huge mound of ice cream almost overflowing the bowl, and applied herself to decimating her tri-color dessert. This didn't slow down the rapid-fire description of her day's travails.

She's sick and tired of splitting her commissions with the travel service where she works, and is thinking of starting her own agency. At the same time she wants to open a shop to sell Big Belles clothing. She's also planning to launch an aerobics exercise place for Big Belles. And she's going to promote a special cruise for Big Belles in the spring. Meanwhile, she's organizing the first branch of the "Big Belles of America" organization.

Of course, she doesn't mention that she's been pestering me to provide the financing for all these fancy ventures. They may be good ideas. But I know she doesn't have what it takes to succeed with any of them.

Suddenly she turned to Martin and said, "Do you think adopted children are any worse than natural kids?"

My brother paused, puzzled. "I think that depends on how the child is treated. Why?"

"Well," said Charlene casually, absorbing more ice cream, "I've been talking to David about our adopting a little girl. She would be wonderful company around here, okay? Look what Cinnamon has done for Uncle Abe."

Martin said nary a word, and I didn't have to guess what he was thinking.

Charlene had another surprising question for Martin. "How would you like a guest next month, Martin?"

"What do you mean?" he asked.

"I'm planning to go up north on a buying trip. To start my Big Belles business, okay? I can use your place in Connecticut as my hotel."

I saw the astonished look on my brother's face as he tried to frame a response. "I don't think so."

Charlene got upset. "You invited me to your house, didn't you?"

"That was a century ago," said Martin gravely. "Too much has happened since then."

"What's the matter?" she growled. "You keep coming here all the time. You stay in *my* house."

"I come here to visit my uncle and my brother. This house also belongs to *them*."

Charlene jumped to her feet. "You come down here to turn David and Abe against me! You just want to break up our marriage!"

I couldn't take that kind of talk anymore. My voice rose. "I want Martin to visit. You don't decide that—I do! He's welcome any time he can come."

"But I'm your wife!" she cried.

"And Martin is my brother!" I'd never spoken to her like this before. I surprised myself.

Her face a mask of anger, Charlene stared down at her ice cream bowl. I had the feeling she was going to throw it at me—or at Martin. Then she twisted around and dashed out of the room.

126

I could sense that sleep would be elusive tonight. So I stayed in my den after everyone else had gone to bed. Too much on my mind, and even Martin couldn't help me sort it all out.

I tried reading, but my brain refused to focus. I tried working on a new short story idea which had popped into my head this morning. It didn't work. My concerns about Charlene kept wriggling under the door of my mind.

Charlene's constant refrain is that we'd have a perfect marriage if only "the family" didn't intrude. Martin has also raised the question of whether he and Rina have interfered with our marriage.

But family isn't the real issue that grates between Charlene and me. I can no longer trust her. I've caught her lying to me more than once on important things. Also, she gets too emotional when I try to discuss our differences. We can't really communicate.

The core of our conflict is her obsession that everything must be done her way. Regardless of my feelings. I can compromise on most things ... just to keep peace. But my family—Uncle Abe, Martin, Rina and their children—are too important to me to give up.

And that's the only thing that will satisfy Charlene. She insists on being top banana.

"Top banana." That's the phrase Lydia liked to use. Her sweet face swam up from the far past and eddied around my mind. I saw her shaking her finger at me. "You're doing it again, David. You're putting family ahead of the one you love."

"We've been through all this, Lydia," I responded wearily. "Why must there be only one kind of love—the love for a mate? What about the love of brother, uncle—whose lives have intertwined with mine for so long? Why can't you see that family closeness can be rich and supportive too? I need both, Lydia. Why do you insist on exclusivity?"

"But isn't that what love really is?" she argued fiercely. "It's intense. It's ultra. It's an island against the world."

How can we two be so alike and yet so different, Lydia? We hurt each other without meaning to. Or do we hurt each other because we can't help doing so?

You want all my thoughts, Lydia, all my desires, all my actions to be your satellites ... to reflect your needs. You insist that I make a choice. But what about my needs, Lydia?

Strange. So many years have passed and yet your image irradiates me with that familiar warm, mushy feeling inside. So many years since I took back the heart I had given to you—covered with scars from your rages and yet still soft from the tender loving you showed.

I tried so hard to reason, to ask for your understanding, Lydia. But whenever we talked seriously, you became ever more suspicious, accusing, blaming. I was speaking into a bottomless canyon.

Why did you make me crawl and suffer and vomit my pain before you softened? Why couldn't you—at least once—say: "I'm sorry. I'm sorry about what happened. I'm sorry I hurt you. Whatever happened is not as important as our being together again...."

I didn't ask you to love my family, Lydia. Just to accept them ... to overlook anything that annoys you ... for the sake of our love

You couldn't do that. You just kept pounding me, needling me, knifing me. Your volcanic eruptions of hatred buried our love as thoroughly as Pompeii.

Until this moment. I suddenly feel your caressing hand on my neck. I lean back and feel your thigh pressing against the back of my chair, warming me and forming a circuit for our feelings to mingle ... and tingle. I find my hand going backwards automatically, as it had done so many times before, to caress your ankle.

Lydia, Lydia, you can be my always—darling.

Show me love. Let the juices of your body yearn for me. Cuddle me to those soft breasts. Baste me with love till I can't see straight. Make me burst with having all of you.

Weave us a spell, my love ... a sparkling new design ... a lovely love ... a loving love ... a really caring love....

My eyes lifted up to the mirror before me. But Lydia wasn't there. Only the chirping of the crickets outside my window.

Before Martin left for home, he and Abe made the rounds to transfer all of the funds and securities into the *Abraham Bloom Trust*. I felt a load off my back once this was done. I could sense from my lawyer that my divorce battle would be bloody.

When Martin dropped in on us again a month later, I spelled out the dimensions of the problem. "Greta says that we must face the vested interest Charlene has in this house. If she gets all or part of my share, she could force me and Uncle Abe out."

My brother mopped his brow. "Okay, so how about giving her the ten thousand bucks she demanded for signing over her share? You remember—in Wertheim and Stone's office."

I grimaced. "I already tried that. I told her that Abe is anxious to have exclusive title. But she's become vindictive. She now wants $25,000. Our total equity in the house is only $30,000."

Martin began to pace the floor. "Are you changing your mind about the divorce and planning to adopt a child?"

I snorted. "Adoption is another of Charlene's fantasies. But I am re-thinking whether I want to go through the tribulations of a bitter divorce trial. I'm getting old for that kind of fight."

"I can't believe you're seventy-one. You act and think fifteen years younger."

"Not that I love living with Charlene. She's unreasonable. She makes Abe's life miserable. And she took out a credit card again—which she promised never to do. I cancelled it when I found out.

"But on the other hand, she's still exciting to be around. And knowing what a tough life she's had, I pity her. So maybe I just have to learn to put up with all her crazy 'shtik'."

Martin stopped pacing and gazed at me. "I understand," he said sympathetically.

I told Martin my one ray of hope was that I finally got Charlene to start seeing a therapist two weeks ago.

Martin looked dubious. "Do you think any therapist could help Charlene?"

"Well, he shook her up by getting her to begin exploring traumas from her childhood. Maybe he can make her easier to live with."

I opened a drawer and took out my stock certificates. "Martin, I need you to drive me over to my bank tomorrow. I want to notarize this letter authorizing the transfer of my stocks to the *Abraham Bloom Trust*. My inheritance from our mother, all I have left. This $35,000 will go partway to make up for what Charlene took from Abe."

Uncle Abe strolled into the den, followed by Cinnamon, and sat down. I told him I was signing over all my stocks to his trust. His face brightened. I knew he'd be pleased that Charlene won't get her hands on the last of my funds. Since I told him that she took $100,000, he calls her "our gold-digger." He now thinks that she started out to milk us right from the beginning, and feels terrible that she's gotten so much already.

Martin asked him that very question. "Do you think Charlene married David just for money?"

Uncle Abe gave a sad smile. "If you have money, you get honey. But sometimes you also get stung."

As we drove to the bank the next morning, Martin asked me if I agreed with Abe about why Charlene married me.

"Not really. I'm sure she wanted a better life, one with frills. But I think she really loves me—in her own crazy way. She really doesn't know what she wants out of life … except that she wants it exclusively."

*I suppose what each of us wants out of life is haunted by the ghosts of our past. Charlene's childhood was a wasteland. Starved for nurturing, her adulthood has been focused on self. She carries painful baggage that she is only dimly aware of, and it drives her. When she is tempted to lift the edge of the curtain, she demands total control to forestall any intrusion. Top banana.*

Once inside the bank, we had to wait. Martin asked, "What's the latest on our tenant, Tobias?"

"Former tenant. He hasn't paid rent for months and I had Barry serve him with an eviction notice. No response. So the Sheriff will be putting his things out on the sidewalk any day now."

My brother scratched his head. "How did such a nice young couple get themselves into such a hole?"

"I heard from a neighbor that they were into cocaine. They just went downhill." I heaved a sigh. "But what can we do?"

"So we're stuck with an empty house again, and we can't sell because Dora shares the title," growled Martin. "I can foresee the day when I'll be battling Charlene over your present house. And be stuck with the same damn problem."

I didn't know how to respond to that.

My brother stared out the bank window. "You know," he said, "I'm still trying to figure out who will be the final survivor in all this—me or Charlene?"

# CHAPTER XIII
# ABANDONED

## *Charlene—Three Days Later*

He left. Finally. The bastard's gone back to Connecticut. He and David had their heads together the whole week, plotting against me.

But what more can they do? They don't know I discovered their secret. Abe left a copy of his new trust on his night table. I found the papers and quick-as-a-bunny made a copy, which I showed to Uncle Mike. He confirmed that my scheming brother-in-law went behind my back to control the family money and rob me of the inheritance I'm entitled to. After all, I'm David's wife.

That fucking trust won't be worth a fart in hell once I attack it in court. Uncle Abe didn't know what he was doing. Dr. Brown will testify that he was incompetent. Alzheimer's. I just wait for Abe to kick the bucket so there'll be no questions. He's far gone already.

I know they changed their wills to cut me out. They don't know that I peeked where David keeps the key to his file drawer, and I made copies of both wills for myself months ago.

Abe's will won't mean shit! All his assets are in joint names, so my husband gets them automatically when Abe goes bye-bye.

I'm not worried about David's will. He'll put me back in. I've always been able to wear him down and lever him where I want him. I'm still his honey child. It's just gonna take more time than before. And I'm learning to be more patient.

Fuck Martin. Cries tears that he wants to be my "brother." Then he tries to screw me out of my house and my inheritance. Even when I ask to stay in his lousy house up north, the prick freezes me out. His promises are horseshit on a bagel.

Well, he's not going to sleep over in *this* house anymore, either. I'm just as much an owner as David and Abe. I got veto power. How the hell can David fight me on this when Martin locks me out of *his* house? Just let him try.

I just wish I knew what they were plotting against me.

131

Hattie knocked on our bedroom door early the next morning as I was dressing to go to work, and she told me that something was wrong.

"It's Uncle Abe," she called out. "I can't rouse him up."

I flung open the door and made a beeline for his room. He's had heart trouble. Could it be that he croaked overnight?

But he was breathing. Breathing with a lot of congestion in his throat. I felt his forehead. He was on fire. I tried to shake him awake. He wouldn't respond. It was like he was in a coma.

"He had a real bad cold yesterday," said Hattie. "When I left he told me he was feeling miserable. Looks like he's got a powerful fever."

"You're damn right," I said, scooting back to fill David in. "Looks serious." I picked up the bedroom phone. "I'm calling an ambulance."

"Maybe it's a touch of the flu," ventured David.

Ignoring that, I gave the ambulance directions and hung up. "David," I said, "the flu is what you and I picked up a few days ago, okay? First you, then me, with our stuffed noses. But Abe's beyond that. He needs a hospital."

"I guess you're right. At his age we don't take chances." David was wheezing a lot and didn't look too good himself.

"I think it's your lousy brother's fault," I said, putting in another dig. "When he arrived here, he was sneezing and blowing into his handkerchief, okay? He planted the bug in all three of us!"

David didn't answer that one, so I dug deeper. "Why the hell does he have to sleep in this house? Is he too cheap to afford a hotel? If he comes down again, that's where he'll be, 'cause I'll be using our guestroom as my showroom for Big Belles clothing, okay?"

This still didn't get a rise out of him. "What's the matter with your tongue today? Get some Krazy Glue on it?"

"I'm not feeling very well," he murmured. "Would you ask Hattie to bring me some hot tea with lemon?"

I became concerned. "Oh, my poor baby, I'm sorry." I pulled the bedclothes up and tucked them around his neck. "I'll bring the tea in for you myself."

As the teapot began to whistle, the ambulance arrived. Shit, those guys are fast. They were also speedy in getting Abe bundled up and into their vehicle. Siren blasting, they took off no more than three minutes after I opened the front door.

The teacup was steaming as I set it down on the nightstand by David. "The ambulance is on its way to Carmel Hospital, and I phoned Dr. Kahn, okay? He'll meet it there."

"Good," said David, still wheezing heavily. "While my tea cools off, would you dial Martin for me, Charlene?"

"Martin?" I asked sharply.

"Yes. We have to let him know that Abe's been rushed off to the hospital."

I saw red. "Crissake! Do we have to phone your fucking brother every single time Uncle Abe takes a piss?"

David didn't answer. He was waiting for me to cool down, but I wouldn't. "That sonofabitch just went home, okay? I don't want him to come running down here again now!"

David reached for a tissue and blew his nose carefully. He needed the second tissue I handed him. Then he cleared his throat enough to talk slowly, through labored breathing. "Look, Charlene, if you won't call Martin, I'll have to speak to him myself. And if he hears how I sound, he'll rush down here by space shuttle."

I got Martin on the phone.

"This is Charlene. David asked me to call you. We just put Abe in Carmel Hospital. He's got a high fever, okay? Some kind of flu bug."

"What did he say?" asked David as I hung up.

"He's taking the next plane down," I said, wishing somebody would sabotage the flight.

Uncle Abe's cat walked in, jumped on the bed near David and squatted with a lost look.

I decided against going to work today. I've got to take care of my Davy. Besides, I don't feel so hot myself. A whole houseful of invalids my fucking brother-in-law created!

The phone rang. "Thanks, Dr. Kahn. We'll be over to visit him soon."

I walked back into the bedroom. "That was the doctor," I told David. "He says Abe has congestive heart failure, but it's under control now, okay? He says it's lucky I got him in the hospital before pneumonia set in.

David looked lots worse. "But it's *you* I'm worried about, Sweetie," I said. "I'm gonna call Dr. Kahn and tell him to stop off here on his way back from the hospital to check you out."

David mumbled something and stretched his head back and forth like he had a crick in his neck. "I can't hear you," I pleaded. "Do you want more tea now?"

No response. I touched his brow. Two hours ago it was hot. Now it was on fire like Abe's.

I grabbed the phone and dialed for the ambulance again. The last thing I need is for Davy to die before Uncle Abe.

I rode to Carmel Hospital with him, holding the oxygen mask over his face. Dr. Kahn was waiting as we pulled into Emergency.

I almost had a pitched battle with the nurses, but Dr. Kahn okayed my coming in while he was examining David. Then the doctor motioned me outside the room and said, "He'll be all right. David has a severe respiratory infection. Lots of congestion. The complication is the damage done to his lungs years ago by polio. They're weak, and pneumonia might set in."

"You're putting him in Intensive Care?"

"It's not that serious. He'll be put in a room on the third floor next to your uncle's, and they'll both be monitored. You did the right thing in getting the ambulance. Try not to worry."

"Are you kidding?" I cried. "You lug my husband in here semi-conscious, tell me he's got bum lungs and can get pneumonia—then you tell me not to worry?"

Dr. Kahn put an arm around my shoulder. "If you want to worry, be my guest. I like to give the complete picture. Neither your husband nor your uncle is serious enough for Intensive Care. But you'll be a case yourself if you don't ease up."

He was right, of course. Once they got David settled in his room, he fell into a deep sleep with his oxygen mask on. Uncle Abe, next door, was also in limbo. I phoned Alice to come over, since she was between jobs. She popped in quick-as-a-bunny and I said, "Am I glad to see you! I need you to stay with Abe so he sees a familiar face when he wakes up in the hospital, okay? And look in on David next door till I'm better."

I leaned on her for support. "I'm feeling like the rat's carcass the cat dragged in. I'm going home to crawl into bed."

When I woke up, I was shocked to find that five hours had escaped. But at least I wasn't feeling like a rotten apple. I dressed in a hurry and was at the hospital in no time.

I just knew Martin would be in David's room, and he was. I ignored him. I grabbed my husband's hand and cried, "Davy, Davy—are you all right? What do the doctors say?" He looked pale and weak, but a helluva lot better than when they brought him in. His voice was so soft I had trouble hearing him. My lousy brother-in-law kept trying to interrupt us, telling me not to come too near the bed.

David cleared his throat and spoke a little louder. "Dr. Kahn just examined me and said I'm getting better. So don't worry. But Martin's right. Better not stay too close to me."

I moved back a bit and gave him a tender smile. "Sweetie, I'm terribly upset over your condition, okay? You know your lungs are weak to start with. I'm sick with worry, okay?"

David squeezed my hand and made soothing comments. "Charlene, shouldn't you be in bed getting rid of that cold so you'll be in shape to care for me when I come home?" Then he closed his eyes and said he wanted to nap. So I kissed him 'bye and went next door.

Alice looked up from her magazine, and we embraced. "Abe's still not conscious," she reported. "But Dr. Kahn says his signs are better."

"And here I thought this would be my lucky day," I said, plunking down into the other seat.

"How's your cold doing, Charlene?"

"It sucks. I'd feel tons better if that Connecticut cowboy wasn't getting in my way all the time. Why can't he catch pneumonia?"

"I can stay on here till Abe's better."

"Thanks, Alice." I stood up wearily. "Call me if anything happens, okay?"

She did, after dinner. Her voice was tense, upset. "David's choking. It's an emergency! Better come quick!"

*Jee-sus!* I tossed a robe over my nightgown and zoomed over to the hospital, through a couple of red lights. Martin and Alice were standing nervously in the corridor near David's room. "Well? Well?" I cried.

Martin took my arm. "They're still working on him." And he tried to shovel on the shit.

I wouldn't buy it. My Davy was maybe dying. I howled as I headed for his door to see what was really going on. As I tried to push my way past the tall Hispanic nurse guarding the door, an aide rushed over and grabbed me from behind. I kept wailing as they pulled me down the hall to the waiting room. Alice managed to quiet me down after a few minutes, and Martin pressed his handkerchief into my hand so I could dry my tears.

"What happened?" I asked.

"Totally unexpected problem," said Martin, and I could see how shook up he was. "David was improving nicely till after dinner. His appetite was good. Then all of a sudden he coughed hard and began to gag. I pounded him on the back. He still couldn't breathe. I yelled for the nurse. She took one look and called for the emergency crew. They've been working on him ever since."

Just then Dr. Kahn appeared at the door, with the look of death warmed over. My heart pounded wildly. The doctor opened his mouth. "We did everything we could to save him. I'm sorry."

I couldn't believe it. My Davy—*dead!* A scream tore from my throat and the world turned black. I was falling, falling, miles and miles downward at a terrific rate, waiting to be smashed flat. But a force caught and held me. I opened my eyes. Alice and Martin were supporting my sagging body. They eased me into a chair.

Martin grabbed Dr. Kahn by the arm. "How can that be, Doctor?" he cried. "You told me David was getting better. You said he'd be home soon!"

The doctor looked grim. "Things happen. Things we don't expect. We did all we could."

As soon as he left, it hit me like a hammer. My husband was dead! I jumped up and dashed down the corridor, wailing at the top of my lungs. I threw myself on the door to David's room, beating it with my fists until they let me in. I collapsed onto my husband's body, crying and sobbing, "Davy! Davy! Why did you leave me? What can I do without you? How will I live?"

Martin and Alice tried to comfort me, but the whole world was spinning away. I felt myself floating, desperately alone in cold, black space.

As I turned my head, I saw Martin's eyes. They were filled with a grief so overwhelming that I could feel it like my own. He felt it, too. He put his arms around me and I clung tightly to him, sobbing my heart out while Alice stroked my back.

Walking back into our house was almost more than I could bear. Everything looked familiar and strange at the same time. Martin insisted I lie down till people arrived, and Alice put up the coffee.

But I was up in a few minutes to cry on the shoulder of my Uncle Mike. He immediately got on the phone to arrange for the undertaker.

The only other person I had notified was Lou Bianca. He greeted me when I opened the door by saying, "It sucks!" Then he flung his arms around me and we both had a good cry.

He limped his way into the kitchen with his arm around me, and I introduced him to everyone. "Lou is a very dear friend—David's and mine."

Lou shook hands all around and expressed his sympathy. "I'm head of the Able-Disabled League, which David and Charlene founded last year. I wanted David to be president, but he insisted I take it. He was such a giving guy."

Lou is the most *simpático* person I know. He limps from a bullet he took in the hip while a lieutenant in the New York City police force. "I've asked Lou to give the eulogy for David at the funeral," I announced.

Everybody was telling little stories about David, showing what a great guy he was. It made me feel better, and my nerves quit jangling. Life must go on. A stupid saying. But anybody got anything better?

Abe's cat, Cinnamon, strolled into the kitchen, looking bewildered by all

136

the people so late at night.

Alice was filling the coffee cups. "What shall we do about Uncle Abe?" she asked.

Martin was opposed to telling Abe about David until his condition improved. Life is crazy. Who would have expected David's funeral to be before the old man's?

"It's going to be a big funeral," I said. I thought of all the people who got to know David over those years of fighting for handicapped rights. Everyone liked and respected him.

"Maybe I'll have Mayor Gomez say a few words," I added. "He came to our wedding—remember?"

Mentioning the wedding was a mistake. I saw myself in that flowing white gown, walking down the aisle on Uncle Mike's arm. I saw myself grabbing David's wheelchair and whirling him around the dance floor. I remembered the men lifting me up in the air, chair and all, then lifting David up in his wheelchair, dancing us around up high while everyone applauded. I burst out crying, and ran sobbing into the bedroom.

Davy, Davy, I loved you. You're the only man I ever loved.


It was midnight, and we were still sitting around the kitchen table, everyone lost in thought. Was there anything else to talk about at a time like this?

Alice called Martin to the phone, and it tore me up to hear him telling his wife Abe was okay, but that David died. Uncle Abe. How come that old geezer lives on while I lost my Davy? It suddenly hit me that this changes the whole ball game. Abe was supposed to die first so we could throw out the trust and deliver all the assets back to David. Then I'd end up with the pot as David's widow. But now what?

I motioned Mike into the den and said, "What do we do about David's will? It cut me out, you know."

"Lose it," he said without hesitation. "Go get it now. I'll make it disappear."

I reached to where David hid the key to his desk drawer. When I handed the will to Mike, he patted it into his pocket and smirked. "The old will counts now. And it leaves you everything."


They were talking about the foul-up when I returned to the kitchen. Alice was asking why David had to die just because he gagged. Martin said they cut open his windpipe, but it didn't work. "What gets me," I said, "is how come just before David died, Dr. Kahn said he'd be well enough to go home soon."

Uncle Mike pounced on that fast. "Sounds to me like malpractice is involved."

I saw red. "*Malpractice?* You mean to say my Davy died because some bastard was negligent?"

"Happens all the time," said Uncle Mike, pointing out that Martin, who was there at the time, could see no reason for David to die. "I'd say you got a case, Charlene. Want me to call Phil now?"

A bitter rage began to churn inside me and I couldn't speak, so I just nodded, and my nerves set up a ferocious jangling again.

Uncle Mike was on the phone a long time with his nephew, who's a liability lawyer. "Phil agrees you have a good case, but we need an autopsy before the undertaker removes the body."

I gritted my teeth. "Let's get those sonsabitches!"

Alice said, "If a doctor screws up and lets somebody die, we've got to go after him."

As Mike headed back to the phone, Lou took me by the elbow and motioned to Martin. He pulled us into the next room to talk to us privately.

"Look," he said, and his tone was grim. "I'm a former detective, and I've seen how gory an autopsy gets. Stop and think. Do you really want David's body cut up into a hundred pieces? Would David have wanted it?"

That stabbed me right in the heart, and I began to cry.

"Then after all that butchery—what if you find no negligence? How would you feel then?"

I knew how I felt right then and there. I was seeing big bare-chested men in black leather aprons and long sharp knives getting ready to slice my husband up like a hog in a butcher-shop.

Still sniffling, I walked back into the kitchen and heard Mike saying, "I was too late with the hospital. The undertaker had already picked up the body, but—"

"Forget all that legal stuff," I said sharply. "I've changed my mind!"

138

# CHAPTER XIV
# SUE, SUE

## *Charlene—The following day*

We arrived at the funeral parlor early. Martin tried to tell me that the Jewish religion doesn't allow the casket to be open for viewing the body, but I didn't care. I wanted to say good-bye to my Davy in my own way.

I walked up to where my husband lay, stone cold and still. I promised myself I wouldn't become hysterical. His face wore the same kind expression I loved so much. Sure I loved him. The only man I *could* love. Whenever I sunk into the dumps, he knew how to lift me back up. And he never put me down, like those other men I got involved with. We didn't always agree, but he respected me, respected my feelings.

And now my Davy is gone. Gone forever. I began to feel in my gut how much I was going to miss him. I took the large red hibiscus blossom I'd brought along from our garden and placed it gently on his chest. Then I leaned over to give him one last kiss.

That was a mistake. The floodgates opened and I burst out with loud wailing cries as I collapsed over the casket. I felt like I was swimming in boiling water, trying to escape from the burning pain all over my body without knowing what way to go. Or was there no escape?

I remember the rest of the funeral, but it's all through a haze. The rabbi made it short, as I asked him to. Lou Bianca made a wonderful speech about my husband. My brother-in-law said some deep things that nobody really understood. What I remember best is that the place was mobbed and everybody came up to me afterwards.

After we lowered my husband into his grave, I tossed some earth on the plain coffin. Then I collapsed.

It seems like a million people stopped over to pay their respects in the next few days. Alice and I cleared up the patio while Martin and Rina did the living room.

"I feel lost," I said.

"I think you really loved the guy," said Alice.

"He was the softest, sweetest person I ever met, okay? That's why I couldn't bear the idea of my Davy being cut up in a thousand pieces." Shit, them hospital bastards would have paid through the nose if I'd gone along with the autopsy. I admit I was tempted. But I just couldn't do it.

Alice shook her head wonderingly.

I shoveled the last of the dirty paper plates and cups into a garbage bag. "I would have had David under my thumb a second time if that stinking brother of his kept his pecker out of our tent. Always interfering to have it his way, okay? Then there's his wife who thinks she's so fucking smart but doesn't know shit from shoe polish."

"You may be down, but you're not out," said Alice, crumpling up the paper tablecloths. "You've bounced back before."

"Yeah. Somebody has to care for Uncle Abe down here. That's me. They think I don't know about the trust. It gives $3,000 a month to Abe, okay? And I'll control that money."

After Alice left and Martin walked into the kitchen, I said, "I've made an appointment for us to see Stone and Wertheim at three o'clock."

I caught him off guard, and could see he didn't like the idea of going to the lawyer who drew up David's will. But I had to know where I stood. "If you won't go, I'll go by myself," I said.

He gave in.

That's when he discovered that David's will was missing and shit!—did that drive him wild! I just played it cool by telling him I had a copy we could bring to the lawyer's office.

Whoops! As I handed it to him, I suddenly realized I was shooting myself in the foot. Mike removed the original so it wouldn't exist. No matter. Later on we can torpedo it when Martin can't produce the original will.

The session was good and bad. I liked Stone, who's a no-nonsense kind of lawyer. He reviewed the copy of David's will and confirmed what I thought: as David's widow, I'm entitled, regardless of what the will says.

Martin pipes up, "There are no financial assets in the estate." And he wins the first round because the joint checking account goes to the survivor, Abe. The rest goes in my favor. I'm now joint owner of the house with Abe, and it goes to me when he dies. I also win on all the furnishings in the house, and the Ford van is all mine.

Martin is clearly surprised that he's been screwed on these things. He thought I wouldn't get a dime under this will. But until Uncle Abe kicks off and we crack the trust, I had to know where I stood. So I played the poor widow to the hilt. "What are you going to do for me, Martin? I'm a sick woman, okay, and David's not around to support me anymore."

He tried to put me off. I insisted on an answer. I've been taking care of Abe, and I'll continue caring for him down here while Martin's up north. But what will my dear brother-in-law do for me?

All I got was promises, promises. He'd better deliver.

Two days later, Uncle Abe was discharged from the hospital. He looked fine to me and I made a fuss over him. Hattie served delicious roast chicken for dinner, but nobody noticed. This was the first time we'd all sat around the table without David. Nobody said much. It was as if we were waiting for David to arrive.

A whole day went by without any action. Martin wouldn't talk about my future. He said he couldn't discuss it with Abe so soon after David's death. But how long can I hold my horses?

That night I tumbled from one nightmare to the next. Martin tying me down on a table and sharpening a long carving knife. Martin sneaking up behind me at the railing of the ship and shoving me over the side. Martin calmly locking the door of the hospital room with a smirk on his face as my husband choked his life away in agony.

Sleeping late, I stared up at the ceiling from my cold, lonely bed. David never expected to die, I know that. He just had a bad cold. Lots of congestion. They had the whole fucking hospital staff in there to clear one man's throat! Why couldn't they do it?

Martin. It must've been Martin's fault. If he'd called them right away, my Davy'd be still alive!

I jumped into my robe, my rage bursting out of me. Yanking open the door to my room, I rushed out and confronted my brother-in law. "You killed my husband!" I screamed. "You killed him—and now I'm all alone!"

Rina and Alice came running over and Rina took my arm. "You can't mean that, Charlene. You know Martin would never do anything to hurt David. All this has been too much for you."

Tears shook me and I tried to smother them. I glared at Martin. "You waited ten minutes before calling the nurse, okay? Alice told me. Then it was too late!"

My brother-in-law looked at Alice, and she just shrugged.

He blew his stack. I had him backed into a wall. I suddenly realized that I was biting off my nose to spite my face. I needed Martin right now. Three thousand dollars worth every month. Maybe more.

I slumped down on the sofa, my shoulders sagging. "I'm sorry," I mumbled. "Let's have some coffee."

I felt shitty all morning. How could David have left me under the control of these bastards? I passed up some real men to marry a wheelchair. I gave up two years of my life to care for that cripple and his fucking uncle. Didn't I deserve something better than licking their boots for scraps?

I seethed all through lunch. I had to know where I stood. But Martin tried to put me off again, saying he wanted to talk to Abe. I got up from the table and stood over him. "Look," I said, "we both know that Abe doesn't have all his marbles anymore. And with David dead, he's even farther out. You make the decisions now, okay? So make 'em!"

"I'm giving it a lot of thought, Charlene," he said evasively, like he was Einstein.

"You're up in Connecticut and I'm here," I said. "I'll take good care of Abe, okay? But what are you gonna do for me?"

He was cornered. "Okay. We'll sit down and talk this afternoon."

As we sat around the kitchen table, I hit him straight out, trying to keep from sounding testy. "What about it?"

My brother-in-law looked at Rina as if he needed her help in answering my question. He cleared his throat and said, "Suppose you tell me what you would need for managing the household and caring for Uncle Abe."

That was more like it. I was completely prepared for that one. Fifteen hundred bucks a month for groceries. Plus all the house expenses. Plus all medical bills. Plus the cook-housekeeper. Plus my car payments, gasoline and repairs. Plus $200 weekly spending money for myself. Sure it came to over $3,000, but what the hell.

"Is that all?" he asked.

"There may be some things I've left out," I said. "I'll let you know, okay?"

The stingy bastard began giving me the third degree, but I cut him off and let him stew. Then I said, "Well?"

My brother-in-law stared down at the table and said, "The answer is no."

That was a surprise. "What do you mean—no?"

"We're just not interested in your proposition," he said calmly, as if he were the King of Shit.

My nerves jangled and I heard Alice ask, "What's your counter offer?"

Martin was as cool as a fucking iceberg. "We won't need Charlene to care for Uncle Abe. He won't be living here."

I was in a state of shock. My shit-ass brother-in-law was tossing me over the side. He went on to tell me I had to sell my house. And he had the nerve to tell me to dump the van, too. The sonofabitch expects to order me around

142

and control my life just like he did with David and Abe.

Hate flared up inside me like a roman candle. I was primed to smash somebody's puss. Then I felt Alice's warning prod under the table. I tore myself away and followed Alice into the bedroom.

"Okay," said Alice, closing the door behind her. "Now it's time for us to play hardball. But let's be smart about it."

"What do you mean?" I found it tough to think clearly.

"First, this is your house. Order him and Rina to get out. Right away. Make it rough for him."

"What if he gets rough with me?"

"Great! That's the trap you want him to fall into. Let's get Martin on the police report for brutality."

"What about Abe?"

Alice smirked. "Possession is nine-tenths of the law. You've been caring for him, and your husband told you he wanted you to continue after he was gone. So that $3,000 a month has to keep coming to you as the trust says."

"But—"

Alice grinned as she interrupted, "But Abe can't live forever. As soon as he kicks the bucket, you get the house and wipe out the trust by showing that Abe was incompetent when he agreed to it."

I thought it over. It sounded perfect. That Alice has a good head on her shoulders. But I probably would have thought of this myself if I hadn't been so crazy upset.

So I grabbed open the door and went storming back. I zeroed in on Martin and cried, "I want you and Rina out of my house! Abe stays here!"

Martin tried to bully me. "This is Uncle Abe's house as much as yours," he said. "And he wants me here."

I didn't give an inch. "If you're not out of here in thirty minutes, my filthy scheming brother-in-law, I'll get the police to throw you out. I'm the grieving widow, and you're making passes at me." I gave a little smile and added, "I have a witness, okay?"

I had him there. He glanced at Alice, threw me a look filled with poison, and stormed out of the room.

"I'm changing the locks!" I called after him.

He twisted around. "Does that mean you're locking me out of visiting my uncle?"

"You'll need my permission," I declared.

I was feeling like top banana when I marched into the guestroom and announced, "Time to go!"

They were closing their suitcases. "Rina's flying home," said Martin, adding as if threatening me, "but I'm staying in town to clear up this mess."

When I saw Abe starting to walk out with them I said firmly, "I won't let you take Abe!"

"Oh," said Martin, "he wants to go to the airport to see Rina off. I can bring him back later."

I took Abe's arm. "Look, Uncle Abe, I'm heading over to the cemetery right now to put flowers on David's grave. Wouldn't you rather come with me to see David?"

He shook his arm free. "Another time," he said, and climbed into the car.

As they turned to leave, I mentally fired a salvo of bullets into Martin and Rina, delighted to see the blood spurting and the bodies writhing in my driveway. Too bad wishing won't make it so.

Alice and I went back in the kitchen for some coffee, and Cinnamon wandered in, looking forlorn. "Don't worry," I cooed at him. "Your Uncle Abie will be back soon."

"You're in the driver's seat," said Alice, pouring. "Even though it hurts, Martin has to pay you three thousand every month to cover Abe's care and expenses.

"Hail Mary!" I chortled. "Martin tried to fuck me with that trust. And he's ending up fucking himself!"

Uncle Mike came rushing over as soon as I phoned him. He was as upset as I was. I told him we hadn't heard a word about Abe since they left for the airport four hours ago.

"Simple," said Mike. "Martin kidnapped him. Took him back to Connecticut to keep you from the money. Let's get it on the record." And Mike phoned the police to report that Abe Bloom was kidnapped by Martin Richman at 4 that afternoon.

"What if they're still at the airport?" asked Alice. "Maybe they couldn't get seats on Rina's flight, and are waiting for the next one."

"Good thinking," said Mike, and he phoned the airport police with the same story, asking them to check the passenger list of the next flight to New York. He also gave descriptions so they could check out people waiting in the terminal.

But it didn't do any good. When the phone rang, it wasn't the police. It was Martin.

"Where is Abe?" Mike screamed into the phone. "What have you done with him?"

After a pause, Mike yelled, "You can't kidnap him! We've notified the police at the airport to pick you up!"

"What did he say?" I asked Mike as he hung up.

"He's got Abe all right. The sonofabitch won't give him back."

I let out a low moan. "He's torpedoed our plan." Tears started to roll. "What do we do now?"

"Sue," said Mike grimly. "Sue the prick for every penny he's got."

We were sitting in Thomas Johnson's office. Johnson handles all the legal work for Mike's company, so he ought to be sharp. He got right down to business.

"I've drawn up these legal papers based on the information you've given me. We are suing your brother-in-law, Martin Richman, on five counts—all of which add up to his swindling you out of your just inheritance."

The sun was bursting out from behind my dark clouds. I was finally getting my hooks into that iron-ass brother-in-law. I was going to pin him down to the mat before a judge and jury. I was going to squeeze the breath and the moola out of him—not just what he tried to hide in the trust, but all his own money, too.

Johnson was explaining. "You are charging Martin Richman and his wife, Rina, with continuous interference in your marriage to David Richman. Right from the start, they attempted to alienate your husband from you. The proof is in the weekly phone calls and constant visits all the way from Connecticut. Their scheming and machinations finally drove you into an emotional breakdown, where you felt your sanity could be saved only by escaping, and you had to leave your husband's house."

This lawyer was good. I listened hard.

"But you soon discovered that flight was no answer. You loved your husband too much. You knew he depended on you. And it didn't take long before you wanted to go back to him. Yet you were filled with shame at having walked away from a disabled husband, a cripple who really needed you. You were so overcome with guilt that you had a full mental breakdown, which put you in a sanitarium for months."

He was telling it better than the truth. No wonder lawyers make so much money.

"After you recovered, you returned and your husband welcomed you with open arms. He missed you as much as you missed him. You were happy lovers once more.

"However, your brother-in-law still loomed over your marriage like Dracula," Johnson continued. "He plotted to do you out of your husband's money. Since all the assets were held jointly by your husband and uncle, he arranged for your uncle to withdraw and transfer everything into an irrevocable trust, with your brother-in-law himself as trustee."

Johnson paused, mopping his brow. "Am I telling everything just the way you told me? Be sure to stop me with any corrections, or if I've left anything out."

I loved the way he told my story. It was like a movie unfolding.

"In other words," Johnson summed up, "your brother-in-law now controlled all of your husband's money by hiding it in a trust in the name of your uncle, Abe Bloom, who was incompetent when the trust was established. The proof of motive is the trust document itself—in which the residual beneficiaries are your brother-in-law, his wife and his own family. No one else. Not even a token for his brother's caring wife."

Johnson sat back with a triumphant expression on his dour face. It was the first time I'd seen him show any emotion. There's more to this dude than shows on the outside. I could see Uncle Mike beaming, and Alice looked as blissful as I was feeling.

"Now we come to the sixty-four-dollar question," said our thin, prune-faced attorney. "How much do you want to sue for?"

"Martin's filthy rich," said Mike. "He thought nothing of flying down every time his brother or uncle farted."

"I want to take the bastard down to his last red cent," I said. "I also want to see that bitch Rina plead for mercy, okay?"

"How about five million bucks?" asked Alice, her glee softened by her feeling of going overboard. I said she was speaking my language.

"Okay," said our solemn lawyer, without batting an eye. "I'll be taking this case on a contingency basis. My office gets forty percent of whatever is awarded or settled for. But I'll need expense money up front. One thousand dollars to start."

"Forty percent!" I exploded. "That would leave me only three out of the five!"

"No problem," Uncle Mike interrupted smoothly, and said we should sue for *ten* million dollars.

"I like that number even better," I said, seeing myself showing off a diamond as big as a walnut.

"All right," said Johnson slowly, "but I'd suggest we make that nine and a half million—only because it sounds more carefully considered."

"This case can make us both rich," I chortled. "Can you imagine the look on my brother-in-law's face when he gets hit with this?" The vision of this made me almost pee in my pants.

Mike wrote the check for Johnson in exchange for my I.O.U. What's a thousand bucks when I'll get millions?

"Take these papers home and let me know by noon tomorrow if you have any questions," said Johnson. "Which brings me to my last question: do I serve Martin and his wife at their home in Connecticut? That will cost you four hundred dollars."

I gave a whistle.

Johnson smiled thinly. "I've got an idea to save you most of that. Richman's lawyer has been in touch with me. He wants a meeting to discuss your putting up the house for sale.

"So?"

"So I tell him you'll agree to talk if Martin and Rina will be present. Then I'll have the process server walk in and serve them personally in their lawyer's office."

"Wow!" said Alice. "That's just like Perry Mason!"

My cup is brimming over. "I just can't wait," I said.

One week later Uncle Mike, Alice and I followed Johnson into this fancy-shmancy conference room with a high ceiling and waxed wood-grain walls. No pictures hanging—just a gold plaque engraved, "Weiss and Weiss." We postponed the timing till business hours were over, so our process server would have no problem getting by their receptionist. Everything was carefully planned.

But my mind was gooey from the time I woke up. It ain't easy to fight, even when you deserve to win. My stomach felt like it was upside down, and my nerves were rubbing themselves raw. This was like the showdown at the O.K. Corral, and I know I can fall apart even when I'm top gun.

Martin, Rina and a young guy named Barry Weiss sat facing us. He mentioned the reasons for this meeting, and asked if we agreed.

"More or less," said Johnson. "The rest of Abe Bloom's clothes are in this carton. We're even returning the family photo album."

"How is my uncle?" I asked, thinking it was a nice thing to say.

My brother-in-law cut me off. "You mean *my* uncle."

His wife said, "Abe is fine."

Uncle Mike turned to Martin and said, "You must be rich—flying back and forth at a moment's notice. We think you're *very* rich. We think you're worth ten million bucks."

Martin buttoned his lip and stonewalled us. Rina sat there looking uncomfortable and not saying a word.

Weiss asked Johnson, "Is your client ready to sign an agreement for selling the house she now owns jointly with Martin's uncle?"

147

Mike stood up and said, "Excuse me, but I forgot to put money in the parking meter." Weiss had to go along to unlock the front door, which was just as we'd planned. Then Weiss repeated his question.

Johnson licked his dry lips and took a long time to answer. "My client feels she has not been treated fairly by her brother-in-law."

"In what way?"

"My client is a poor, sick widow. She insists on getting what she is entitled to."

Weiss was going crazy trying to pin Johnson down. Then, just like we planned, Mike walked back in. He was followed by our dude. He went straight to my brother-in-law.

"You Martin Richman?"

"Yes. Who are you?"

The guy jabbed our papers into Martin's hands and turned to Rina. "You Rina Richman?" She nodded in surprise, and he pushed another set into her lap before marching out.

What happened next was better than a fuckin' orgasm. Martin glanced at the packet and passed it to Weiss like a hot potato. Weiss took one look and yelled, "What the hell! You've been served! Right here in my office!" He turned to Johnson. "You dirty bastard!"

Weiss began skimming the pages, getting madder by the minute, and growled to Johnson, "I'm going to bring you up before the Board for this dirty trick!"

At the last page Weiss turned to Martin and Rina. "Your sister-in-law is suing you on five counts. A total of nine and a half million dollars!"

I never felt so great. The looks on Martin's and Rina's faces was worth a million bucks in itself. God—did we shaft 'em!

We stood up and slowly strolled out, grinning from ear to ear. Except for Johnson, of course, who hardly ever changed from his usual glum expression.

Martin and Rina were slumped in their chairs like jumbo-sized inflated balloons right after somebody had pulled the plug.

# CHAPTER XV
# STAY, STAY

*Martin—One Day Later*

"What the hell is all this legal garbage?" I challenged Barry, slapping the complaint document down on his desk. "I read it three times last night. I understand the words. But what do they really mean?"

Rina and I were in the offices of Weiss and Weiss. "Yes," added my wife, "since we're being sued for nine and a half million dollars, I assume we're entitled to know."

"Ten million if you count lawyer and court costs," I added bitterly.

Barry Weiss glanced down. "The way this complaint is written is a joke. It's full of legal errors. But I don't mean to minimize what you're up against. The essence of their claim is too serious to expect a dismissal ... or an easy case."

A sobering thought. "Okay," I said. "Let's let it all hang out." My pencil was poised to take notes.

"The first count charges that both of you conspired and inveigled David and Abe Bloom into appointing Martin as their fiduciary with full control over their money, taking advantage of their advanced ages to deprive Charlene of her spousal rights."

"No problem," I said. "The Abraham Bloom Trust was set up in a completely legal manner. Abe will testify to that. He appointed me as trustee." I became emotional. "Charlene has no right to that money. My uncle worked hard for it years ago. David had no money left of his own."

"The second count—'malicious conversion'—ties in with the first. You are charged with setting up the trust in a manner that allows you to convert funds to your own use, as well as assuring that all benefits accrue to you and your heirs ... and Charlene demands a full accounting."

I snorted. "Ridiculous. My records clearly show where the money goes and I get no compensation—not even expenses. She's just fishing for something to hang me on."

The phone rang and Barry told his secretary to hold all calls. Good, but I was annoyed by his habit of caressing a hard candy in his mouth.

"The third count involves defamation, charging you and Rina with making fraudulent statements to undermine Charlene in the eyes of her husband and others, making her suffer humiliation, embarrassment and mental anguish. It says here you called Charlene a 'degenerate'."

I chuckled. "There are many things I'd call her, but that would be an odd word for me to pick."

"Did either of you ever say she was 'a stinking businesswoman who doesn't know how to handle money?'"

"We may have thought so," said Rina, "but we're not the kind of people to say things like that."

"What about: 'Charlene ran off with a sailor, and had a sailor in every port'?"

"You know," Rina said with a small smile, "each of these quotes sounds like Charlene's voice—not ours. It's what Charlene thinks we say about her. She's put her own fantasies into this legal document."

Barry grinned, then said, "The fourth count involves 'emotional distress'. Charlene charges you both with malicious schemes and stratagems to harass and intimidate her, to make her husband mistrust her and to cause such psychological damage that she was forced to run away from house and home. After undergoing treatment, she was able to return to her husband in six months, but you continued the same lies and pressures to estrange her from her husband."

"That's a neat trick," said Rina. "Charlene leaves her elderly, disabled husband for another man, secretly running off with $100,000 of his uncle's money—and she has the nerve to blame it all on us!"

Barry drooped his eyelids and said, "There's more 'emotional distress'. She's actually accusing you of murder, Martin. It says here that you failed to call a doctor or nurse 'during the crucial ten minutes when David, Martin's own brother, was choking to death in his hospital room.' And she goes on to say you deliberately prevented her from having an autopsy performed to see whether your brother's death was due to a natural or unnatural cause."

I rolled my eyes up and around in exasperation. "I'd call Charlene hopelessly paranoid, except that there's too much of the clever 'big lie' in this venom."

Barry heaved a sigh. "The last count involves 'invasion of privacy'. That's a cute way of saying you both conspired to destroy their marriage. She claims you were constantly flying down to interfere with their lives, bad-mouthing her to her husband and trying to persuade him to divorce her."

"False," I said, my face flushed with anger. "We tried in every way to make her feel part of the family. Even after she deserted David for a ship's officer and reconciled six months later, we wanted their marriage to succeed for David's sake. We would have done anything to make David happy."

Barry flipped his manila folder closed. "My first step is to file a preliminary response. I've already drafted nine motions to strike and dismiss their complaint on the basis of legal errors. But don't get your hopes up. Johnson will simply re-file a corrected complaint."

"You know," said Rina, "being sued for ten million dollars is quite a thrill. I'd say that our entire life's savings comes to one percent of that." She turned to me and said, "Have you been holding out on me, Martin?"

"You forgot to count our house. Charlene will be glad to take that too!"

As I kissed Rina good-bye at the airport early next morning, she gave me a comforting smile. "Charlene doesn't really have a case. I'm not worried. So don't you worry."

Easy to say. As soon as she was out of sight, depression set in. I felt violated, even a bit devastated. I was living a bad dream.

*You don't have time for such feelings,* I told myself. *Too much to do.* I had circled about a dozen "Furnished Apartment for Rent" ads in the newspaper, and started on my rounds to find a suitable place for Uncle Abe and Hattie, the latter having agreed to live in and take care of him.

Late that afternoon I found the right one. The apartment building looked no more than three years old, and I was shown a two-bedroom layout on the ninth floor with a lovely view. The furnishings were crisply contemporary. The building had a swimming pool and a shaded area where several residents about Abe's age were relaxing on outdoor chairs and lounges. I left a deposit, explaining that my uncle would be living there with an aide.

As soon as I entered our suite and saw the crease lines on Hattie's face, I sensed something wasn't right.

"What's wrong, Hattie? Where's Uncle Abe?"

"Oh, nothing really wrong, Mr. Richman. He's napping in the bedroom."

"Come on. What is it?"

"Well," she said, drawing it out, "he ain't his old self. Nothing hurting him. But his mind ain't all there today."

I walked into the bedroom. Abe's eyes opened and when he saw me, he sat up. "Where have you been?" he asked.

"I took Rina to the airport. She had to go back to work—remember? And I have good news—I found a very nice furnished apartment for you and Hattie."

"Why do I need an apartment? What's wrong with the house we've been living in?" He looked around, puzzled. "Where's David?"

I sat down on the bed next to him and spoke gently. "David isn't with us anymore. He died last month—remember?"

It took a few moments, but he remembered, and his mouth drooped.

I put my arm around him. "You said you didn't want to live with Charlene, so you and I checked into this hotel. You said you'd like to have your own place. And Hattie has agreed to stay with you … to cook and take care of things."

I could see that he was groping around in his brain to bring himself up to date. At last he spoke. "I don't want to be with Charlene. She yells at me. Take me to my own place."

I smiled and took his hand. "Your apartment won't be available for three weeks, and I'll stay with you till then. But first, I want to be sure you'll like living there. Let's take a ride now to check the place out."

Abe was pleased when he saw the apartment, and signed the lease. But as he handed me back my pen, he looked perplexed and said, "I have no money. How can I pay the rent?"

I assured the rental agent that I was handling all of Abe's financial affairs. Back in the car, it became obvious that my uncle had lost all recollection of the Abraham Bloom Trust, as well as other vital facts. He did remember that Charlene deserted David and ran off with their money. He also remembered that Charlene was suing us. Battered by the shock of David's death, the ejection from his home and a multi-million-dollar court case, Abe now had a swiss-cheese memory.

Not exactly suitable for the witness stand in my defense.

*David, David, I miss you in more ways than one.*

The next morning we opened a checking account in Abe's name at a nearby bank. This was not just to reassure him. I planned to send Hattie weekly checks from Abe's trust which would cover her pay, groceries and other necessary expenses.

Checking out of the hotel, I helped Uncle Abe get settled in his new apartment. I slept in the second bed in Abe's room. Hattie moved her stuff into the other bedroom, and arranged for her sister to come on Sundays so Hattie could have a day off.

I made a big thing of the view with Uncle Abe. "You're on the ninth floor," I said, "so you can see the whole town, practically. That's something you didn't have when you lived in a house all those years."

He seemed suitably impressed. But he was even more impressed when I lugged up the big new 23" TV set I had just bought and placed it opposite his recliner.

I knew it would be traumatic for Abe if Charlene suddenly showed up, so I posted a note in large letters on the inside of the front door:

DO NOT ALLOW CHARLENE OR ALICE TO COME IN

Now I could return to Connecticut with peace of mind. Well, not exactly. When you're being sued for millions, no matter how crazy the case, you can't feel happy-go-lucky. But Hattie is like family, and knowing that Uncle Abe is in good hands at last was like enjoying a warm fire after a freezing hike.

Back in Sarasota a month later, I rode the elevator to the ninth floor and rang the doorbell marked "Bloom." Hattie greeted me with her mighty smile and bear hug while Uncle Abe looked up from his newspaper with expectant eyes.

"I told you I'd be back very soon. How's the old Uncle Abe doing?"

He smiled up at me. "If I'm old, how much harm can I do?"

"Come on," I poked him in the ribs, "you're not that old. You haven't even hit ninety yet, and I'll bet you're still ogling the cute gals on television."

I asked if he was happy in his new surroundings. "Hattie takes wonderful care of me, just as always," he said. "And I like this place. But tell me," he leaned over and asked softly, "how did I get here?"

Slowly and in simple terms, I began a recapitulation of the past. Yes, he remembered that David had died, but he was upset because he didn't remember the funeral. "You were too sick at the time to go," I reminded him. He nodded his head. But the rest was a blank. All he could remember was that Charlene was out to get her hands on his money.

"He keeps asking me that same question," said Hattie. "He likes it here, but don't remember no-how how he got here or why."

So I took a pad and wrote out a summary: Charlene marrying David ... running off with Abe's money where her name had been added to the accounts ... evading David's attempts to divorce her, returning and being accepted back by David ... refusing to sign over her share of the house and van as she had promised ... and now, after David died, suing me and Rina.

I read it all to him, and said I would leave the pad alongside his easy chair so he could refresh his memory any time. But I shouldn't have mentioned that nine and a half million dollars. It upset him, and he slid down into a vale of depression for the rest of the day.

At breakfast, he joshed and seemed back to normal. Then I heard him ask Hattie, "How did I get here?"

I suppose it's fortunate the human brain can repress painful memories.

"Barry," I said, plunking myself down in front of his desk, "What's happening?"

"As I told you on the phone, Martin: nothing. Haven't heard a peep out of Johnson in response to my motions. I don't know why you insisted on seeing me now."

"But it's six weeks," I said earnestly. "How long can they keep us hanging?"

Barry popped a hard candy into his mouth and told me there was no legal deadline for their response. He would let me know as soon as something happens.

"I can't accept that," I said. "I don't want this sword hanging over my head for years. They have no case. You said so yourself."

"No case is ever won until it's over. I can't predict what Johnson will pull out of a hat. And since we can't deny your sister-in-law a jury trial, we'll be battling the 'poor, defenseless widow' syndrome." Barry sucked on his candy. "There are no guarantees."

"Meanwhile," I said, "how come Charlene can simply go on living in the house which is half-owned by Uncle Abe? How long do I keep paying the mortgage, taxes and insurance?"

Barry pondered that and said, "You can stop making payments starting now. I shall notify Charlene that Abraham Bloom desires to sell his interest in the house immediately. I'll tell her that since she has the exclusive use of the property, she is responsible for all expenses henceforth."

"What about my uncle's cat? He misses Cinnamon."

"I will demand its return to Mr. Bloom in the same letter."

I was upset by Barry's lack of initiative, and didn't hesitate to tell him so.

He gave a wan smile. "My initial strategy is simple. Since they are suing for such an outlandish amount, Johnson is obviously hoping to scare you into making a settlement. He'd like to make a quick killing—say, a million bucks, to save your valuable time and your large legal costs."

"So?"

"So," said Barry, shifting the candy in his mouth, "in my opinion, we've got to play it slow and cool. He's stalling before he invests a lot of time in revising his hasty complaint. After all, he's on a 'contingency' basis."

"Contingency?"

Barry explained that since Charlene has no money, Johnson gets paid only if he negotiates a settlement or wins an award for his client. "Let's make it tough for him, Martin."

I stroked my chin. "Right. That's why I'm not satisfied to be a defendant, Barry. I want to go on the offensive."

Barry showed mild surprise.

"Charlene stole my brother's will," I said hotly. "I want you to challenge her in Probate Court now."

Barry put his palms together and advised against it. He reminded me that I'm paying him $300 an hour, and he's glad to take my money. But isn't this an expensive way to vent my anger?

I laid out my own strategy. Charlene and her uncle Mike will deny in court they took David's will. Since I don't have the original, they will claim David's prior will applies—where he left everything to Charlene before she abandoned him.

"But all that's irrelevant," said Barry impatiently. "Our whole case rests on the fact that David had no assets of his own, so his will is moot."

"But I know something you don't know. What if we can catch Charlene and Mike with perjury in Probate Court? Wouldn't that help torpedo their case against me?"

Barry's eyes widened.

I smiled indulgently. "I've got a witness who will testify that he heard Charlene and Uncle Mike conspire to steal my brother's last will on the night my brother died."

There was a pause. "Bingo!" said Barry.

I went home to Connecticut. Abe settled into a comfortable routine with Hattie. Barry filed suit in Probate Court for the establishment of David's lost or destroyed will, claiming it was last in the possession of Charlene or her uncle. And, of course, they contested it.

It was now time to put on the heat. My lawyer arranged for Charlene and Uncle Mike to appear at his office for the taking of depositions. I flew down to be an observer, and to make sure Barry wouldn't miss asking any important questions.

Barry and I watched as they filed in with their lawyer, looking more like a funeral party than they had after my brother died. The court reporter sat nearby to take it all down.

Mike Fox was brusque and condescending. He declared that he had an important business appointment in thirty minutes, and should be questioned first. After being sworn in, he announced he was acting as his own lawyer.

Barry established Mike's relationship with Charlene and David and his presence at the house shortly after David's death. Then Barry bore in.

Q: During the course of that evening, was there ever a time when you saw the last will and testament of David Richman?

A: No.

Q. Did you and Charlene have any discussion about a bequest in her husband's will?

A: No.

Q: Do you know what happened to the original of David Richman's will?

A: No.

Q: Let's be absolutely clear on this, Mr. Fox. You are saying that you did not discuss such a will with Charlene Richman that night, nor did you take this will out of the house or destroy it?

A: You are badgering me, Mr. Weiss. I already answered those questions. I know nothing about a will. I didn't hide anything. I didn't destroy anything. And I demand you withdraw the complaint against me.

Q: We feel the complaint is justified, Mr. Fox.

A: I'm trying to control my temper, but I must warn you that your client may be counter-sued for taking frivolous action against me!

Q: Okay, okay. Just stop shouting, Mr. Fox.

A: No, it's not okay! My niece has no money for food or the electric bill. She has nothing. I can't believe that Martin would do this to his own sister-in-law. How can a man of wealth be so greedy? Why—

Q: Just a minute, Mr. Fox. No speeches here! This is MY deposition. I ask the questions. And I'm finished with you.

"Shit!" said Mike, stuffing his papers into the folder in front of him. Then he quickly turned to the reporter to say, "I'm off the record. Right after Weiss said he's finished with me."

As he got up, he glared at Barry and growled, "But I'm not finished with you! You're wasting the time of an important businessman. If you don't drop your complaint against me, I'm gonna slap you with so many motions that you'll beg for mercy." He smirked as he paused on his way out. "I've fought lawsuits for years. You're trying to intimidate an expert!"

Barry and I looked at each other. He shrugged and stated we were now moving on to take the deposition of Charlene Richman. He reminded her that, having been sworn in, she was still under oath. I noticed this put her visibly on edge.

Q. On the date your husband died, did you visit him in the hospital, Mrs. Richman?

A. I was sick at home myself, so I could only visit him for a little while. His last words to me were that he loved me very much.

Q. Let's focus on what happened after your husband died. You and others gathered at your house?

A. Yes. It was a very traumatic time for me, okay? We sat around the kitchen table drinking coffee. Uncle Mike called the funeral parlor to make arrangements. We talked about what a wonderful person my husband was.

Q. Did there come a time that evening when Martin left the group to speak on the phone in another room?

A. Yes. His wife was calling.

Q. While Martin was busy, did you take David's original will out of his desk?

A. Not that I recall. My memory is very fuzzy about that night.

Convenient memory loss, just as I anticipated. Barry pinned Charlene down tightly with specific questions, getting on the record her denial that she and her uncle discussed David's will or removed it from the house that night. If Charlene and Mike only knew that their conspiracy was overheard by Lou Bianca.

Q. I now want to direct your attention to the events which occurred on the Tuesday after your husband died. You set up an appointment with Benjamin Stone in the law offices of Stone and Wertheim?

A. Yes, I met Martin there. His wife too—he never made a move without her.

Q. What was the purpose of that meeting?

A. Mr. Stone prepared my husband's will, and I wanted to know where I stood, okay? Then Martin produced another document which he claimed was a later will. It was written to deprive me of all my rights as David's wife.

Q. Isn't it a fact that you yourself provided that copy to Martin that very day?

A. No, sir.

Q. Did you object to the will as not being valid?

A. No, I didn't know it was a fake, okay? But my husband would never sign anything like that.

Q. Mrs. Richman, didn't you take the original copy of that will from your husband's desk on the night he died and give it to your uncle, Mike Fox, so that he could conceal it?

A. I've answered you three times. You're hassling and harassing me, okay? You're making me lose control....

Charlene began sniffling into a handkerchief and Barry gave up. After he ushered her out, I asked, "What do you think?"

"Let's go talk to your Lou Bianca. If he'll testify like he told you about their conspiring to steal the will—we'll have their nuts in a wringer."

As Barry and I drove over to Tampa General Hospital, I mentioned that Bianca was still suffering from the wound that put him on disability. While

157

a detective with the Chicago police department, he was on a drug bust when he took three bullets. One had lodged near his spine and gave him trouble from time to time, which was why he was now in a hospital bed.

He liked the fragrance of the flowers I brought, and told us his doctors couldn't decide whether to try another operation, because of the high risk. But he assured Barry and me that he was well enough to answer our questions.

"Just tell us in your own words what happened the night that David died."

"It was a rough time," he said. "Everyone was way down in the dumps when I arrived at the house. Then suddenly this Mike character—I didn't know whose uncle he was till the funeral—starts a big thing about suing the hospital and the doctors over malpractice. He gets on the phone with a lawyer—by this time it's after midnight—and now he's laying it on that there must be an autopsy of poor David's body."

"Did anyone object?" asked Barry.

"That's what got me so mad. Mike was railroading everybody along ... except Martin here. I looked at Martin's face and I knew he was horrified by the thought of his brother being sliced up. And so was I."

Lou moistened his lips. "So I took Charlene and Martin into the next room and talked to them like a daddy. Charlene began to cry when I described what an autopsy is like. She agreed with me that David would never have wanted to be cut into pieces, and Martin backed me up. So she stopped Mike cold."

Barry asked what happened later when Martin was called to the phone.

"Well, as I was passing the den on the way to the bathroom, I heard something about a will. It was Charlene's voice saying, 'That will is poison.' Or something like that. Then Mike said, 'We'd better get rid of it.' Then Charlene told him to put it in his pocket and take it out of the house."

"They said all this in front of you?" asked Barry.

"They didn't notice me there, just outside the den. I didn't know what that talk was all about till Martin called me to say he was being sued. And he mentioned David's will was missing."

Barry stood up. "Lou, would you be willing to testify for Martin in court—simply relating what you told us here today?"

"Of course," said Lou. "It's nothing but the truth."

The wheels of justice must be square or octagonal, because they certainly don't turn smoothly. It took three months before the Probate Court hearing came up. And this was just a preliminary to hear motions.

I flew down to Sarasota and spent that afternoon with Uncle Abe and Hattie. We sat outdoors in the shade and chatted. Uncle Abe seemed to be thriving. "But he be getting lazy," drawled Hattie. "He be napping too much in his easy chair."

"You're just jealous," responded Abe, "because I have you working all the time while I take life easy."

Then he turned to me. "The trouble with Hattie is that she's too good a cook. That's why I'm getting so fat and lazy."

It was comforting to see Abe contented and like his old self. But his memory was still undependable. When I mentioned the house with the swimming pool where he had last lived with David and Charlene, I drew a blank. He asked about Rina and our kids, but the mention of Charlene drew a negative expression. The Abraham Bloom Trust and other memories seemed to be blocked out.

Early the next morning I was in Barry Weiss's office as he pulled together papers for our hearing on David's lost will. "Mike Fox wasn't kidding," he told me. "I was flooded with a blizzard of counter-motions intended to scare us into excluding him from our case."

"Mike's motions are coming up this morning?"

"Just a smokescreen," said Barry. "I'll have no problem countering them with the judge."

The hearing was held in the private chamber of the Probate judge. He was quick and impatient. He disposed of Mike Fox's motions with cool disdain: "Chuckleheaded."

He then told us that he had carefully reviewed Johnson's motions to dismiss, as well as Weiss' responses, and saw no need for oral arguments.

He went on to say there were insufficient grounds for a motion to dismiss. "However, in view of the pending suit in another court charging fraud in connection with the estate, I am staying these proceedings until the other case is adjudicated."

I blinked. A stolen will. Documented perjury. Why put off for tomorrow what must be done today?

"Your Honor," protested Barry, "we have made a serious charge: that a will has been stolen. We will show convincing proof of this. We are charging Charlene Richman and Mike Fox of lying under oath about it."

Judge McInerny said tersely, "I see no reason to become involved at this time."

"But Judge, this is a probate matter."

"I am *staying* this proceeding!"

I sat there stunned!

# CHAPTER XVI
# CAN'T LOSE

## *Rina—3 Months Later*

"It's about time," said Martin as he swung our rented Buick Century onto Route 41 and headed north to Tampa. The Southern Able/Disabled Organization announced they would bestow a posthumous citation on David to recognize his life-long achievements on behalf of the handicapped. We had accepted their invitation to attend the ceremony and receive the plaque.

"Better late than never," I said. "It's nice of them to remember."

Martin snorted. "David founded that organization. When they rejected him, they tore away his spirit. Losing that election was like ripping his heart out."

I remembered. Outwardly David remained his smiling self, open to anyone whose problems he sensed. But we knew that he felt adrift, struggling to find new bearings in his life. That's why we were so pleased when he decided to make a last grab for happiness with Charlene. Even though he was almost twice her age.

"Look," I said, "you can't blame the present leaders—they weren't involved in that crisis. Alex Crowne, the president, told me this should have been done long ago."

It's hard to realize that nine months have passed since David died. Martin still broods about it. It isn't just Charlene's lawsuit. Martin has lost his best friend.

*Charlene! Would she be there—fighting us for David's plaque? Relax. Charlene and David had avoided S.A.D.O. since the debacle. Most of the current members know David only from his reputation.*

Crowne greeted us warmly as we walked into the pastel pink Community Outreach Center. We followed his electric wheelchair as he introduced us around, and the ceremony opened with about fifty in the audience.

David was lauded as the group's founder and mentor:

*"He never stopped fighting. Accessible public places ... accessible housing ... accessible transportation...."*

*"He was the first to set up sheltered employment for the disabled."*

*"He got us a concrete ramp across the sand so we could enjoy bathing—the first in the country."*

*"David Richman was soft-spoken but as determined as steel. He would never let anything stop him. He was hell on wheels."*

Martin was obviously touched as he accepted the plaque. "David would have been proud of how this organization has developed."

As refreshments were served, an elderly woman limped over to us and introduced herself as an old friend of David's. "I cried and cried at his funeral," Molly Keller said.

Molly was surprised to hear of our problem with Charlene, and revealed a surprise in return: David wasn't Charlene's second husband—he was her *fifth!*

"My God!" I said, "Did David know that?"

"Sure," said Molly. "I told him when I heard they were engaged. I met Charlene years before. I warned David she was a slut. But he was in over his ears with her, and wouldn't listen."

I saw the hurt look on Martin's face and knew what he was thinking. *David and I were so close, and yet he never told me. I wonder what else he never told me?*

"Who were those other husbands?" I asked.

Molly knitted her brow. "I don't know the details. They're all dead. I do know that the second, third and fourth husbands were in their sixties when she married them. Just like David. It seems that Charlene makes a profession out of widowhood!"

Martin's eyes lit up excitedly and he grasped Molly's arm. "Would you be willing to testify at our trial what you know about Charlene?"

Molly smiled. "Of course. It's time somebody put a crimp in that money-grubbing bitch."

The trial was starting in a month. We were sitting in Barry Weiss's office telling him what we'd learned yesterday.

He shrugged. "I can't get too excited. After all, your brother *knew* he was husband number five. If we could prove that he *didn't* know about the three other husbands, we could develop a pattern of deceit by Charlene."

"But what about the 'professional widow' angle?" persisted Martin.

Barry offered us his jar of hard candy before slipping one in his mouth. "That has some possibilities. I'll arrange to depose Molly Keller right away. And I'll hire an investigator. He may turn up something solid."

"So where do we stand now?" Martin demanded.

"I'm cautiously optimistic," said Barry. "They've dropped their charge that Martin willfully contributed to David's death. It gets into the criminal area—ticklish."

Barry saw trouble in their charges that we had interfered with and helped break up their marriage. "Alice Henry will back up Charlene's accusations on the stand."

"How can we counter those lies?" I asked.

"Credibility," said Barry flatly. "I'll call up Greta Townsend, David's divorce lawyer. Can't put your Uncle Abe on the stand, but I'll call Hattie to describe Charlene's relationship to David, and to you two. I'm of the opinion it will really come down to how convincing you both are."

Barry slid yet another hard candy into his mouth. "I'm also counting on Charlene being less convincing. When I deposed her a few weeks ago, she was rattled by my questioning. I have the feeling she won't stand up under cross-examination."

"Let me tell you what worries me," I said, from my psychological background. "Charlene is more than a high-strung personality. Under high stress, she's unstable and unpredictable. Pushed over the edge, she could easily become violent. I think Martin should wear a bullet-proof vest when he's in court."

Martin humphed. "Sweetheart, this is real life—not Hollywood." He turned to our lawyer. "Barry, I'll tell you what's bothering me. I thought you said we had a strong case. Sounds to me like we're rolling dice ... when there are millions of dollars at stake."

Barry put on an enigmatic smile. "I never gamble. But we are dealing here with a jury trial. In my opinion, when you have a grieving widow blasting at you, you never know where the missile will land."

Back home in Connecticut, as the trial date approached, Martin was showing the stresses and strains of the already condemned. He would drop objects. He tossed and turned in bed night after night. And he began snapping impatiently. This was not the husband I knew.

One day I sat him down. "Martin, I'm just as concerned as you are. But I want you to come out of that fog and think. Are you digging yourself into a pit where you'll have a hard climb back into the courtroom? Or will you face that jury with the relaxed self-confidence that comes from being positive you're in the right?"

"Oh sure," he cried. "I just snap my fingers and the world turns rosy again. Just yesterday Hattie forwarded the foreclosure notice Abe received. It's from the bank holding the mortgage on Abe's house. Charlene keeps living there, but hasn't made mortgage payments for nine months. She won't agree to sell, but she won't cover the costs. It's the same goddam problem we've got with Dora on the old house my parents left us."

I put my arms around Martin's shoulders and eased him into decompression. "You've got every reason to feel angry and upset. All you did was try to help your brother and protect your uncle. You're feeling mutilated by lies and threatened with the loss of all we've saved for our later years."

I held him close to me. "Just remember that I'm in this boat with you. I'm feeling the stress and the pain too. But we're going to beat it. We're going to beat it because we're two smart people—and because we're right!"

His head was on my shoulder and I ran my fingers through his hair. "Remember when we were hijacked to Cuba with our children years ago? I was shaken to pieces, while you buoyed us both up. Now it's my turn to remind you that as long as we're together, we can ride out any crisis."

Martin lifted his head and spoke to nobody in particular, "What do people do who don't have the special relationship we have?"

I laughed and told him that we psychologists have been working on that problem for years. If couples would only realize that the partnership connections they build together is what puts the real meaning in life.

Martin gave a small smile. Then he put his head close to mine and whispered in my ear, "I love you."

*"What did you say?"* I heard Martin yell into the phone. At his nod, I rushed to pick up the extension. The voice at the other end was Barry from Tampa. He was telling Martin to calm down and listen. He said that as our attorney, he felt it his duty to explore a settlement. It might save us a very expensive trial.

Martin sucked in his breath, but he listened.

"I ran into Johnson when I stopped at the courthouse," Barry said. "He asked me if my clients would be interested in a settlement. He mentioned a high figure, and I told him he was crazy."

Martin started to respond, but caught himself.

Barry continued. "I told Johnson: 'Come off the cloud and be real. I might be able to get my clients to agree to $50,000 if you get the okay within an hour.'"

The line seemed dead for a whole minute, prompting Barry to ask, "Are you there, Martin?"

I could sense that my husband was throttling himself to keep from exploding. His voice came low and angry: "Did I ever mention any interest in a settlement, Barry? Did I ever ask you to discuss it?"

Barry sounded flustered. "What's the harm in sounding them out?"

"Damn it!" Martin's voice crackled. "I make no deals with gold-diggers! That's admitting I've done something wrong! You should've turned him down flat!"

"Look," Barry said defensively, "I was only thinking of your interests. I'm of the opinion this trial could cost you a hundred thousand dollars. That's if you don't lose. It can run you a helluva lot more if you do."

"We'd better *not* lose!" cried Martin. "Now you just call Johnson up right now. Tell him you were in error in even discussing settlement—that your clients are completely opposed to the idea!"

The silence at the other end of the phone was deafening.

Funny how a small incident like that can make a big difference. It stiffened Martin's spine and injected him with fresh determination. He shrugged off our failure to locate the ship's officer with whom Charlene had run off. He took action when Barry advised us that his private investigator had been unable to track down Charlene's first husband and had turned up nothing special about her other husbands. Martin saw this as a challenge. He felt that if he went to Florida, he might unearth something himself. So I got a leave of absence and we headed south again.

As the plane breezed along at 35,000 feet, I felt strangely isolated. Martin, as always when confronted by a goliath problem, was drowned in thoughts, freezing out conversation.

I gazed out the window and began to appreciate the virginal beauty of the cloud formations below. Some majestic Greek god had blown cotton fleece across a plain of sun-washed blue sea. I marveled at the haphazard pattern of ice floes and wispy plumes, ruffled and rippled, in this serene panorama.

Standing up in the aisle for a broader look, I noticed the indifference and boredom of my fellow passengers, sated with the experience of flying. I suddenly had a flash vision of Orville Wright, and tried to imagine the thrill he felt as he winged his puny craft up into the sky, exulting in the freedom of the birds.

My mind jumped to a concept I ran across recently: to look at things "diachronically." Examining events through the lens of time can yield fresh perspectives. I imagined I was on a rocket instead of an airship. Not very long ago the first rocket rides offered at $25,000 created a pandemonium rush of excited ticket seekers. Yet today the jaded passengers on our rocket shuttle from New York to Melbourne hardly give a glance out the portholes.

Funny how we take the wonders of our civilization for granted. We are born into a world where we didn't have to build the houses, the roads, the factories—they were here. The technology was already figured out by Newton, Lavoisier, Edison and a long line of innovators. The first man in space and the first man on the moon were passing marvels. Maybe the weltschmertz that haunts so many people comes from being focused too tightly inward, instead of seeing the big picture of humanity's climb upward from the caves.

Suddenly the plane lurched and I grabbed wildly for balance. The captain's voice blared forth the order for passengers to take their seats and buckle up. I slipped down into my chair before the announcement was finished and the aircraft rode a washboard course, bumping and thumping. It was over within sixty seconds and I took a deep breath. Then we heard the pilot's voice say: "Sorry about that, folks. We hit the back of a front. Please excuse the rough ride."

Martin disembarked with a detailed plan in his head. He got on the phone and checked with everyone he could find who knew David and Charlene. He had the odd feeling that, as we couldn't get any facts on Charlene's first husband, this might hold the key to our case.

No luck. He heard lots of negative comments about Charlene, but nothing we could use in court. Then someone mentioned that Lou Bianca was in the hospital again, which explained why Barry hadn't been able to reach him. So we drove over to Tampa General for a visit.

Lou looked pale and drawn. As I arranged the flowers we brought, he recounted his tribulations with the medical profession. He had been inside the hospital far more than outside. Two prolonged operations had accomplished nothing. "I feel like my ass is in a sling," he said.

"Do you hear from Charlene?" Martin ventured.

"It's a funny thing," Lou wrinkled his forehead. "We were so close before David died. She was dying to sleep with me. And now she freezes me out like I'm in Siberia."

Martin and I both stiffened, and Martin leaned over. "Did you sleep with Charlene before David died?"

Lou grunted. "What kind of person do you think I am? I could never do that to David. My friend. A prince of a guy."

I explored gingerly, "What made you think Charlene was dying to sleep with you?"

"She told me so. She tried all her tricks to get me into bed."

Martin and I exchanged looks. Here was a new twist we hadn't anticipated. We pressed Lou for details.

"Charlene began making eyes at me before she left David, but I gave her no encouragement. Then a few months after he took her back, she kept asking me to escort her to places when David couldn't go."

"Did you go with her?"

"Only once to a meeting. She made me uncomfortable on the way home, nuzzling up to me and making suggestive remarks. Like how lonely she was. And that David didn't understand her anymore."

"Would you consider that as asking to sleep with you?" I used my professional tone.

Lou grunted again. "She got specific when I didn't react the way she wanted. She propositioned me. She said that David was now too old for sex. He knew she had a passionate sex drive. So he urged her to get satisfied elsewhere—he wouldn't mind."

Lou winced from some subterranean pain and added, "That's what *she* said he said. Then she suggested we go to my place and spend the night."

Martin and I waited breathlessly for him to continue.

"She got nasty mad when I turned her down. I told her I couldn't do that to a good friend like David. She just wouldn't understand."

"Did you ever mention it to David?"

"Why would I want to hurt him? Anyway, he probably suspected, because she kept flirting with me even when he was around. Sex was in every conversation. She just wouldn't give up trying to get me into bed with her."

Martin put his hand on Lou's shoulder. "Would you be willing to repeat all of this in court? You could be of tremendous help in our case, Lou."

"Why not?" he answered with a weak smile.

Barry became a born-again attorney when we told him about Lou. "Now we've got the kind of contradictory testimony we need to shake up the image of the devoted, grieving widow."

Yesterday's heartache had become today's smiles. Then Martin had another thought. "But what if something happens to Lou in the meantime to prevent his testifying? He didn't look good to me, and even the doctors don't seem to know how bad he really is."

"I could depose him tomorrow," said Barry, "which would give us sworn testimony to introduce if he was unavailable. But that would discount our advantage."

Martin and I looked puzzled.

"For any deposition," he explained, "I'd have to notify Charlene's lawyer, so he could be present. Then Johnson would know the trump card we're holding. He'd have time to figure out a defense, and maybe blunt the impact we need."

Martin and I chewed that one over. Then I pointed out that life often doesn't have clear-cut choices. "We can minimize our risks by checking on Lou daily. If we hear that he's taking a turn for the worse, Barry can arrange for a deposition session at the hospital on an emergency basis."

"When did you study risk theory?" asked Martin with a chuckle. And it was agreed that we would phone Lou every day.

Martin looked up at the ceiling and mused, "It's still hard for me to accept that my wise, thoughtful brother would take up with a grasping, narcissistic person like Charlene."

"Not so strange," said Barry. "Aristotle, in his dotage, fell for Phyllis. And when she ordered him to get down on all fours so she could ride on his back, the world's greatest philosopher did just that."

"Charlene reminds me of the Wife of Bath in Chaucer's *Canterbury Tales*," I said. "She described each of her three husbands as 'elderly, rich and pliable.'"

As Barry showed us out, he said, "Most people believe the stereotype that it's the woman who is taken advantage of by the man. My job is to convince the jury that women like Charlene are in a special class."

"Yes," I said. "Charlene was two husbands up on the Wife of Bath."

I felt it was important for us to spend as much time as possible with Uncle Abe while we were down south. We roamed Busch Gardens. We looked in at the Ringling Brothers Circus winter campground. And since Abe wasn't up to going into the ocean, we spent many an afternoon with him around the kidney-shaped apartment house pool.

It was paying off. There was new verve in his movements. He somehow polished up his memory banks for access to most subjects. But the Charlene/David file was still too painful. He simply repressed it.

One thing that galled me was the loss of Cinnamon, his cat. She'd be a comfort to Uncle Abe. Charlene stonewalled our plea to give her back. Plain spite. Barry said there was nothing we could do.

Driving back from Barry's office, I spotted a dumpster with an odd inscription:

DAINTY RUBBISH SERVICE

I pointed it out to Martin. "Doesn't that oxymoron somehow sum up the crazy thing we're going through?"

167

On the eve of the trial, Scott called from Denver, full of concern, asking if there was something he could do to help us; "anything … anything at all." Annabel, in Minneapolis, rang in with a positive note: "You can't lose. It wouldn't be fair!"

After Abe had gone to bed, I interrupted Martin's reading. "I don't see how we can lose either. But how would you feel if we did? Think. I want to know."

He put his palms together and let the seconds drift by. Then he said, "I'd feel like I had fallen into a vat of shit and was drowning. But then I'd realize that it wasn't *my* shit. So I'd grab you and we'd fight our way out. Then after we washed ourselves clean, I'd just ignore that we had no clothes, nothing. We would survive."

"Damn right," I said.

# CHAPTER XVII
# BUTTERFLIES ARE FREE

## *Charlene—3 Days Later*

My stomach is in no-man's land. I'm scared shitless when it comes to trials. My brain is still shell-shocked from Ed's shooting all those years ago.

But then I think about that snake Martin and his slimy wife, and how we're going to shaft them. And how I'm going to be bathing in all those shekels once this fracas is over. That keeps me going.

Once I focus, I see that the trial is riding smooth. Johnson laid my case out in his cool style, but with all the soap opera flourishes that held the jury hanging on his every word. He poured it on about Martin conspiring with his wife to cheat me out of my widow's inheritance. He's good ... even better than I thought.

Martin's lawyer, Weiss, said he would show I had no claim to any money, and that Martin and his wife had nothing to do with turning David against me. He cried crocodile tears for me, and sounded so sincere that I felt like taking up a collection for him.

For his first witness, Johnson called on Alice. She testified how lovey-dovey David and I had been all the days of our marriage. How we always went everywhere together, both of us dedicated to the cause of the disabled. How I always took such loving care of David. Alice was a perfect witness—she really laid it on thick.

Then Johnson zeroed in on my fucking brother-in-law and his wife.

Q. Mrs. Henry, do you know the defendants, Martin and Rina Richman?

A. Yes. Martin would come down from Connecticut about once a month. Sometimes both came. They'd stay for a week at a time.

Q. Was there a reason why Martin came so often?

A. I heard him say that he wanted to protect his brother. He was always saying that his brother was too soft, and had to be told what to do.

Q. How did David's brother act toward Charlene?

A. He made nice on the surface, but he was always interfering in their lives, making Charlene look bad. Charlene suggested they move to a new house which was wheelchair-accessible, because the place they lived in was a hardship for David. Martin was dead set against it.

Q. So Martin talked David out of it?

A. It was too late. They already put down the money. But Martin never stopped harping on it as Charlene's mistake.

Q. Were there similar incidents?

A. Plenty of them. David inherited some Chinese art objects from his parents. Martin's wife Rina said she didn't want Charlene to have them, and demanded them back. She has them now. And when Charlene went back to work because she didn't want to be a financial burden on David, Martin torpedoed her beauty parlor career. He pushed David into selling the beauty parlor business which Charlene was running.

Q. Did David make a profit when he sold the business?

A. Naw. He took a big loss because of selling it fast.

I knew I could depend on Alice. She has the gift of gab, and sounds like the little girl next door. Naturally, she expects to get a chunk out of the dough I get, friendship or no friendship.

She was even better when her testimony continued the next morning.

Q. Mrs. Henry, you mentioned yesterday that Martin was always turning his brother against Charlene. What did you see or hear to make you feel that way?

A. One day while I was helping Abe to the bathroom, I heard Martin telling David that Charlene was only interested in his money, and that he should divorce her.

Q. Was there anything else?

A. Once as I was coming into the den, I overheard Martin saying to David, "Your wife, Charlene, is a degenerate. She runs around with other men."

Q . What did David say?

A. He said nothing. He never argued with his brother. From what I saw, David went along with just about everything Martin said.

Q. How did Martin's wife act toward Charlene?

A. Rina was always antagonistic, always backbiting Charlene. I once heard her tell David, "Charlene spends a fortune when she goes to the supermarket." Rina always had her head together with Martin, like they were plotting something.

Q. How did Charlene react to all this?

A. She became upset and frustrated, as you can imagine. She knew that the brothers had a close connection. But she was David's wife! She loved him, and knew it was unfair for their decisions to be made by Martin. And she found out that Martin was pulling every trick in the book behind her back to get rid of her.

Q. What did Charlene do about it?

A. What could she do? She tried to set her husband straight, to help him see what was going on. But every week Martin would have David on the phone for an hour. And he kept running down from up north so often that he kept David under his spell. He turned Charlene into such a nervous wreck that her spirit broke down and she ran away. It took six months before she worked her way back to normal.

*Hah. Now let them try to drag out that crap about my running away with a sailor. Alice has the jury convinced that you can't go through torture like that without a nervous breakdown. She showed I just couldn't take it anymore. Right on.*

Q. Her husband accepted her back even though he had made plans to divorce her?

A. Of course he took her back. He loved her and she loved him. And Martin wasn't there to interfere when she and David got together again.

Q. What was Martin's reaction when he found out?

A. Fire and brimstone. He came rushing down from Connecticut and put Charlene through a third-degree. After that he made life miserable for her.

*Can you imagine my smart-ass brother-in-law trying to con me into believing he would forgive and forget everything that happened? Guess he thought I was born the day before yesterday. As soon as I let my guard down, he went for my soft underbelly. I'll get that motherfucker if it's the last thing I do.*

Q. Mrs. Henry, David had an uncle living with him for many years: Abe Bloom. How did Charlene get along with Uncle Abe, in your observation?

A . Uncle Abe is a sweet old guy. He and Charlene hit it off swell right from the start. He's a great kidder. But he's in his eighties, and developed Alzheimer's. His memory looped, and he did things that were off the wall. He became difficult to handle.

Q. Did Charlene take good care of him, just as she did her disabled husband?

A. I'll say! No nurse could have done more. When he went wandering the streets in a daze, she spent hours frantically trying to find him. She cleaned up after his shit—excuse the expression. And she always treated him gently and lovingly.

*Abe was a lot of fun, before he went off his rocker. If I'da known the money in the family was his, he's the one I'da married. Now he's still alive, and my Davy's dead. Crazy world.*

The judge adjourned for lunch. As the three of us sat in the greasy spoon

171

down the street, I said to Johnson, "Why won't you let Alice testify that Martin beat me up?"

"Yes," said Alice, "I can do that."

"You didn't go to a doctor or report it to the police," said Johnson. "Besides, I heard you telling Alice what to say. I don't want to be involved in that sort of thing."

"I don't know what you mean," I said, curling my lip.

He ignored me and said to Alice, "What I want is for you to show the jury how stone-hearted Martin and his wife are. I'm calling you up again to describe how they cast Charlene out in the cold and told the grieving widow to fend for herself. Better finish that burger—we're due back right quick."

Q. Mrs. Henry, I want you to recall the last time you met in Charlene's house with the defendants, Martin and Rina Richman. David had died several days earlier. Please describe what happened that afternoon.

A. The four of us were sitting around the kitchen table. Charlene was trying to sort out her life. She volunteered to continue taking care of Uncle Abe—Abe Bloom—just as she had in the past. Martin turned her down cold.

Q. Then what happened?

A. Charlene couldn't believe that her husband died and left her no money to live on. That's what Martin told her, and she believed him then. She pleaded with Martin and his wife to help her until she could get back on her feet.

Q. What did they say?

A. They wouldn't give her a red cent! Martin's wife said, "You can go on welfare and get food stamps!" They deserted her, and took Uncle Abe away with them.

Weiss stood up to attack her story. He tried to rattle Alice by charging that I ordered them out of my house. But she turned the tables by saying: wouldn't any woman get mad if she suddenly became a poor widow and was cast adrift by her scheming brother-in-law?

Then he tried to trap her about the time I went away.

Q. You testified, Mrs. Henry, that Charlene and David never stopped loving one another?

A. Yes, from the time they became engaged to the day David died.

Q. Isn't it true that Charlene left David's house for a period of six months, telling him she was getting a divorce?

A. Not so! She told me she had to get out of that house because Martin had made her life unbearable. She left and had a nervous breakdown. I mentioned that earlier.

Q. Mrs. Henry, isn't it a fact that Charlene Richman ran away at the time on the cruise ship *Fantasy* in the company of a sailor she met on board?

A. I know nothing about that. I only know that she sent me postcards from different places saying how sick she was, and that David was not answering her letters. When I phoned David about it, Martin answered the phone and said no letters ever arrived. That's what he said.

Q. Mrs. Henry, didn't Martin tell you at the time that David had filed for divorce, and didn't he ask you where Charlene Richman was?

A. I didn't know where she was. And I didn't believe Martin about the divorce. The proof is that when Charlene came home, David took her back and was very happy with her to the day he died!

Alice really twisted Weiss's tailbone on that round. Everyone was feeling that he had socked himself on the jaw. It did my heart good to see that smart-alec Weiss stymied. My fear pangs were evaporating.

Johnson next put my Uncle Mike on the stand to dig the grave deeper, and also to cover our asses.

Q. Mr. Fox, how well did you know David Richman and Abe Bloom?

A. David married my niece about three years ago. Abe had been living with David, and stayed on with them. My wife and I would get together with them every couple of months.

Q. How would you characterize the marriage?

A. Beautiful! It justified my faith to see two people so much in love. Especially David finding happiness so late in life. And they complemented each other so well.

Q. How would you describe Charlene's relationship with Abe Bloom?

A. Close. She took such good care of him that you would think she was his daughter instead of his niece. He even told me once that he thinks of her as his daughter.

*That was when I found I couldn't get rid of the old geezer and David wouldn't go along with putting Abe in a nursing home. So I played up to him again till he put me in his will and added my name as we rolled over his C.D.s at the bank. More than one way to skin a cat. But it got to be too long for me to wait and I hightailed it with the hundred G's. Funny how fast money goes when you're loaded.*

Q. Mr. Fox, do you recall attending a meeting, several months before David died, at the law firm of Stone and Wertheim?

A. Yes. Charlene phoned me to say that Martin was seriously interfering with their marriage ... "trying to break it up," she said. I told her I'd be glad to come down and help smooth things out.

Q. Did she tell you what it was about?

A. I knew that Charlene had suffered a nervous breakdown, and had gone away to recuperate. She'd had some very rough deals in her life, but I didn't know until then that Martin was the cause of this problem.

Q. What problem are you referring to?

A. Charlene told me that Martin and his wife were doing everything they could to turn David against her, to get David to divorce her. Now they were asking Charlene to cast aside her financial security.

Q. What did she mean by that?

A. They wanted to force her to give up her share of the house they live in, as well as their van. I told her, "Nobody's gonna force you to do anything while I'm around."

*Uncle Mike has been great. He's been reading me the riot act all my crazy life, but he hasn't given up on me. I'll give him half a million or so, depending on how much of the ten million bucks I get.*

Q. What happened in Stone and Wertheim's office, Mr. Fox?

A. First I tried to patch things over. After all, here are two kids who love each other. So there were some mistakes made. Let them go home and talk it over without lawyers, without outside interference.

Q. Did it work?

A. David didn't say a word. I guess Martin had his claws in too deep. So I tried to solve the money question

Q. What did you do?

A. I said that Charlene would agree with what they asked if she wasn't bankrupted. My compromise was that they pay her a fair price for her share of the house and van. "Let's get this mess behind," I said, "and let the two lovers live in peace."

Q. Did they accept the compromise?

A. Naw. When push came to shove, they just backed off and didn't bring it up again. I guess Martin had other schemes up his sleeve.

Weiss objected to that, and the judge sustained it. But Martin's lawyer could see there was no use challenging Uncle Mike's testimony. So he tried to trip him up over the will.

Q. Mr. Fox, on the night David died, you came to Charlene's house?

A. Yes, we gathered in the kitchen to comfort her in her sorrow.

Q. Did the subject of David's will come up while Martin was out of the room?

A. If it did, I don't remember it.

Q. Mr. Fox, did you see Charlene take her husband's will from the desk that evening and did you remove it from the house?

A. No.

Q. Mr. Fox, are you certain that you have no knowledge of this will? Remember, you are under oath.

A. No. Definitely not.

*Weiss was blocked again. What a dumb lawyer. He's shot himself in the foot. Why bring up David's will if he's claiming David had no assets?*

*His whole case is on a Jello foundation. He's claiming that all of the assets belong to Uncle Abe. That's so stupid. The assets were all in joint names—David's and Abe's. Then a little while before David died, Martin takes Abe to set up a trust with Martin in complete control. Abe lives on Cloud 9. So everyone can see that the trust was just to freeze me out.*

That was Johnson's next step. He called Uncle Abe to the stand and demonstrated that the uncle had air between the ears. Abe couldn't answer any questions about wills or trusts. He even flunked simple things, like the name of the President of the U.S. and what today's date was. Uncle Abe turned out to be *our* best witness.

Johnson then torpedoed Uncle Abe's trust by calling Dr. Brown to the stand. Our psychiatrist testified that he hospitalized Abe more than once for mental trauma, and that he had diagnosed Alzheimer's long before the date when the trust was established. Weiss didn't even bother to cross-examine.

Now it was my turn. I was pumped up by all the rounds our side had won. But as I stood up on the stand to be sworn in, I could feel the butterflies taking off in my stomach.

I was wearing a simple black suit, and carried a few black kerchiefs in my purse. Johnson started off with powerful concern, making it clear how much he sympathized with the grieving widow.

He led me through my first meeting with David, and how well we meshed right from the start. He pictured David as my Sir Galahad, rescuing me from a brutal, wife-beating husband, and how this led to a deep-rooted love and marriage so strong that it bridged our gap in years.

Johnson smeared it on thick. How David and I worked shoulder to shoulder to improve conditions for the disabled. How we went everywhere together, with my driving the van because of his failing vision. How dedicated I was to his every need, like my sleeping over in the hospital corridor when I almost lost David under the surgeon's knife.

Uncle Abe? I loved the old gent, with his kidding ways. Johnson had me talk about my taking him everywhere with us until he became senile. About how I would watch over Abe once he developed Alzheimer's and would wander off the deep end. About how I would shepherd his pills so carefully, and get him to the hospital as soon as he developed dangerous symptoms.

Q. Sounds like you had a perfect marriage, Mrs. Richman. What caused the disruption?

A. David's brother and his wife, Rina. The funny thing is: when I first met them, they seemed so likeable, okay? But as time went on, they were always interfering with our lives.

Q. In what way did they interfere?

A. In many, many ways. For example, David and I had decided the house we lived in was too small for David to get around in an electric wheelchair. Martin and his wife didn't want us to move, and they got furious when we did. Then Martin kept blaming me for problems which came up with the old house, okay?

Q. How else did they interfere?

A. David knew I wanted to work, so he bought a successful beauty parlor, which I managed. When Martin heard about it, he persuaded David that it wasn't a good investment and David sold it, okay?

Q. These actions seem to be directed against you?

A. No question. Martin and Rina were always criticizing me in front of David. And I heard from others that they told David terrible lies about me behind my back, okay? No question they were trying to destroy my marriage and drive me away. Why else would they come down so often?

Q. What lies did they tell?

A. That I was cruel to Uncle Abe. That I was spending a fortune on groceries. That I ran around with other men.

Q. Was there any truth to any of these allegations?

A. No.

Q. But you did leave your husband?

A. Martin and his wife forced me out. I had to get away because I was losing my husband. I was afraid of losing my mind, okay? I actually suffered a severe nervous breakdown after I left. It took months to get better, to gain the strength to return to my husband and fight back.

Q. What happened when you came back, Mrs. Richman?

A. My husband was overjoyed to see me, to have me taking care of him again. He understood what made me go away. Then we had a long talk with Martin when he came down and agreed to let bygones be bygones. To start with a clean slate.

Q. Did it work?

A. Only for a month or so. Then Martin persuaded my husband into pressuring me to give up my ownership share in our home. He forced me to go to a lawyer's office, okay? If it weren't for my Uncle Mike coming to my defense that day, Martin would have swindled me out of my rights as David's wife.

I surprised myself at how well I was doing on the witness stand. The butterflies weren't all squashed, but my stomach had stopped quivering.

Johnson then asked me questions to confirm key points in Alice's and Uncle Mike's testimony. How the letters I sent while I was away were blocked from reaching my husband. How Martin deliberately talked me out of having an autopsy performed right after David's death—when I couldn't think straight.

Q. Mrs. Richman, you are now a destitute widow?

A. Yes. Since my husband died, I've been too sick to work. Martin has taken control of all of my husband's assets. He refuses to give me a penny, okay? I can't even pay the mortgage.

Q. Didn't your husband leave a will?

A. Yes, leaving all his assets to me.

Q. Your Honor, I submit this document entitled, "Last Will and Testament of David Richman," which is dated 2 March 1991, as Exhibit A. Now Mrs. Richman, please read from this document article III, paragraph B.

A. Okay. "I give, devise and bequeath all of my estate to my spouse, Charlene Richman."

Q. What is stopping you from getting your husband's money?

A. My brother-in-law went to court to block the will. He claims he has a later will which cuts me out completely. My husband would never do that, okay? He loved me.

Q. Did your husband ever mention a later will to you, Mrs. Richman?

A. No, sir.

Q. Is there anything else impeding you from getting your husband's money?

A. Right after my husband's death, Martin's lawyer told me that there were no assets in my husband's estate, okay? He said all the money was in a trust fund.

Q. What do you know about this trust?

A. I discovered that the trust was set up only weeks before my husband died. All of my husband's bank accounts and stocks and mutual funds were withdrawn and transferred into the Abe Bloom Trust by Martin.

I was watching Martin's face, and man, was he sweating bullets! Rina just sat there looking like a broomstick was stuck up her ass. I felt like gloating, but I forced my face to hold my woebegone widow's expression.

Q. How could Martin withdraw your husband's assets?

A. Uncle Abe's name was listed jointly on all funds, okay? But he has Alzheimer's, so how could he know what he was signing?

Q. In other words, you believe that your brother-in-law, Martin Richman, arranged to transfer your husband's assets into a trust in the name of his uncle, Abe Bloom, thereby depriving you of them?

A. Yes. Martin is set up as the trustee of this trust. He is also the primary beneficiary, okay? Other beneficiaries are his wife and children. I have no access to my husband's money.

Q. And your brother-in-law has given you no money to live on since your husband died?

A. Not a red cent! They treat me as if I never married their brother … as if I never existed!

Johnson was wearing a satisfied smile as he sat down. I was feeling pretty good myself until I saw Barry Weiss slink toward me like a panther about to pounce. I waited for his first question, but he just stared me in the eyes like he was searching my brain. Then the little monster stepped back and purred ever so gently in his first few questions, as if he felt just as sorry for me as Johnson was. He thought he could make me look primitive, but I had some snappy answers for him

Q. Mrs. Richman, please describe your education.

A. I have got approximately—well, the equal of—three years of college. I have practical nurses training. I also have training in law enforcement, okay?

Q. What was that in preparation for?

A. I was the first female patrol officer in the U.S.

Q. That's very commendable. Were you married before you met David Richman?

A. Yes, several times. I've suffered through some very rough times in my life. Every one of my husbands is dead!

I burst out into tears and Weiss rushed to hand me his handkerchief, making all kinds of sympathetic noises. Man, he sure spreads his shit on thick before he gets down to business.

Q. Mrs. Richman, you testified that you left your husband David because you felt a nervous breakdown coming on. Where did you go first?

A. Puerto Rico. I went by ship because the ocean calms my nerves, okay?

Q. On that voyage on the cruise ship *Fantasy,* did you meet a man named Manuel Martínez?

That stopped me. How much did Weiss know? He couldn't know much. Manuel wouldn't talk—not after I paid him to seal his mouth. I'll play it cool.

A. Yes. He was one of the ship's officers.

Q. Isn't it a fact that you ran away with Mr. Martínez just one week after you met him?

A. That's a lie! I didn't run away with anybody! Mr. Martínez noticed on board how upset I was, and he took pity on me, okay? He talked to me and was very sympathetic.

Q. Isn't it a fact that you slept with him and spent considerable time with him afterwards, sailing around the Caribbean?

A. No! No! I never slept with him! That's why he lost interest in me—I refused to sleep with him! I wounded his Spanish pride!

Weiss paused, like he didn't know what to say next. After all, he couldn't prove anything, could he? So he attacked from another direction.

Q. Mrs. Richman, you testified that you felt forced to leave your husband because you were losing your mind. Isn't it a fact that you withdrew large sums of money to take away with you?

A. I needed money to live on. So I took money from my own accounts, okay?

Q. Isn't it a fact that you cashed in every one of the Certificates of Deposit where you had recently persuaded your husband to add your name? Didn't you run away with over one hundred thousand dollars?

A. I don't recall what the total was.

Q. Didn't your husband tell you that the monies in these C.D.s actually belonged to Uncle Abe, that David's name was listed jointly only because he handled the family finances?

A. No.

Q. Mrs. Richman, how do you justify taking off with such a large sum of money?

A. I was David's wife. I worked my fingers to the bone taking care of him. And Abe too. And I needed money to get back to myself, to get well, okay?

Q. Mrs. Richman, you took away over one hundred thousand dollars. What happened to all that money?

A. I used it to get my health back. I was in a sanitarium for a long time.

Q. What's the name of that sanitarium? Where was it located?

A. In Mexico someplace, okay? I don't remember exactly.

Q. You said you recovered and came home. Surely you recall the name of the place which helped you get better? Or any place it was near?

A. I told you—I don't remember.

That didn't sound good, I know. But so what? The important thing is showing that Martin was causing all my troubles, and was trying to rob me of my rightful inheritance. But Weiss kept boring in.

Q. Mrs. Richman, when your husband accepted you back in his household after your long absence, did he ask you to agree to certain conditions?

A. The only conditions were that I try to control my headstrong impulses, and that I don't leave him again.

Q. Mrs. Richman, I remind you that you are under oath. Didn't you agree, as part of the reconciliation, that you would give up your interest in the house and in the van to Abe Bloom as partial make-up for his monies which you took and spent?

A. No! That's the story that Martin was putting out, okay? Why would I give up my financial security?

Q. Do you recall a meeting at the offices of Stone and Wertheim a couple of months before your husband died, where your husband declared, in the presence of witnesses, that you made such promises as part of the reconciliation, and where he asked you to live up to these promises?

A. I've told you over and over again that my husband was hypnotized by Martin to say all kinds of things against me, okay? You're trying to trap me. You're getting me all flustered!

At this point the kind old judge called a recess. He saw how upset I was, and he took pity. I was also glad that the jury could see how Weiss was tormenting me.

When they put me back on the stand my intestines were still in a bind, but I had the feeling that the worst of the tempest was over. I'm sure the jury was buying my story of Martin the Monster, brainwashing his brother David into shoving me out of the picture.

But Weiss wasn't through with me. First he tried to trip me up about the missing will, asking me the same questions he asked Uncle Mike.

Then Weiss got to his point:

Q. A few days after your husband's death, did you go to the Stone and Wertheim law offices along with Martin and Rina Richman?

A. Yes.

Q. What was the purpose of that meeting?

A. I was a new widow. I had no money, okay? I wanted to know where I stood financially.

Q. Did Mr. Stone consult papers which he identified as a copy of 'The Last Will and Testament of David Richman' and did he give his interpretation of the terms?

A. I think so.

Q. And did the terms call for the whole estate to go to David's uncle, Abe Bloom?

A. Yes—but that will wasn't genuine. The signature wasn't really David's. My husband would never make a will that cut me off, okay?

Q. Mrs. Richman—did you object or say even one word about its being invalid that day?

A. Look, I was all mixed up—okay? My husband had just died unexpectedly. I was in shock!

Q. Mrs. Richman—

Weiss was now snarling at me, closing in. I suddenly noticed that he looked like my father coming at me with that mean look before he whammed me. Now he's grabbing me and it hurts. He won't let me go. His eyes tell me he's got that awful thing in his mind. Now he's on top of me, forcing me back, his hand over my mouth. He's pressing hard into me, hurting, piercing, pumping, paining....

Q. Mrs. Richman, please answer my question—

A. Wha...?

Q. Mrs. Richman, my question is: why didn't you object?

A. Questions, questions! Look—I lost a husband, a lover, a wonderful companion. I'm a sick woman. All this pressure you're putting on me is flaring up my diabetes!

Q. I'm sorry, Mrs. Richman. I didn't mean to get you so upset.

A. If you haven't lost your spouse, you can't understand.

Q. I understand—

A. You don't understand! You don't know what it feels like to suddenly find yourself without a cent in the world! My brother-in-law is still trying to take advantage of me right here in this court!

I had the jury's sympathy. Weiss slunk off with his shoulders folded down. But then he swiveled around and reserved the right to call me back to the stand.

I wasn't too happy about that. Especially when I noticed Lou Bianca in the courtroom as I took my seat.

He knows too much. He'd better not tell.

# CHAPTER XVIII
# NOTHING BUT THE TRUTH

## *Martin—One Day Later*

"Truth is mighty, and will prevail." There's nothing wrong with this statement except, as Mark Twain pointed out, it just ain't so.

Can you blame me for being cynical? Yesterday's court performance made it seem like truth has become an alien life form. The prosecution painted me as the archetypical swindler and marriage-wrecker, with Rina as my chief assistant. Then they smugly rested their case.

My badly-needed lift came from our kids. Scott and Annabel flew in last night, saying they had to be with us during these trying days. Not easy for them to take time from their jobs. How heartwarming are the family ties that bind.

Today it's my turn. To tell it as it really was. As I walked up to the witness stand to lead off for the defense, I glanced into the eyes of the jurors. Not very friendly—to say the least.

Barry Weiss, my lawyer, took great pains to set the record straight. First, he led me through my close relationships with David and Uncle Abe, so I could demonstrate how strong and deep were my feelings toward them. This led us to Charlene.

Q. How did you feel when you first heard that David was getting married?

A. I was delighted. David was always doing for others. At last he was finding personal happiness.

Q. How did you and Charlene get along?

A. Fine, at first. I welcomed her into our family with open arms. So did my wife and kids. We did everything we could to make her feel part of the family, instead of an in-law.

Q. What was Charlene's attitude toward you and your wife?

A. She was friendly at first. But once they bought the new house, we sensed that Charlene was building a wall between us.

Q. What gave you that feeling?

A. She became cool and reserved, and we couldn't understand why.

*We were the same people. It was Charlene who changed. Maybe it was that one innocent comment I made at the time that derailed her. I can't remember now what it was—but I remember that look on her face.*

Q. Were you opposed to their buying a new house?

A. On the contrary, I agreed that my brother needed the extra comfort and convenience.

Q. Did you oppose David's buying into the beauty parlor business for Charlene, and persuade your brother to get rid of it?

A. Absolutely not. I didn't know about the beauty parlor until after they bought it. Later, David told me he had to sell it because it was a losing operation.

Q. Did you ever tell your brother that Charlene was only interested in his money?

A. No.

Q. That he should divorce her?

A. No.

Q. Did you ever say: "Charlene is a degenerate. She runs around with other men?"

A. Absolutely not.

My rebuttals were crisp and sincere. As Barry said, credibility would be the decisive core of this case. The truth and nothing but. *So simple if only Pinocchio were alive. Then the jury would merely have to check whose nose grew longer—mine or Charlene's.*

Q. After David and Charlene were married about a year, what unusual event occurred?

A. My brother phoned me to say that Charlene had deserted him and run off with another man.

Q. Your brother was totally surprised?

A. He was astounded and hurt. Particularly when he discovered that Charlene had cleaned out their checking and savings accounts, and cashed in seven Certificates of Deposit.

Q. How much money did she take away *in toto*?

A. Approximately $100,000.

Q. What did your brother say about this?

A. He was terribly upset because this was all Uncle Abe's money. David had no assets except for two small mutual funds he inherited.

*If it hadn't been so easy for Charlene to run off with all that moolah, she would have had to make the marriage work. Or was it doomed from the start?*

Q. After Charlene took off with the money, did David go for a divorce?

A. Yes. But his lawyer, Greta Townsend, couldn't serve Charlene because she concealed her whereabouts. Even her uncle and her best friend maintained they didn't know where Charlene was for six whole months.

Q. Did you ever intercept or block any communication from Charlene to her husband?

A. Absolutely not! How could I? I live in Connecticut, and spent only a few weeks in Sarasota during the six months in question. Besides, if I had heard from Charlene, David's lawyer would have known where to serve the divorce papers. *I never did understand why the divorce couldn't be filed against Charlene. After all, she deserted my brother. Florida has no-fault divorce, so why did it matter if she couldn't be found? How different things would have been today!*

Q. What happened about six months after Charlene disappeared?

A. I had a phone call from David saying that Charlene had returned, and that he had taken her back.

Q. What was your reaction?

A. I was speechless. But my brother said she was a changed person. She promised to pay back the money she had taken. She promised to sign over the title to the van and her share of their house. She said she loved only David, and he believed her.

Q. Did you believe her?

I described how I flew down and tried so hard to establish a new and friendly relationship with Charlene, how I wanted to become the brother she never had. I spoke with the intensity of the heart.

*I've always wondered why it didn't last. Was it a mistake to remind her of the promises she made? No—the house and the van came from Abe's money, and she should have turned them back.*

Then I described how David tried to get Charlene to sign a reconciliation agreement, and how she insisted on getting $18,000 more of Uncle Abe's money to do what she promised to do six months earlier.

Q. What happened next?

A. My brother called up his divorce lawyer and told her to re-institute his suit, now that Charlene could be served.

*Everyone has a limit. No matter how obliging the disposition. David's legs were useless, but he still had a backbone.*

Q. So David filed for divorce again?

A. He didn't foresee the problems. Because he accepted Charlene back into his household, he would have to build a new case, and Charlene would surely fight it tooth and nail.

Q. Did he take any action against Charlene?

'A. No. My brother finally decided he was too old and tired for such a battle. He gave me a copy of the new will he made when Charlene left him—where he specifically disinherited her. Uncle Abe's new will also eliminated any bequest to Charlene.

Q. Did David and Charlene separate?

A. No. My brother told me he no longer loved her, but would have to tolerate living with her. He felt he had no choice.

*David was right. Sometimes in life you have to settle for the lesser evil. My brother learned to grin and bear it. Well, not really. They had some real battles before the end. Maybe it bothered him more than he showed. Maybe this conflict and stress hastened his death.*

Q. Mr. Richman, tell us what happened three months later on January 12.

A. I had an emergency call and flew down to Sarasota. My brother and uncle were both in Carmel Hospital. According to the doctor, neither condition was serious. My uncle Abe recovered, but David died. They couldn't save him. It was completely unexpected.

*What an understatement. One moment the person turns his head, talks, feels, breathes. Some fleeting moments later the head no longer moves, speaks, thinks. The body is there, like before. But the intrinsic personality—where did it go? Decades in development. Evaporated in a flash.*

Q. Mr. Richman, was setting up a trust for Abraham Bloom your idea?

A. No. David proposed it as a protection for the balance of Uncle Abe's money, and had his approval. David asked for my help in arranging the details with a trust lawyer.

Q. Did Abraham Bloom ask for that trust?

A. Abe often told David that he worried about the rest of his money falling into Charlene's hands. Abe favored anything that would protect his assets so they couldn't be taken from him. And he went willingly with me to convert everything into his new trust.

Q. Are you saying that Abraham Bloom was fully aware of what this trust was all about?

A. Absolutely. He was 87, but he was lucid on important things. His condition has deteriorated considerably since that time.

Q. How come?

A. Abe had two severe shocks in quick succession. One: he lost my brother, who was a son to him. Lost him very unexpectedly. Two: he learned that Charlene is suing in court, and may get all his money after all. His mental health was devastated.

Q. Did you cut off your brother's wife without a penny?

A. Not at all. One week after my brother's death, Charlene ordered us to leave the house—even though Abe Bloom was part owner. We paid all the accumulated bills, including a $600 physician's bill for Charlene. We also continued paying the home mortgage for three months—even after Charlene instituted this suit against us.

I looked to where Rina was sitting, and I saw in her eyes that I was coming across like a solid citizen. I was watering down each of the negatives the opposition had introduced.

Barry gave the jury a brief nod and a confident smile before sitting down. Then it was Johnson's turn, and he wasted no time going on the attack.

Q. Mr. Richman, how often did you visit Sarasota after your brother married Charlene Richman?

A. About every two months.

Q. Your home is in Connecticut. That much travel adds up to a mighty big expense. You expect us to believe that you've been spending all that money without a thought of the fat estate you stand to inherit if Charlene Richman were not in the way?

A. That's insulting. You apparently haven't heard about loving families, Mr. Johnson.

Q. I see. You loved your brother David so overwhelmingly that you resented Charlene's intruding herself into your selfish relationship—is that it?

A. That's not it at all! Number one for me was David's happiness. Rina and I did everything we could to make Charlene feel fully accepted in the family. We did nothing to interfere with their relationship.

Q. Nothing? When Charlene and David began finding Uncle Abe difficult to handle and they talked of putting him into a nursing home where he would have the best of care—didn't you object vigorously?

A. Yes, but—

Q. Just answer "yes" or "no," Mr. Richman

A. Abe is my uncle, too—

Q. Your Honor, please direct the witness to answer my question.

A. Yes.

*That's the trouble with testifying in court. You tell the whole truth, but the inquisitor can bend and twist your words into boomerangs. There ought to be a law....*

Q. Mr. Richman, did you and your wife conspire to convert assets in the name of David Richman to your own use?

A. Absolutely not!

Q. Isn't it a fact that for many years there had been assets in the name of David Richman valued at hundreds of thousands of dollars? Yet you testified your brother David had no assets!

A. My brother never earned that money. All of the assets in the Abraham Bloom Trust came from monies earned by Abe Bloom through the years. My brother's name was jointly listed prior to the trust as a convenience for handling financial affairs, in deference to Abe's age.

Q. What happened to the two mutual funds which David Richman inherited?

A. David signed those over to the trust shortly after it was set up. He told me the $35,000 would go partially toward the $100,000 Charlene had taken of Abe's money.

Q. Let's not confuse the jury, Mr. Richman. Didn't you just say that $35,000 of David's money is now in the Abraham Bloom Trust—instead of going to his impoverished widow?

A. Yes, but I've explained that—

Q. And doesn't that contradict what you just told the jury a few minutes ago? Let me quote you: "All the assets in the Abraham Bloom Trust came from monies earned by Abe Bloom."

A. I meant—

Q. Mr. Richman, I hope you'll get your facts right as we go further along. Particularly when they are vital to the outcome of this case. Do you expect us to believe that your brother transferred his last remaining funds to a trust, leaving his wife and himself without a penny? Or did you somehow persuade him to carry out this stupid action?

A. It wasn't stupid. My brother was getting $3,000 per month from the trust to cover all expenses, including Charlene's. And the executor is authorized to provide additional monies as needed.

Q. Ah—but who's the executor? Who is in control—David Richman? Oh no. It's Martin Richman. The beneficiary of the trust. The one who wants what remains in the trust to be as big as possible!

A. Not so—

Q. No more questions of this witness!

It's lucky the judge called a recess. I thought I didn't have a temper, but I felt like strangling Thomas Johnson right there on the courtroom floor. As we walked into the hall, I marveled at how this attorney had managed to find and bore in on the weak chinks in my testimony, twisting little things into big. No wonder this country has so many lawyers. We need one to counteract every one of the Grand Inquisitors in court who hold the lighted faggots against the soles of your feet.

I headed for the men's room. My brain was churning with all the things I should have said on the witness stand. I was feeling like a mop that hadn't been fully wrung out. Then I looked down and saw that I was pissing on my left shoe.

The white-haired man two urinals down hadn't noticed, so I rectified my aim and then darted into a stall for toilet paper. After cleaning my shoe and the puddle, I carefully soaped my hands and stared at myself in the mirror. *This too shall pass.* I took a deep breath, and joined the others waiting outside the courtroom.

Barry was saying that we have to expect more of Johnson's clever tactics, only worse. But we've got some surprises for him, too, added Barry. Rina asked if Lou Bianca was next, to expose the stolen will and to reveal Charlene's attempted seduction. Barry gave a secret smile and said he was saving Lou for the climax.

Barry built our defense slowly and methodically. First he put up an accountant who is president of the local C.P.A. association. Alex Greene stated he had been retained to research income tax returns filed by Abraham Bloom and David Richman. He testified that in going back twenty years, the only annual income reported by David Richman (about $3,000) was from two mutual funds, whose latest value is approximately $35,000. All the stocks, bonds and bank holdings were listed in the Bloom tax returns as yielding interest and dividends, and Abe Bloom paid the taxes due.

Q. In other words, Mr. Berger, the social security number used for those stocks, bonds and bank holdings belonged to Abraham Bloom, so that the earnings were reported on his tax returns?

A. Correct.

Q. Does that mean, even though the assets were listed in joint names with David Richman, that the ownership was truly Mr. Bloom's?

A. Yes.

Q. Did this pattern change after David married Charlene?

A. No. Except that the couple filed joint returns, and their total taxable income was still too low for any income tax to be owed.

Johnson rose pensively, pencil poised under his chin, to undermine the testimony.

Q. Mr. Greene, are you telling us that simply because the interest and dividends were reported on the Bloom tax returns, this is sufficient proof that the stocks, bonds and bank account funds belonged solely to Bloom?

A. I would say so.

Q. Ah, but you are being paid by the defense. As an accountant, Mr. Greene, have you run into cases where people have chosen to list earnings from joint assets according to where there is the smallest tax liability?

A. Yes, but—

Johnson cut him off and sat down with a smug smile. Barry jumped up and had the witness point out that it would be illegal to do as Johnson cited. Barry also showed that David had been on disability income for fifteen years, and that a watchmaker's income before that wouldn't be adequate to purchase the stocks and bonds in question.

Barry then called a succession of witnesses to prove that Uncle Abe was legally qualified to set up his trust. Dr. Klein, the neurologist, testified to Abe's lucidity at the time he examined him, contradicting the Alzheimer's diagnosis of Charlene's psychiatrist, Dr. Brown. Charles Jacobs, the trust lawyer, related how he carefully qualified Abe and made sure he was fully aware of the provisions of the trust as each page was explained and initialed. Dr. Kahn, the internist who treated our uncle at the time of David's death, indicated that he saw no aberrant behavior while Abe was in the hospital. Johnson had no success in shaking any of these witnesses.

The judge called a lunch recess. Our family and Barry took Lou Bianca along to a nearby pizza parlor where we could order low-cholesterol pies. I bit into a hot slice and said, "After all that, I think we've blocked Charlene's charge that I swindled David's money from her."

Rina agreed, but Barry cautioned, "You can win all the points, and lose on the count. Can't predict juries in cases like this." He wolfed down his pizza slice and added, "We still have to block those alienation charges. That's why your testimony is so important, Lou."

But before putting Lou Bianca on the stand, Barry called Greta Townsend. David's divorce lawyer confirmed that she was unable to find Charlene for six months to serve the divorce papers David wanted. She also testified that after David reconciled with Charlene, he expressed regret over it. However, he had no stomach for renewing what would have been bloody divorce proceedings.

Hattie came next.

Q. You cared for David Richman and Abe Bloom as a full-time housekeeper and cook for a year and a half?

A. That's right.

Q. Think back to the month before David died. Did Abe Bloom understand everything you said to him? Did he understand what was going on around him?

A. Oh, he was in his right mind, if that's what you mean. Like other old men, he was slow to catch your meaning. And he forgetful much of the time. But he understand the important things he heard. Not like now.

Q. Abe Bloom is different now?

A. Yeah. He been knocked by all that's happened since. Memory very bad. Sometimes don't know where he is. Broods a lot. I try to jolly him.

Q. How did Charlene and David get along after she went away and came back?

A. Fine, for a month or two.

Q. What happened after that?

A. I'd hear them disputin'. David was usually soft, but she mighty upset at times. I could hear her yelling through two closed doors.

Q. What happened in the month before David died?

A. They'd be a fight every day. She'd raise her voice to the limit, but he wouldn't back down. He'd answer her quiet like, and she'd get madder. Sometimes she just storm out of the house.

Johnson stood up and approached the witness on cat's feet. He studied her till she became uncomfortable.

Q. Hattie—I may call you "Hattie?"

A. Call me whatever you like.

Q. Hattie, did you like your boss, Charlene Richman?

A. We got along.

Q. How did she treat you? Was she tough? Was she unfair? Come on, Hattie—tell us the truth!

A. She was unreasonable at times.

Q. In other words, you didn't like her. Maybe you even hated her at times—right?

A. I do my job.

Q. Maybe you hate her enough to make up stories to get her in trouble—isn't that right, Hattie?

A. I do my job. Period!

Q. And right now what is your job, Hattie? You're working for Martin Richman over there—right, Hattie? He's paying your wages right now as you testify up here, Hattie. So maybe you're not exactly an objective witness, Hattie—

A. Lookee here, mister—

Barry objected heatedly, and Johnson sat down with a smirk pasted on his face. I hoped the jury would see through these tactics.

And now for our top gun, Lou Bianca, whom I saw limping his way to the stand. Here's where Barry torpedoes Charlene's story.

Q. Mr. Bianca, you were a close friend to both David and Charlene Richman?

A. Yes. I was invited to their wedding. I went to their home frequently. We founded the Disabled Citizens of Florida organization together.

Q. What do you know about a beauty parlor business they were involved in?

190

A. David told me they were losing money. He was aggravated over it. He finally sold it at a loss.

Q. Mr. Bianca, was there a time when you heard that Charlene deserted David?

A. Yes. He phoned me one evening, very upset. "Charlene left me," he said, "for a sailor."

Q. What else did he tell you?

A. He said she took a lot of money. "I was very stupid," he said. "I trusted her." It was sad.

Q. Later you heard that Charlene returned?

A. Six months later. David called and told me he took her back because she promised to give back the money.

Q. You saw them both after that?

A. Oh, yes. We continued close friends.

Q. You saw Charlene the night David died?

A. That's right. Charlene phoned to tell me. What a shock. She asked me to come to the house that evening. She needed comforting.

Q. What happened later that evening in reference to a will?

A. Martin was on the phone speaking to his wife and I was passing the den on the way to the bathroom when I heard Charlene telling her uncle to steal David's will.

Q. Did Charlene Richman actually talk about sneaking the will out of the house?

A. Maybe not in those words. But they didn't want the will left there. And the uncle said he'd take care of it.

A stunned silence fell upon the courtroom. We got 'em. Perjury. Direct contradiction of Charlene's and Mike's sworn testimony. Where there's a will, there's relatives. *Lying* relatives.

Q. Mr. Bianca, I'd like to take you back to two months before David died. Did you have occasion to drive Charlene to a meeting?

A. Yes, David wasn't feeling well. She phoned and said, "Lou, Baby, take me to the meeting tonight." She always called me "Lou, Baby" or "Honey."

Q. Did anything unusual happen that evening, Mr. Bianca?

A. On the way home, Charlene kept nuzzling up to me in the car. And she made suggestive remarks.

Q. Let's be more specific. What sort of things did she say?

A. Like she was very lonely. Like, "I'm having a rough time with David" and "David doesn't understand me anymore." She kept telling me how much she liked me. "I'll bet you'd make a great lover," she said.

Q. How did you react?

191

A. I didn't. I wouldn't think of hurting David in any way. But then Charlene came right out and propositioned me.

A gasp went up in the courtroom. I looked over at the jury. They were wide-eyed. I glanced at Charlene. She was bug-eyed.

Q. What did she say?

A. "Lou, Baby, let's go to your place and spend the night. I've got the hots for you."

Q. What did you say?

A. I told her David was my best friend. And she said David wouldn't mind. He was now too old for sex. He knew she had a high-octane sex drive. "Honey, he wants me to be satisfied," she said.

.Q. What did you do?

A. Look—just because she said David wouldn't mind doesn't make it so. I turned her down and she got nasty. She just couldn't understand.

Q. Did she stop talking to you?

A. Naw. She kept flirting with me even when David was around. She never gave up trying to get me into bed with her.

I savored my moment of sweet triumph. But it didn't last very long. Johnson had some poison-tipped darts left in his blowgun.

Q. Mr. Bianca, you look like a pretty virile young man. Would you say you have a normal male sex drive?

A. Sure.

Q. So how can you expect us here to believe that an attractive woman like Charlene Richman would beg you to jump into bed with her—and you would turn her down cold?

A. But that's what happened, dammit!

Q. And you say she continued ogling you and making passes at you in front of her husband. What did he say about it?

A. Nothing.

Q. Nothing? Are you trying to tell us that a wife tries to seduce a family friend right before the eyes of her husband and the husband doesn't say a word?

A. David was too much of a gentleman to talk about it.

Q. I see. But you're not, are you, Mr. Bianca? Now let's get to the night David died, when you stood outside the den to eavesdrop on the conversation between Charlene and her uncle.

A. I didn't eavesdrop.

Q. Oh? Then what were you doing standing there just outside the door?

A. Uh ... I don't know. I was just there.

Q. I see. You didn't know what you were doing, but you listened. Just

192

how well did you hear, Mr. Bianca? Please tell us the exact words you heard.

A. Well ... Charlene said, "What can we do about this paper?" And her uncle said, "Get rid of it." And she said, "Put it in your pocket and take it with you." And he did.

Q. And those were the exact words you heard?

A. Well, pretty close.

Q. In other words, neither Charlene nor her uncle mentioned the word, "will" or "David's will?"

A. Mmn ... I think they mentioned a will. I don't remember for sure.

Q. There seems to be a lot you don't remember very well, Mr. Bianca. Let me read you your earlier testimony: "I was standing just outside the den when I heard Charlene telling her uncle to steal David's will. Maybe not in those words. But they didn't want the will left there." Do you remember saying that, Mr. Bianca?

A. Yes.

Q. How come you were certain that they mentioned a "will" when Mr. Weiss questioned you ... and when I asked you what you heard, you simply called it a "paper?"

A. It was a will, all right.

Q. Oh, now you're certain the paper was a will, eh? Mr. Bianca, you were a detective for many years. What did you think of a witness who told two different stories of the same event?

A. I know what I heard.

Q. If your memory isn't so reliable, Mr. Bianca, maybe you have the same problem remembering what happened in your relationship with Charlene, who was your friend as well as David's. Is it possible what really happened is that you were trying to seduce HER—instead of the other way around?

A. That's a crock—

Q. And maybe she spurned your advances, Mr. Bianca. And you're just trying to get back at her on this witness stand, perjuring yourself out of your jealousy and hatred!

Barry jumped up and objected heatedly before Johnson completed the sentence, but the damage was done to our key witness. The jury was told by the judge to "disregard." But you can't undo the emotional impact of wounded testimony on twelve average human beings in the jury box who really don't know who is telling the truth.

# CHAPTER XIX
# GOD LAUGHS

## *Rina—That Evening*

Our case is beginning to look pretty bleak. As a professor of psychology with three degrees, I pride myself on understanding people's behavior. So I can empathize with Charlene. She has no support system—no husband, no circle of caring relatives. I feel sorry for her. But that in no way excuses what she is doing to us.

After the court recessed and we walked out into the hall, Barry summed up the day. "I hate to say this, but when the jury doesn't know whom to believe, they usually side with the poor widow."

Martin's fists were white and I could sense how tightly his teeth were clenched. His anger unfurled slowly, but with rising intensity till it swelled with more impact than if it had surged forth in a rush. "Lies!" he spat. "Her whole case is built on lies! And the world believes them!"

We headed back to Barry Weiss's office for a council of war. But there the cloud of gloom befogged our brains. We felt dead in the water, drained of ideas.

Martin tried to find some silver lining. "How can the jury believe that Charlene and my brother remained lovey-dovey after she deserted him for six months? David's divorce lawyer testified that David wanted to proceed with the divorce after Charlene reneged on her promises for reconciliation."

Barry popped his ubiquitous hard candy into his mouth and said, "I'll be the devil's advocate. Number One: David took Charlene back. Number Two: Martin and Rina kept interfering in their lives, turning David against his wife—forcing her to run away, and then poisoning their marriage after she was accepted back."

"What about Hattie's testimony that Charlene had many fights with David?" I asked. "Doesn't that confirm David's intention to divorce Charlene?"

Barry shrugged. "This only confirms Charlene's case against you. You two conspired to make her husband distrust her, turned her husband against her and undermined their marriage."

194

Maybe I'm beginning to believe it myself—that Martin and I interfered in their marriage. Our intentions were good, but if we had stayed at arm's length, maybe their marriage would have worked.

"Whose side are you on?" snorted Martin when I voiced my doubts. "Everything Charlene did had a single purpose. She set about building a wall as soon as she saw us as a threat to her controlling David and Uncle Abe. We were in her way. Why can't you face it?"

"Mom, how can you worry whether Charlene was right or wrong when you can lose everything you own?" asked Annabel.

"I wish I had a lightning bolt to toss into court tomorrow morning," said Barry. He shuffled his papers impatiently. "I'd better get started on working up a knockout summation."

But nobody made a move. Giving up was an awful alternative. Brainwaves reached out in frantic circles. Finally I ventured, "What about the mystery of Charlene's first husband?"

"What about it?" said Barry. "How could that help us now, at the edge of a cliff?"

Brow furrowed, I said, "When you're hanging over a cliff, it's wise to grab at anything. I'll bet he's connected with that weird statement she made about being a police officer."

Barry looked puzzled. "Give me that again."

"When you asked Charlene on the stand yesterday about her background, she said she had practical nurse training. Then she made the astounding statement that she was 'the first female patrol officer in the country.'"

This set off a pregnant silence.

"Well," I turned to Barry, "Firsts always get publicized. Did you have your investigator check this out as I asked you to?"

Barry began thumbing through the phone messages his secretary had left on his desk. "Ah, Wilbur did call me at 3 today."

Barry dialed and got into animated conversation with his investigator, firing questions and taking feverish notes. Martin and I became increasingly infected with his excitement while tingling with suspense. Barry finally hung up just as I felt like wringing the story out of him.

"Forget Perry Mason," said Barry exuberantly. "This is believe-it-or-not real life. We found Charlene's first husband. He's dead, like all the others. But this one she killed herself!"

*"What!"* yelled Martin, unbelieving.

Barry read from his scribbled notes: "Charlene at age 20 married Edward Osborne, 39, who was the police chief of a small town in Georgia called Edson. She was sworn in as a deputy police officer one year later. Four

195

months after that she shot and killed her husband in their home one Sunday. She claimed self-defense—to stop her husband from beating her to death. She was sentenced to nine years for manslaughter and served six before being paroled."

"Wow!" cried Martin, jumping to his feet. "Can this whole story be presented in court?"

"I think so," said Barry thoughtfully. "Now it pays to introduce the fact that Charlene had four husbands before David. It's relevant to demonstrate a pattern of her marrying men much older than she, who each die off. We can't prove that she withheld these facts from your brother. But the pattern and the killing will help undermine whatever sympathy she built up with the jury."

"What's wrong?" Martin asked me as we walked up the steps of the courthouse the next morning.

"Nothing important," I said.

"Come on, Rina. We've been together too long. I know when something has you on edge."

We came to the top step. I sighed. "I've got some mixed feelings about this Charlene killing."

His eyebrows shot up. "She's torpedoing us and you're still feeling sorry for her—?"

"No, not that part. When it comes to brutality against women, you know how upset I get. I imagine Charlene, a young thing of 21, getting beaten up time after time by her husband. Finally she can't take it anymore. Desperate for her life, she pulls out her gun and tells him to stand back. He laughs and comes at her. She shoots. And she goes to jail for nine years."

"She got out after six—"

"That's not the point," I countered. "We are using this poor woman's unfortunate experience to blemish her in the eyes of the jury. Isn't that taking unfair advantage?"

Martin quietly led me to an alcove in the corridor. "I understand how you feel, but we're not going to re-try her case here. We are not condemning her act. Barry will simply bring out the facts from Charlene's own mouth."

Now that I started, I was standing stubborn. "You know, Martin, if Charlene's case were tried today, she would win or get off with a very light sentence. Killing in self-defense is now an accepted plea in most wife-beating trials."

Martin stared at the opposite marble wall. "Rina, you don't know all the facts in this case. Barry told me that Charlene did the shooting not just to stop her husband. She emptied her revolver into him. All six bullets. Some into his back."

That didn't really relieve my discomfort. When a woman shoots to protect herself, fear and excitement can press the trigger till the gun runs out of bullets.

Martin saw I wasn't satisfied and he added, "Charlene didn't call anybody until seven hours after she shot him. Seven hours."

I saw Charlene sitting there holding the smoking gun, young and dazed. The shock after the act of killing can immobilize the brain for a long time. Were we being fair in dragging in this act of desperation?

Martin shook his head sadly. "Aren't you overlooking the main point here, Rina?"

"What's that?"

"Charlene is charging us with a conspiracy to destroy her marriage by making her husband distrust her and become alienated from her. Now you know that's a goddam lie! But how do we convince the jury of the truth? By rolling out every fact we know. Do we really have a choice?"

*Life is often like that. No simple choices. Somebody's got to be hurt.*

"Rina," Martin added softly, "I hope you'll erase that guilty look before we get to the courtroom. We didn't lie about anything. Matter of fact, what we're doing today is telling the whole truth—and nothing but."

When Barry recalled Charlene to the stand, she seemed confident and even cocky. He set the stage by asking her to describe how she met David, and how their acquaintance blossomed into marriage.

Q. So, Mrs. Richman, you were married to someone else when you first spent the night in David Richman's home?

A. I was desperate that day, and David took pity on me. My husband was a wife-beater, okay? I was afraid to go home.

Q. Had you been to David Richman's home before that day?

A. No.

Q. Had you spent any time with David Richman outside his home before that day?

A. No, but—

Q. In other words, you spent the night in the home of a perfect stranger. If you feared for your life, why couldn't you have stayed with a relative? Your uncle appeared in this court, and you must have others.

A. I couldn't stay with relatives.

Q. What about friends? Alice Henry appeared in this court, and you must have other friends.

A. I had no place else to go, okay?

*Many abused women have no place to go. Staying with a friend or relative only encourages the wife-beater to come after them with a vengeance. It's time for society to protect these battered women.*

Q. Mrs. Richman, David was 69 when you two were married? How old were you?

A. I was 39.

Q. Did you feel any hesitancy about marrying a man of such advanced age? After all, you were still a vigorous young woman, in the prime of your life.

A. I loved David, okay?

Q. The fact that he had a big house and seemed well-heeled didn't influence your decision to marry a man almost twice your age?

A. No. I marry for love—not money!

Johnson had objected to the last question, but the judge allowed it. Johnson kept jumping up to object through the rest of Charlene's testimony, but Judge Lewin ruled that Mrs. Richman had opened up this line of inquiry by denying that money was any consideration in her marriage.

Q. Mrs. Richman, you were previously married to Vincent Badillo. He was 66 when you married. How old were you?

A. I was 38.

Q. Whom were you married to before Mr. Badillo?

A. (pause) A man named Rudolph Carter.

Q. How old were you and he when you married?

A. Uh, I was 34.

Q. How old was Mr. Carter, Mrs. Richman?

A. He was 68.

Q. You were also married before that, weren't you? What happened to your marriage with Mr. Goodman?

A. We were married about a year when I became a widow.

Q. Please tell us how old you and Mr. Goodman were when you married.

A. I was 30. I think he was 67.

Q. Are any of your many husbands alive today, Mrs. Richman?

A. No.

Q. That's very interesting, Mrs. Richman. In every one of these four marriages, you selected men in their sixties—men who were twice your age. Do you consider this normal for an attractive, healthy young woman in her thirties?

A. You're badgering me. When you're in love, age doesn't count.

*If that homily were only true. Some age-gap couples have long and*

*affectionate marriages. Others I've known grew apart as they matured on
different paths. I wonder what path Charlene will take with the Truth or
Consequences question coming up.*

Q. Mrs. Richman, how many times were you married in your life?

A. Four.

Q. Richman, Badillo, Carter and Goodman. What about Osborne?

A. Who?

Q. Edward Osborne. I'm sure you'd rather forget about your first
husband, Mrs. Richman. I see you're having difficulty answering my
question, so I'll reword it. Did you marry Edward Osborne on May 4, 1972,
when you were 20 years old?

A. Yeah.

Q. Please speak up. The jury can't hear you.

A. Yes.

Q. That means David Richman was your fifth husband—right?

A. Yes.

Q. Getting back to your first husband, what was his occupation?

A. He was the police chief of Edson, Georgia.

Q. Did you divorce him?

A. No.

Q. How did he die? I remind you, Mrs. Richman, you're under oath.

I saw the beads of perspiration forming on Charlene's forehead. She could
tell where this was heading, and her chin began to quiver like the wings of
a hummingbird. But no sound came forth. And the air of suspense hung in the
courtroom like the momentary hush before a squall.

Q. We're waiting for your answer, Mrs. Richman.

A. You're ... you're trying to confuse me!

Q. Let me help you. He was shot, wasn't he, Mrs. Richman?

A . Yeah.

Q. Who shot him? I repeat—who shot him?

A . I did.

Q. Please speak loud enough for the judge and jurors to hear you.

A. I shot him.

Q. Why did you shoot your husband, Mrs. Richman?

A. He was always beating me up! I just couldn't take it anymore, okay?

Q. You testified earlier that Vincent Badillo abused you the same way.
Were all of your five husbands wife-beaters, Mrs. Richman?

A. No! Ed was really vicious! I had to stop him before he killed me!

Q. I see. You felt your life was in danger, so you shot your husband. But
help the court to understand why Edward Osborne was found with six bullets

in him that evening. You told us you took professional training as a police officer. If you were trained to fire a gun with accuracy, why did it take six shots at close range to stop your husband from hurting you?

A. I was frantic with fear.

Q. But what did the jury decide at your trial, Mrs. Richman? They didn't believe the killing was self-defense—did they? You were sentenced to nine years in prison for manslaughter—isn't that right, Mrs. Richman?

A. I was innocent! I never murdered anybody!

Q. Could it be that the jury didn't believe your story because two bullets were found in your husband's back as well as the four in his chest? And because you failed to report the shooting for seven whole hours after Police Chief Osborne lay bleeding on your rug?

Charlene broke into tears and collapsed. Judge Lewin banged his gavel and called a recess as Johnson and the bailiff fanned Charlene with legal pads. My heart went out to her. I couldn't help it, although I knew Martin was right. Even if Charlene had no choice in life, we also had no choice in this trial.

When Charlene took the stand again later that afternoon, she still looked pale and uncertain. But Johnson used his cross-examination to build up her confidence and self-esteem as he painted over Barry's gory scenario with gilded strokes.

Q. Mrs. Richman, I'm sorry we have to put a grieving widow through such travail, especially after life has treated you so harshly. But if you'll be brave and strong, I have some questions which can put to rest the injustice which you endured in prison many years ago.

First: You didn't serve time for nine years, did you?

A. No. I was paroled after six.

Q. In other words, you must have been a model prisoner. Maybe, indeed, someone who really didn't belong in prison. You were quite young when you first married?

A. I was only twenty.

Q. And having a police chief ask you to marry him seemed an answer to a young girl's dreams?

A. Ed was very strong and handsome. It was very romantic.

Q. What happened to change that?

A. When we were married six months Ed suddenly lost his mother, who lived with us. It changed him, okay? It seemed like he loved her more than he loved me. After that he began to drink heavily.

Q. Didn't that affect his job?

A. Not much. He was a man who could hold his liquor. But he became real mean, okay? The more he drank, the meaner he got. So by the time he came home, any little thing I said would drive him crazy. And he'd beat me.

Q. What did you do?

A. Well, I loved him, so I'd try to cozy him and get his mind diverted. I even ripped off my clothes and begged him to love me, okay? Even that didn't work after a while.

Q. Why didn't you leave him if he continued brutalizing you?

A. I thought about it a million times, okay? But it would be no use. He'd go after me till he found me, and I wouldn't survive his revenge. Ed was too macho to let a woman have the last word.

*Classic wife abuse syndrome. Male beats female again and again. Desperate, she leaves. Feeling cheated, he frantically searches and finds her. Enraged, he inflicts greater pain and damage. No way out. Some choose Charlene's way. But there's got to be a better way.*

Q. Mrs. Richman, please tell us what happened on Sunday, September 2, 1973.

A. Ed came home drunker than usual that night. I pretended I was asleep, but he dragged me out of bed by my hair and screamed at me for not having his dinner ready. It was almost midnight, and never before did he want food when he was potted, okay?

Q. He beat you up?

A. He slammed me against the wall and knocked the breath out of me. Then he stomped all over me with his big boots. He raised welts and put me in agony all over. When I squirmed to get away, he landed a hard kick in my face and my nose spurted blood all over the carpet. I passed out right after that.

Q. What happened the next day?

A. Ed was still snoring at eleven o'clock when I finished cleaning up the mess. When he awoke, he started drinking again without a word, okay? When I finally asked him if he wanted me to fix some lunch, his arm lashed out and knocked me over the chair.

Q. You were hurt badly?

A. I was aching so much in every part of my body, I could hardly move. I finally felt I couldn't take it anymore, okay? I quietly threw a few of my things in a suitcase and then Ed saw me coming out of the bedroom.

Q. He tried to stop you?

A. "Where the fuck you think you're going?" he yelled. When I didn't answer, he grabbed me from behind as I reached the door and yanked me so hard I thought my arm came off, okay? Then he whammed me on the side of the face. And as I staggered sideways he slammed me with his fist and I hit the floor.

Q. I can see how much these memories pain you, Mrs. Richman. Please tell us what happened next.

A. He wouldn't stop hitting me, even though I begged him. I was sure he'd kill me this time, okay?

Charlene had the habit of using that "okay?" as a challenge to the world, her voice climbing to the top of the musical register. Now it had a hysterical ring which plucked at the heartstrings.

Q. Then what happened, Mrs. Richman?

A. I finally squirmed out of his reach behind a table and found my purse. I warned Ed I'd kill him if he hit me again, okay? He just laughed, so I took out my gun and told him I meant it.

Q. Did you intend to shoot your husband?

A. I just wanted him to stop beating me. I couldn't stand any more pain, okay? But he just kept laughing and coming at me. So I pressed the trigger. He looked surprised, so I pressed it again and again and he went down.

Q. Why did you continue shooting after he went down?

A. It's all a blur after that. I suppose I couldn't believe he'd stay down, okay? Ed was so strong that I thought he'd get up and come after me again if I didn't put him down for good.

Q. Here, use my handkerchief, Mrs. Richman. We can all understand how difficult it is for you to re-live this nightmare you suffered. I have just one more question: why didn't you notify anyone till hours later?

A. I told you. Everything was a blur. I was in shock. I didn't want to kill my husband—I just wanted to stop him before he killed me! I couldn't believe he was dead, okay? I was in a state of shock! Can't you understand that?

I glanced at the jury box. There were seven women and five men. I don't know about the men, but I'm sure all the women understood.

Judge Lewin recessed the case for the weekend and Martin muttered, "Well, we played our ace in the hole. And we were trumped by wife-beating!"

"Look at the bright side," said Barry Weiss as we stood outside the courthouse afterwards in a despondent fog. "99% says their first two counts will be dismissed. We've proven that the family funds belonged to Abe Bloom, and we have solid testimony that he knew what he was doing when his trust was set up.

"That leaves the other three counts—defamation, emotional distress and invasion of privacy—where it's your word against Charlene's. So the most she can win is three million dollars."

Martin heaved an expressive sigh. "Thanks. You just saved us six point five million bucks, Barry. Now advise us how to scrounge up the paltry few million we'll need on Monday."

"I know it's no laughing matter," said Barry. "But it may not be as bad as it looks. I'll be spending my weekend preparing the finest summation ever heard in a Florida courtroom."

Barry hailed a taxi and we parted like pallbearers after the casket is lowered into the grave. As we walked toward the parking garage for our rented Buick Electra, Martin's arm was jostled from behind. He turned and Alice Henry was standing there. "Can I talk to you, Martin?" She sounded highly agitated.

"What is it?" he said guardedly. She was the enemy.

"I mean privately," she persisted. "Just the two of us. It's something very important. Won't take long."

"Does it involve the case?" asked Martin.

She hesitated. "Yeah."

Martin's eyes caught mine, and I nodded. We'd wait for him at the coffee shop across from the garage.

I was so overcome with curiosity that I unthinkingly put sugar in my coffee. I never take sugar. Scott and Annabel were each launching wild speculations on what Charlene's best friend was hatching, stirring up whirligig thoughts in my mind.

Fifteen minutes later Martin joined us looking strained and anxious. "More bad news?" I asked.

"I don't know what to call it," he said, mopping his brow. "Killing with kindness? The lady or the tiger? No—I guess it's 'Mephistopheles Rides Again'."

"Stop talking in riddles," I said impatiently.

"I need some black coffee first," he said, motioning over the waiter. And then he let out a prolonged sigh.

"Alice Henry tells me she's got a humongous problem. Her 17-year-old son Jimmy totaled a borrowed car and is seriously injured. He's completely paralyzed."

"That's terrible," said Annabel.

"Alice says there's a 95% chance he'll die unless a top surgeon is flown here from New York tomorrow."

"I feel sad for Alice and her son," I said, "but what's that got to do with us?"

203

Martin took a sip of his coffee. "It'll cost twenty thousand dollars for this specialist. *Payment in advance.* And Alice has nowhere to turn for that kind of money."

"You mean ... you mean she's asking *us* for twenty thousand dollars, Martin?" I was more than incredulous.

Martin's expression reflected the irony. "Yep. The friend of our enemy wants to be our friend now."

Scott jumped in. "Why in hell should you help her? She lied through her teeth to put you in this hole."

Martin said, "Ready for the good news?" and took another drag on his coffee. "Alice Henry is now ready to recant. She told me she now realizes she did wrong in lying about us. She confessed that Charlene offered her five hundred thousand dollars from what the jury would award against us. Alice says she's willing to tell all in court even though she'll face perjury charges."

"Wow!" cried Annabel. "Who said there isn't a Santa Claus? This'll blow the case wide open!"

"There's more bad news," said Martin dryly.

"I know what's coming next," I said tersely, "but tell me."

"You're right," said Martin. "If we don't give the twenty thousand, Alice don't get religion. She didn't exactly say so. But look who her best friend is. Or was."

"Then you're going to give her the money?" asked Scott, wide-eyed.

"Hold on," said Martin. "There's a lot more to this than meets the eye. Better to use the nose."

I snorted. "Your father means that this whole thing smells bad. In law, I think they call it bribery to suborn a witness."

"I don't understand," said Annabel. "You'd never offer anyone a bribe, Dad. But this is different. The woman is desperate to save her son. She came to you, and you're willing to help her—even though she was digging your grave!"

Martin gave a grim chuckle. "Do you think I should give Alice Henry the twenty thousand right now with no strings attached?"

There was a silence at the table as all the ramifications of this new development sunk in. Scott suggested that Alice testify when the case resumes on Monday, and then we give her the money. But the surgeon must be flown in tomorrow. Annabel felt we should give the money to save the boy and take our chances that Alice would do the right thing.

"How did the accident happen?" I asked.

"Alice told me her kid had been doing drugs for three years, getting deeper and deeper. She couldn't handle him. Then she got a call that he went impromptu drag racing with a stolen car and cracked up."

"What are you gonna do, Dad?" asked Scott finally. "With Alice's testimony, you can't lose the case."

Martin quietly drained his cup, his eyes clouded and distant. Then he turned to me. With one look, he knew he didn't have to ask where I stood.

"We can't give Alice the money," Martin said. "Even if I handed her a check tonight 'for humanitarian reasons', once she testified in our favor we'd be tainted with bribery. Who could believe that we would bestow a twenty thousand dollar gift on the person who put nails in our coffin—unless the money was to escape from the coffin?"

Martin looked around the table. "We shouldn't even think that way. Alice was bribed by Charlene to lie about us. Now Alice is asking us to bribe her to tell the truth about it. That's an ethical swampland."

I said, "When we really think about it, there's really no choice to make. We're not rich, so we'd never give twenty thousand dollars for a boy with whom we have no connection."

Martin took Alice's phone number from his pocket. As he looked to see where the pay phone was, he said, "Bribery—no matter how you slice it—is still baloney."

Martin walked off and I summed up our crazy day for our kids. "Dad's mother—your grandmother—had a favorite saying: *'Der mensch tracht ... und Gott lacht.'* In Yiddish, that's an ironic way of saying that a person plans and plans. And God only laughs."

# CHAPTER XX
# WHEN ALL ELSE FAILS

## *Martin—One Day Later*

Sleep was a stranger last night. Every phase of our case replayed in my mind. I thought of all the things I should have said when I was on the stand. I thought of all the things Barry might have tried. It still added up to only one thing: the jury must be leaning in Charlene's direction.

What popped into my mind was the fortune cookie message I cracked open at the Hunan Wok restaurant where we ate last night:

> *Life is a tragedy for those who feel,*
> *and a comedy for those who think.*

Maybe if I think hard enough I'll find something funny about all this.

About two o'clock in the morning I decided that a little fresh air might derail my festering concerns. I slipped out of the hotel bed and dressed quietly without waking Rina. And as I prowled the almost deserted streets of downtown Tampa, a line from an old song flashed into my head and kept revolving like a carousel:

*It's a Barnum and Bailey world,*
*Just as phony as it can be.*

At least it smothered the monkey on my back for a while.

I didn't notice her till she was directly in front of me, and the blast of her perfume suddenly overwhelmed my nostrils. Twelve inches from my face she murmured, "Looking for a good time, Mister?"

I shook my head sadly and pushed past her. At the corner ten feet ahead, it hit me that she had the voice of a child. I turned slowly and stared at her, as she stood at the curb to accost an approaching car.

What I saw was a woman-child, in heavy paint. Amazingly attractive— not my vision of a prostitute. She was wearing a fluffy white blouse over a tight black miniskirt. Sleek pantyhose made her slender legs look like shiny pencils narrowing into high spiked heels. Hips thrust forward, she grunted a casual "fuck you" when the headlights flashed by after stopping briefly.

She was uncommonly pretty. Tempting, even at my age. Then I wondered about her clients. Do they see Death lurking between those smooth thighs? Do they think about how AIDS could spring a painful closure to their lives?

Yet, like Charlene, she does what she does because life steered her that way. Some man had disappointed her, hurt her, damaged her. She'd like to wish upon a star, but brutal reality has tossed and turned her into a Black Hole, whose powerful gravitational pull sucks in and envelopes anyone who comes too close.

I turned and headed back to the hotel. When I slipped back into bed, I dozed, but very fitfully. As I dressed the next morning, it felt as though I hadn't slept at all.

At the Flamingo Restaurant across from our hotel, we tried to perk up our spirits with a pancake breakfast. Scott had a positive attitude. "Dad, the game isn't over till it's over."

"Our family is together," said Annabel. "And pulling together, we'll beat this thing somehow."

Their brave generalities were trite, but it was the deep sincerity behind them that warmed my spirits. Where in life do you find a substitute for family?

Scott had picked up the Tampa paper for the sports scores, and as he unfolded it a front page headline caught his eye. "My God," he cried, "your case is in the news!" My heart looped as I saw the headline:

## DISABLED WIDOW BROKE, SUES FOR INHERITANCE

It was obvious that Charlene had initiated the story. She was quoted all over. The reporter, Jason Gardner, indicated the dispute was whether the widow was entitled to certain assets. The facts weren't wrong. But the spin was all toward Charlene. The article ended by saying that Martin and Rina Richman were "unavailable for comment."

Livid, I seized the payphone and dialed the newspaper office. Gardner took my call, and I exploded over his not getting our side of the story. He explained that Charlene Richman had approached him after the court recessed, and he couldn't reach us before his 9 p.m. deadline.

I muttered bitterly, "If only your apology could be made personally to every juror on my case who reads your article."

Back at our table, Annabel said, "Charlene really likes to play dirty, doesn't she?"

Scott grimaced. "She's not the only one who feels winning is everything."

Stopping back at the hotel, we found a letter waiting for us from Rina's brother Bob. After wishing us well in court, he described the poignant story of his 9-year-old granddaughter and her head lice:

> *Even though Debra is extremely careful in her hygiene, she just discovered that lice had invaded her hair for the third time. Disgusted, she said: 'I would run away if I thought it would do any good. But I don't think it would help me or anybody.'*

I chuckled. "I know just how she feels. I've been invaded by a louse too."

"Time to head over to see Uncle Abe," said Rina as we piled into my rented Buick Electra.

Hattie greeted us at the door to the apartment with her typical exuberance. As always, Abe was buoyed up to see our kids, and showed great interest in their activities. But his attention span was limited, even when we reminisced about happy family memories. He remembered that David was gone, but shied away from talking about it. Finally he brought up the one thing on his mind: did Charlene get her hands on his money?

"Your money is safe," I said. Charlene may get our assets but it seems likely he'll have his to live on. He looked relieved, and Hattie led him into his bedroom for a nap.

Of course, this whole debacle involves more than money. How could an intelligent guy like David have tied himself to a grasping, self-centered woman like Charlene? How could he take her back after she deserted him and ran off with a huge chunk of Abe's money?

Then I remembered some of the dumb things I've done myself. Yes, even the mighty do fall.

Scott's voice brought me back to my family. He was suggesting we hold another council of war. "There may be something we've overlooked. Look what happened when you checked that 'female patrol officer' testimony."

"We've investigated every lead we have," I said wearily.

"But we're desperate," said Annabel. "Why not make a list and check off each one to see if there might be something worth probing more deeply?"

Nothing better to do. I got a pad and began listing all the people with any connection to David or Charlene, followed by any points which might bear on the case. Rina filled in what I missed. Scott and Annabel were even able to add some points they knew about, such as Charlene's odd behavior in asking Annabel to share her hotel room on the eve of her wedding, and then being so cold on Annabel's visit.

One hour later, having drawn out no new threads with our fine-tooth comb, I glumly thanked Rina and the kids for their persistence. "Let's head out for something to eat."

"Don't you do that," called Hattie from the kitchen. "I been fixing a nice lunch for all of us. Be ready soon." Then she stuck her head in the room. "Meanwhile, maybe one of you can go to the drug store. We need the refill on Uncle Abe's prescription, and it's just two blocks from here."

Scott headed off. Then Annabel said, "That's one point we missed. Uncle Abe's drugs."

"What do you mean?" asked Rina.

"Didn't you tell us you suspected that Uncle Abe was being overdosed by Charlene to fuzzy up his mind?"

"Why ... yes."

"Did you check that out with Dr. Kahn? He might know something we don't."

I couldn't see how Dr. Kahn would know if it was Charlene, or whether Abe was overdosing himself. Besides, the strongest medications were prescribed by Dr. Brown, the psychiatrist. And Dr. Brown, who didn't even bother to check for an overdose when Abe was rushed into the hospital, was clearly in Charlene's corner.

"But when all else fails," persisted Annabel, "why not try Dr. Kahn and see what he says?"

So I did. And I drew a blank. All he could tell me was that in his opinion, the dosage specified by Dr. Brown was higher than he felt was necessary for Uncle Abe's condition. No, the dosage level prescribed by Dr. Brown posed no real danger to the patient.

Dead end.

"Just a minute," said Annabel. "Wasn't there another doctor before Kahn? Remember that right after the wedding, I developed some rashes? The doctor who was caring for Uncle Abe at the time treated me for poison ivy."

"Yes, that was before David and Abe moved from the old to the new house," said Rina. "I can't think of the doctor's name."

After a minute I said, "It was 'Spencer.' Dr. Jason Spencer. He was on my original list and I phoned him."

"Another dead end?" asked Rina.

I stared out the window. "I left a message and he never called me back. That was months ago. He's probably on Charlene's side too."

"What makes you say that?" asked Annabel.

"Charlene picked him," I said. "Before Charlene joined the family, David and Uncle Abe used a different internist."

"What do you lose, Dad? Call Dr. Spencer now...."

"I know," I said, picking up the phone book to get his number, "When all else fails...."

I gave my name to the receptionist, and there was a long wait at the other end. At least Dr. Spencer was in his office on Saturday. When he picked up, he sounded strangely tense and said he wouldn't answer questions over the phone. But then he abruptly told me to come to his office right away. Taken by surprise, I said I'd be there in ten minutes.

"Folks," I said, "Maybe we shouldn't get our hopes up. But this is just wild enough to maybe mean something."

Dr. Spencer was a white-haired version of Robert Taylor with a small paunch. As Rina and I were ushered into his private office, he shut the door with grave deliberation.

I said, "Your time is greatly appreciated, Doctor. This matter is of extreme importance to us."

"I know," he said solemnly. "I read about the trial in this morning's paper."

"Doctor, did you treat my uncle, Abe Bloom, about two or three years ago?"

"Yes. Charlene brought him in. He was my patient for almost a year."

"Why did he stop coming?"

Dr. Spencer rubbed his chin, his hand covering his mouth. Then he spoke in a subdued tone: "Mr. Richman, I'm going to tell you something startling. I knew Charlene for a long time as an old patient. But I feel I can't keep this confidential any longer. Your sister-in-law once tried to bribe me in connection with your uncle."

"*Bribe* you?"

"She suggested that I provide medication which would help her put Abe Bloom out of the way. Medication which would avoid any suspicion. She said it would be worth fifteen thousand dollars to her." The doctor's voice had dropped to where it was barely audible.

"My God!" said Rina. "What did you do?"

A wan smile touched Dr. Spencer's face. "I told Charlene she was crazy. I'm only interested in saving lives."

"Why didn't you tell my brother David?" I demanded.

"I didn't want to get involved. I thought maybe Charlene wasn't really serious about it. But she pressed me hard and I got really upset with her. Nobody in the family contacted me again. I heard later that they moved."

"Didn't you tell *anybody* about this plan to murder?" I asked incredulously.

"Oh, I reported it to the police that day. I had to. To protect myself. I wanted the bribe rejection on the record."

"So what did the police do?" Rina asked.

"Nothing. They simply made notes. They said they'd file a report. For the record."

I couldn't believe it. "They did *nothing*?"

The doctor shrugged. "They said they hear lots of death threats. Mostly one spouse threatening to kill the other. Hardly anyone is ever serious."

"A fifteen-thousand-dollar bribe to kill isn't serious?" Now Rina was incredulous.

Dr. Spencer sighed. "What more could be done? I had no witness. And I couldn't believe Charlene really meant it. She's not the murderer type."

A silence settled while all this sunk in. "What made you decide to tell us about this now, Doctor?" Rina asked.

"I read about the trial in this morning's paper," he said. "I knew the kind of person your brother David was. And I know Charlene—maybe better than she knows herself. I began to feel very sorry for you and your husband. When you happened to phone, I simply had to get it off my chest."

I looked Dr. Spencer squarely in the eyes. "So now you *are* involved. That means you'll testify for us on Monday?"

He looked torn and sad. "What kind of doctor leaves his case hanging?"

Back at our hotel suite, I ordered champagne brought up as Rina described the unbelievable turn of events to Scott and Annabel. I then grabbed Annabel and danced her around the room. "You remembered Dr. Spencer!" I cried gleefully.

"What a great memory zoologists have!" said Scott. "Must come from working with elephants." And he began to whirl his mother in a joyous two-step.

Rina disengaged and said, "Before we do too much celebrating, shouldn't we call Barry and assess how valuable Dr. Spencer will be?"

I dialed our lawyer's home number and gave him a detailed rundown. The line was quiet for a few moments. Then Barry said: "You know, it sounds like your problem has just stumbled onto a solution. I'm heading right over to Dr. Spencer's office to fill in some small gaps, and to be sure of the best way to direct my questioning."

"But won't this kill Charlene's case?"

"Ever meet a lawyer who wasn't conservative?" asked Barry. "Remember what happened with Lou Bianca's seduction testimony, and with Charlene's first husband? But Doctor Spencer could end up being our savior."

So we tempted fate and celebrated in anticipation. The champagne cork popped and the stream gushed into our glasses. Flicking on the radio, I danced with Rina. Scott flung Annabel across the floor in his version of the Lindy. Scott danced with his mother. I danced with Annabel. Then we all joined arms and did an impromptu *hora* to the rock-n-roll beat blaring from the speaker.

Improbable? Sure. But we had no other tune at the moment. Our personal messiah had come.

# CHAPTER XXI
# SWEET DREAMS

### *Charlene—One Day Later*

Cinnamon was mewing like crazy. I'm glad I didn't give her back. She could tell I was fixing her dinner up on the kitchen counter. As soon as I set her bowl down on the floor she hopped to it with gobbling gusto.

Not too different from people. Put a big dish of goodies in front of us and we go for it like a tiger pouncing on a rat. Law of the jungle. We see it all around us.

That's the doorbell. I let Craig, my new roomer, answer it. Never know when Martin may come crashing in. But it was Alice, and I dashed to the front door to comfort her. She'd phoned me from the hospital last night to say that her Johnny had made it.

Arms around each other, we both had a little cry. "He's alive. Thank God. Thank God." Alice was sobbing with relief.

I poured the coffee. "Lucky he came through without that brain specialist from New York."

"The chief surgeon here in Carmel Hospital did a great job. My Johnny opened his eyes this morning and I was crazy for joy. It was a thousand-to-one shot."

"But you said he's paralyzed. Can they fix that?

"No. The top of the spinal cord was crushed. He's a quadriplegic."

"Oh shit!" I said. "Isn't there something they can do to heal it? Remember —you'll be getting half a million bucks from my case against Martin. Money can do wonders."

"Doesn't seem likely. Not unless they develop donors for spines."

The doorbell rang again and Craig opened the door for Uncle Mike. After Mike settled behind a cup of steaming coffee, he asked: "Who was that big black man who let me in?"

"Craig is my bodyguard," I said. "I rented one of my bedrooms to him. On the condition that he answers the door for me, okay? I can't take any chances that Martin may bust into my house one day to beat me up."

"You still have your other bedroom rented out?" asked Alice.

"Yep. To that fancy-dress Cuban lady. She's hardly ever home, so it's no sweat."

"Well, the rents pay for your groceries anyway," said Mike. "And maybe by this time tomorrow, the jury will award you so much money that you can tell your boarders to get lost."

"Really, Mike?" I grew excited. "How much do you think I'll get?"

My uncle rolled his head on his thick neck. "Who knows how juries figure it? But since you started by asking for ten mil—they can't end up with small change. At least a couple of million."

I smiled smugly. "I'd like to squeeze every penny out of that motherfucker. After the way he treated me. His own sister-in-law!"

Alice had something else on her mind. She closed in on my uncle with hate in her voice. "Mike, I'll never forgive you for turning me down on Johnny."

"Look," he said, "I was sorry to hear about your son's accident. But I don't loan twenty thousand bucks to anybody. I don't even loan money to relatives."

I supported Alice. "The loan was only for a few days. You know I promised Alice half a million from the award I get."

"I'm no bank," said Mike blandly. "Besides, I heard your son came through anyway."

Alice had no answer, so I shifted the talk back to happier subjects. "I'm planning a victory party," I said gaily. "I'll take the ballroom at the Royal Poinciana and invite everyone I know, okay? Except Lou Bianca, of course. I'll send him a special telegram saying: 'Traitors Keep Out.'"

Mike was in a wet blanket mood. "Just remember there's a difference between the judgment you're awarded and what you'll be able to collect. Martin and his wife may not have that much."

I guffawed. "They're loaded. But I won't take it all. I'll leave them a few thousand for funeral expenses, okay?"

Alice was concerned for Uncle Abe. How would he get along without any funds?

"Oh, he'll be taken care of in a nursing home by Medicaid, okay? And I'll send him a little spending money." I snorted. "I'm not hard-hearted Hannah, you know."

"What are you planning to do with all that cash, Charlene?" asked Mike.

"All the things I've dreamed about. I'm gonna get me a wardrobe of the fanciest designer duds to make me look svelte. I'm gonna book myself on the Concorde, and then flit around Europe in the top-drawer hotels before taking a cruise around the world."

"Where are you planning to live?" asked Alice.

"I dunno. I'll probably buy one of those posh oceanfront villas on Sanibel Island or Marco Beach. And if I get Martin's mansion up in Connecticut, I can use that as my summer place, okay?"

Uncle Mike turned to me. I've been turning to him for help all my life. Now for once he was asking me for something. "You're taking care of Alice, Charlene. What are you going to do for me—your favorite uncle?"

I thought about that. Then I said, "I'm going to buy the fanciest, most expensive car you sell, okay? And I'm going to pay you full ticket price!"

I was only kidding.

# CHAPTER XXII
# SCREW-UP

## *Martin—One Day Later*

"Your Honor," said Barry Weiss, addressing Judge Lewin, "this morning was scheduled for summations, but some vital new evidence has come to my attention over the weekend. "With the court's indulgence, I'd like to call a new witness to the stand for the defense."

Johnson immediately objected on the grounds that the surprise testimony gave him no opportunity to prepare.

"Your Honor," said Barry, "I believe this case will stand or fall on the credibility of the principals. The testimony I am about to present goes to the heart of the case. These proceedings would be incomplete without it."

Judge Lewin allowed it and Dr. Stanley Spencer was sworn in. I was watching Charlene as his name was called. Her shoulders jerked spasmodically; her face turned ashen.

Q. Dr. Spencer, you are an internist and general practitioner?

A. That is correct.

Q. When did you begin treating Abe Bloom, David Richman's uncle?

A. November of 1990. Charlene Richman was a patient of mine and brought him in. Actually, she wasn't "Richman" at the time—she married David a month later.

Q. What were Mr. Bloom's medical problems at that time?

A. The usual aches and pains for a man of 85. Arthritis. About a month later, just before Charlene's wedding, he suffered an incident of depression.

Q. How serious was it?

A. Charlene called in a psychiatrist to handle it, a Doctor Brown.

Q. Did you treat Abe Bloom again after that?

A. For seven or eight months, as his internist. He showed some beginnings of senility, but his health was unusually good for a man of his age.

Q. Did he suffer from Alzheimer's?

A. Charlene described symptoms to me which fall into that syndrome. But during his visits with me, I observed no sign of Alzheimer's disease.

Q. Dr. Spencer, are you aware of any reason why Abe Bloom ceased being your patient?

A. I think I am.

Johnson objected that the witness was being asked for an opinion on a non-medical matter. "Trying to assess another's motives is conjecture, which is inadmissible," he argued. Barry said that he would show facts to corroborate the doctor's statement, and Judge Lewin allowed it.

Q. Dr. Spencer, please tell the court what occurred on the afternoon of June 8, 1990, which was about eight months after you began seeing Abe Bloom.

A. Charlene Richman brought him to me for a routine visit. His vital signs were fine. I recommended a decrease in the dosage of the drug prescribed by Dr. Brown some months earlier.

Q. Did anything unusual happen during that visit, Dr. Spencer?

A. Yes.

Q. I see you are reluctant to talk about it, Doctor. Why is that?

A. Well, Charlene was a patient of mine for many years. I hesitate to reveal what would be harmful to her.

Q. But what I am asking you does not invade your doctor-patient relationship, does it?

A. No. It doesn't touch on Charlene's relationship to me as her physician.

Q. Dr. Spencer, please tell the court what unusual thing happened during that visit on June 8, 1990.

A. While Mr. Bloom was dressing after my examination, Charlene had a talk with me in the privacy of my office. She described the problems she was having caring for Mr. Bloom: his erratic behavior, his incontinence, and other such difficulties. She told me she was concerned about her safety as well as her husband's. She said that she had awakened in the middle of the night smelling gas. The kitchen was reeking with it, and after she opened all the windows, she found that all four of the gas range jets were wide open without being lit. She said: "We all could have been asphyxiated."

*Surprise. Charlene is now saying Abe almost killed them all, yet she never mentioned that incident to us. Can it be that Abe grabbing her breasts and all those other bizarre episodes were strictly fantasies conjured up in Charlene's brain?*

Q. What was your reaction, Doctor?

A. I sympathized with her problem. Speaking as a friend, and not as a physician, I suggested that if she and her husband saw no other alternative, Mr. Bloom could be placed in a good nursing home.

Q. What was her response?

217

A. She said her husband wouldn't agree. She said David's brother from Connecticut was opposed and controlled her husband.

Q. What happened after that, Dr. Spencer?

A. Charlene asked me whether a heavy overdose of the pills prescribed for Abe Bloom would be fatal.

Q. What was your reply?

A. I said it would depend on dosage and frequency. Continued excessive dosage could debilitate his brain, and would surely hasten death .

Q. Dr. Spencer, did Charlene Richman make a request at that time which surprised you?

A. It wasn't a request. It was a proposition.

Q. Kindly tell the court what she proposed.

A. She said that Mr. Bloom would be better off dead. And she asked me to help her put him away. For good.

The courtroom reverberated with gasps of astonishment, and the judge banged his gavel. I glanced over at Charlene. Her eyes were bulging, and globules of perspiration were glistening on her forehead.

Q. Dr. Spencer, are you saying she asked you to *kill* him?

A. I laughed at her. I thought she must be joking. But she said that Abe Bloom had nothing to live for anymore. He should be put out of his misery, she said. And she offered me $15,000 to overdose him in a manner that would avoid any suspicion.

Q. She tried to *bribe* you?

A. I turned her down cold, of course. No physician could do a thing like that.

Q. Was there a witness to this conversation, Doctor?

A. No—I told you it was private. But after she left with Mr. Bloom, I filed a statement with the police. I felt I had to be on record as rejecting a bribe. I'm sure it's still on file.

Q. When did you last see Charlene Richman or Abe Bloom?

A. They ceased being my patients and dropped out of sight after that visit. Charlene left in great anger. And I felt sorry for her. You see, as an old patient of mine she would confide in me on personal matters. I was aware that she has a highly disturbed personality, stemming from an abused childhood and from being a battered wife. She looked upon me as a father figure, and was bitter over my rejecting her—

Charlene suddenly sprang up from her chair and rushed toward Dr. Spencer screaming, "You promised you'd never tell!"

The judge pounded his gavel and the court attendant dashed from the rear to restrain her. But before he was halfway there, Charlene whipped a pistol from her purse. Then she whirled around and aimed it squarely at me at the defense table.

"You fucking bastard!" she yelled. "You screwed up everything!"

I had just enough time to grab my briefcase from the table and shield my head. Then I heard shots and felt searing pains in my chest. I heard Rina scream as I crumpled and my world went black.

I was alive. It smelled like a hospital. In the left corner of the ceiling were some small fragments of scaling paint. Then I saw the suspended I.V. bottle with its lethargic drip, and it seemed vaguely familiar. Oh yes, that was when I flew down in a hurry to find both David and Uncle Abe in Carmel Hospital. Just before David died.

Someone was talking to me, and it was an effort to focus my brain circuits to make sense of the words.

"I'm so happy to see you awake, Martin." The lovely, loving voice of my wife. It sounded like a phrase of familiar music. Now I could make out her face above mine as she leaned over the bed to kiss me.

"You kissed me back," she said. "Now I know you're getting better."

I tested out my voice and it worked. "I know you. You're Rina, one of the angels up here. Tell me what happened."

"You were shot. By Charlene."

"I remember that part. How bad?"

"Her first two bullets were blocked by your briefcase, fortunately. But then she got two into you before Johnson knocked her down."

"How bad?"

"One was a flesh wound. The other just missed your heart. But the surgeons here fixed you up beautifully. It'll take weeks to recover, but no permanent damage." Rina heaved a big sigh. "I can't tell you how relieved I feel."

"You and me both. How long was I out of it?"

"Two days. Scott and Annabel are still here, of course. They're in the waiting room. Let me tell them you're awake."

Family. This is the time they count: when you're flat on your back, helpless. When it feels that in this whole big world you're so insignificant. When you have that aching hole that needs filling.

They came flowing into my hospital room brimming with affection, sending it washing over me in waves to warm my heart and my head. How I loved them all. Some people say that getting well is sixty-five percent happy attitude. It must be so. I could almost feel my flesh and bones mending in the midst of this merry effervescent flock.

After I took a nap and polished off a lunch that tasted remarkably good, they were all back in my room and the conversation inevitably turned to Charlene.

"Your case was dismissed, of course," said Rina. "And Charlene is in the hoosegow for attempted murder."

"Charlene is a dangerous bitch," I said bitterly. "I'll see to it that she gets locked up till her teeth fall out!"

"She deserves it," snapped Scott. "She lied. She cheated. And she almost put you six feet under!"

That thought sobered us into some quiet reflection. Then Rina said, "I know it's not logical, but I can't help feeling sorry for Charlene. Her life was practically pre-programmed to end badly."

"What do you mean?" asked Annabel.

"I had a long conversation yesterday with her friend Alice. Charlene grew up seeing her father beating her mother. He was from Spain. And he wouldn't forgive his wife for giving him a daughter instead of a son."

Scott looked puzzled. "What has that got to do with her shooting Dad?"

"There's lots more. Her father hated Charlene for being female. She constantly wore black-and-blue marks to school from his beatings. Then one night when she was twelve, he came into her room and raped her. She endured this sexual abuse and battering till she turned fifteen, when she ran away from home."

Knowing how involved Rina was in women's issues, I could sense how deeply moved she must be by Charlene's catastrophic childhood.

"She lived off the streets. And I'm sure you know how women live off the streets. The only men she knew wanted only one thing. And so men became her mortal enemies … as well as her meal ticket to survival. Her whole life taught her that everyone is out to get you unless you get them first."

Scott said, "Sure. But I can't feel sorry for her. Not after the way she made Uncle David and Uncle Abe and the rest of us suffer."

Annabel saw the other side. "You have to admit she brought Uncle David a pile of happiness, too."

I remembered once thinking that Charlene wasn't all bad. That was on the night David died. Once she heard that David would have to be cut up for an autopsy, she gave up suing the doctor and the hospital for negligence.

I remembered other things, too. How she devotedly kept watch in the hospital corridor all night when David had that kidney operation. How she called the ambulance promptly when Abe came down with congestive heart failure, rushing David to the hospital soon after.

"I don't get your point, Mother," said Scott. "Are you saying, like those bleeding heart liberals, that it's not Charlene's fault? That she's simply a product of our 'repressive system'?"

"No," said Rina firmly. "I believe every person must be responsible for his or her own behavior. My point isn't really about Charlene. It's about us."

Puzzled looks all around, and Rina continued, "We've won. But winning isn't everything. We've come through a tough, grueling experience. What has this done for *us*? Are we full of blind hate, or have we grown in our understanding?"

I felt I was hearing something profoundly important. But lying there with two holes in my chest had me in an emotional fog.

The long silence was shattered by Barry Weiss's sudden entrance and thunderclap announcement: "Charlene is dead!"

We stared at one another. "How did it happen?" I asked.

She went into a diabetic coma in her cell. It must have happened after dinner, but they didn't discover it till this morning. They rushed her to the hospital and worked on her, but it was too late."

"Don't the guards check the cells on a regular basis?" asked Rina. "How come they didn't find out at bed check time?"

"There'll probably be an investigation. But the official I spoke with said that she had been screaming and carrying on since they put her in a cell, abusing the guards and yelling that she'd been framed. She was hysterical. I suspect that when she had her seizure, the guards were relieved that she finally quieted down, and so they kept away from her cell."

As that sank in, I said, "How ironic. Dug her own grave."

"Maybe she had a death wish," said Annabel.

"I've thought about that, too," said Barry. "She shot Martin because she saw no way out. She might as well be dead, so she wanted to take him out first. Then imagine how she felt when she learned he didn't die."

"We'll never really know," I said. And I watched the I.V. bottle above my head as the drops dripped monotonously and oozed into my arm.

# CHAPTER XXIII
# CATCH A FALLING STAR

## *Martin—Three Weeks Later*

There were more stars out tonight than I can ever remember. And they seemed brighter, somehow. Maybe it's because I haven't looked at a Connecticut night sky in some time.

Rina took my hand and we began our stroll. "This is the first walk you've taken outdoors, Martin. Why do you insist on doing it now, after dark?"

"The doctor said I could start today. I was napping when you came home from classes and you resisted waking me. By then it was time for dinner. And I was determined not to let another day go by."

Rina chuckled and said, "Okay. But don't let your enthusiasm make you overdo. 'The fault, dear Brutus, lies not in our stars, but in ourselves....'"

That brought back a long-forgotten memory, rising up from my mind like a porpoise breaking water. It was David saying, "Maybe the meaning of life is like the stars. We will never reach them. But they can provide points by which to steer our lives."

As we sauntered along the near-deserted sidewalks in our neighborhood, I told Rina about that long-ago philosophical discussion with my brother, and his proverbial aphorism. She pondered it and said, "But didn't David suddenly switch stars?"

Interesting. "I see what you mean. David, in the winter of his life, made a last grab for happiness when Charlene appeared in his sky. He began navigating by other stars, which were in conflict with his familiar constellation of Judgment, Honesty and Family Connections."

A lone pair of headlights flashed by. "How do you see Charlene?" asked Rina.

"Charlene found new meaning in life when David appeared, glittering in the firmament like a savior. She felt he was her last chance for finding her way to Ease, Luxury, and most important: Control.

"She was surprised and dazzled along the way by some points of light she'd never paid attention to: Affection, Tenderness, Warmth, Understanding. But they were soon outshone by her old warped beacons

222

which wouldn't allow her to trust anybody—especially men."

I could feel myself beginning to tire, so we turned homeward.

"And how do you see yourself?" asked Rina.

I didn't know how to answer that question because I don't think I've really changed much. Except that I have passed the point of hating Charlene. Or of hating anybody. This doesn't mean I forgive, any more than I could forgive Nazis for the Holocaust. But I seem to have developed a higher level from which to view such things.

As though to echo my thoughts, the sky suddenly brightened. "Look!" I exclaimed in wonderment. "A shooting star."


## THE END

Printed in the United States
18857LVS00002B/163-252